I0676307

Also by Fount Adams

A Pirate Born

PORT ROYAL

Book Two of Pirate's Life Series

Fount Adams

Evem Press

PORT ROYAL
Copyright © 2019 by Fount Adams

All rights reserved. No part of this publication may be
reproduced, distributed, or transmitted in any form or by any
means, including photocopying, recording, or other electronic or
mechanical methods, without the prior written permission of the
author, except in the case of brief quotations embodied in critical
reviews and certain other noncommercial uses permitted by
copyright law.

This is a work of fiction. Names, characters, places, and
incidents are either products of the author's imagination or used
fictitiously.

Manufactured in the United States of America

Evem Press
Palm Beach Gardens, FL

ISBN 978-0-578-48176-0

2019937370

PORT ROYAL

For

my Aunt Nancy

a lover of pirates and pirate lore

Prologue

July 1690

T he *Tetrarch* sliced through teal water, plowing sprays of white foam. Thunderheads built up out of dark underbellies into white billowed tops cutting against blue sky. A line of brown seaweed ran just off to starboard, and the green and yellow bodies of the fish the Spanish called *el dorado* flashed soft smears in the sunlight that pushed just below the surface of the sea.

Nick, standing at the bow of the ship, held his gaze steady across the pale water at the land that drew closer.

"Ah, lad . . . . it's a lovely day to find riches," Leesh said, appearing at Nick's side. His teeth gleamed white against dark skin that wrinkled richly into his smile. His once-red cap had now faded under the tropical sun.

We'll see if this is the day, Nick thought, and saw Leesh catch the twist of lip that betrayed his mind.

"Now there," Leesh said. "Don't you be worrying."

"We'll see," Nick said aloud this time.

Stuart shouted orders from the helm, and Nick turned to do his part in bringing the ship to a halt where the water changed from its already pale shade to a near-yellow where it ran shallower still. Nick worked quickly and expertly, no longer a neophyte.

1

Once the ship had halted and anchored, the boats were lowered and the men armed themselves. Nick strapped his two pistols into his sash along with his rapier.

"Come along, Nicky," Edward Corbyn beckoned toward one of the dinghies being lowered into the water.

Nick made his way down into the boat along with others. Rowing together they quickly brought themselves in formation with the captain and pulled toward shore where the waves rolled peacefully onto the sand. The beach formed a white strip against a dense line of green over which rose palms swaying in the steady but soft breeze. It was the kind of scene Nick would have enjoyed stopping to appreciate, but they came here on a mission.

As planned, the Captain's boat reached shore first. As the rest arrived, jumping into the shallow water to drive the boats onto the beach, the Captain marshalled them. He did not need to tell them to be quiet or to remind them to be cautious.

Stuart led them into the dense growth, several in the front hacking their way through with cutlasses, the heavy swords that did not require much skill to wreak tremendous damage. Nick walked along just behind them, with Captain Stockett and Leesh. They knew there were paths through the jungle to their destination, but they hoped to surprise by an unexpected approach and did not want to risk encountering someone along the way.

The humidity draped over the men like the wanton drunken ladies so many of them had been with over the past month. The jungle rose above a green cathedral filled with hot, dead, sopping air. Nick felt sweat rimming his lip and trickling in beads down the side of his face under the thin scarf he wore. He looked over to see Leesh smiling grimly. The heat was breathtaking, even in the shade.

They pressed on.

Finally they stopped, Stuart's hand jerking up to halt them. Just ahead the jungle opened against blue sky, and Nick could see through palm fronds the stone walls of a village.

His pulse quickened. He watched Stuart's eyes shift in the green light as they searched for the stronghold. Nick himself could not see, but Stuart indicated its general direction.

The routine was set. Attack the village, rush the stronghold, take gold and silver. No reason to think there should be any problem.

No reason except . . .

Stuart gestured to tell the men to ready themselves, then looked at them, nodded, and raised a yell as they charged the village, racing into the melting hot sun.

They crashed onto the streets, the people rushing away from them.

But just as last time they attacked a small village purported to hold a treasure horde, here again the people did not scatter the way they would if they were surprised. They seemed not afraid at all. Their movements were methodical— more than that, predictable. It would not be hard to find the stronghold of the town, even if Stuart had not already located it, because everybody was running in that direction. Women dragged children by the wrists or snapped them up and carrying them. Older men make their way slowly. Young men put up no resistance.

All clearly by design and even rehearsal.

Nick felt his stomach sink. The ground inclined up to the stronghold that rose gray-white above the palms. It was made of coquina, or rock made of tiny impacted shells, a tough building material the Spanish loved to use for their military structures. It stood on the highest point in the village, and Nick felt his calves tighten against the slope. Sweat runneled into his eyes, and he blinked it away.

When he and the rest of the crew reached the building, they did not have to kick the thick wooden door in. It stood open, as if taunting them. The inside was completely empty, the shelves and hooks that should hold guns and swords naked against the wall.

"Go," Stuart said half-heartedly, and Nick went with the rest of the crew to search the building, already knowing they would find nothing. Anxiety coursed through him as he thought about the implications.

Now there'll be the Devil to pay

As he made his way through the rooms, he envisioned the scene outside. The Captain and Leesh would now be making their slower way to the fort—they were the oldest men in the crew—and Stuart would nod silently and then point out that the open door was a new touch. The Captain would look at it and then at the entire population of the village massed around him, all lined up in a semicircle, their dark eyes innocent and blinking. Nick knew the Captain would be weighing what best to do. His mind cast back to a week ago when he first learned about certain techniques of torture that would make people talk. Maybe Captain Stockett was considering one of those. Nick well knew what the man was capable of.

But there were bigger problems than just how to make this particular foray pay. Now large questions loomed not about those villagers but about the crew of the *Tetrarch* itself.

Of course the building was empty, and he and the rest of the men who searched with him arrived back at that open doorway at the same time.

Leesh was already talking to one of these men as if they were all at a country dance and he was telling a joke of some sort he found outrageously funny. His hilarity contrasted with the rest of the crew, in whom frustration and now

4

suspicion was rising. Even Nick felt himself wanting to knock the smile off Leesh's face.

But there was not time to do that or anything else, for now sounded the same call-out he had heard last time:

"Hombre!"

Nick watched the semicircle of villagers part roughly in the middle. A man stepped out with a rapier at his side. He was short and thin, but his arms nevertheless showed strong ropes of muscle. His beard formed a triangle on his chin, and his eyes squinted coldly in the bright sunlight. Otherwise his face was undistinguished, as if it were impossible to bring the features into focus.

A man had stepped forward in the last town the *Tetrarch* attacked to challenge Nick. Nick had defeated him handily. Clearly the script included singling Nick out for a *duelo*.

What does this mean? How can they know we are coming? And why set up this challenge?

Nick watched the man draw his sword, and, just as the previous challenger had done, he saluted the gathered crowd, including the crew of the *Tetrarch*. Nick followed suit, hearing the snickers of his mates. "Cut his bloody throat, Nicky, and let's get on with it," John Black called out. It was ridiculous to stop and fight a duel—strange that a bunch of pirates (for there was no denying what they were, Nick well knew) should actually halt for this little contest. Nick figured to dispatch this man quickly as he had done with the other.

But something immediately felt wrong as he settled into his stance, which was the defensive French-style he had learned from his (never-admitted) father, Lord Furth, and from the treatises he had managed to get his hands on.

The Spaniard remained standing straight up, simply raising his sword to shoulder height and pointing it at Nick's throat. No stance at all, really—just a man standing there holding a sword. Nick's first impression was that the man was lazy and inexperienced. But the squint of those eyes did not suggest inexperience at all.

Nick advanced quickly, his point aimed low at the man's exposed right flank, testing to see if he was simply stupid or if he was actually inviting an attack there in order to set up his own attack. The answer came immediately.

But not in the way Nick expected.

As Nick attacked, not only did the man drop the point of his own rapier to parry, he also stepped to the side and forward, moving in a circular direction. As he did, he pulled the sharp edge of the rapier from the parry across Nick's stomach.

The move caught Nick completely off guard. With youthful reflex he sucked in as best he could but not enough to avoid the blade's slicing through his thin shirt and flesh. He felt immediate pain as he heard his mates gasp. He managed to spin around as the Spaniard circled back for the kill, his parry just catching the Spaniard's deathblow with an awkward clanging crash.

The Spaniard did not flinch, but moved again in that awful cold revolving way, the blade reorienting with smooth, deadly rapidity as the man stepped forward not thrusting but simply following the sword's point toward Nick's throat.

Nick parried the point away just in time, but now his legs were tangled under him as he tried to follow the Spaniard. He tripped over his own feet and fell into the dirt, dizzy, feeling blood seeping out of his wound. He could not tell how deep the cut was.

Again the man came on him, smooth as before, and yet, even though he seemed not to have increased his speed, he arrived before Nick could process it. This time, Nick's parry was too late—he did divert the blade from a fatal blow to the heart, but he could not halt the point, which stabbed into his left shoulder, knocking him on his back.

The sensation of the steel in his body was a terrible new one to him. He felt the blade withdraw quickly, and he knew the point would find its way to his heart next. Images, emotions, fears, disappointments all washed over him in a single powerful deluge. He could not see the outer world anymore, had no idea when the deadly strike would come as he turned inward and faded out of consciousness.

I

Don Diego Pedro de la Figueroa sipped the glass of tawny port his second cousin had smuggled out of Portugal. Don Diego had a low view of port—the bottles of albariño from his own family vaults were far superior—but he doubted any Englishman could appreciate a truly fine wine. So he brought this bottle for the man sitting across the table in the Governor's Mansion in Port Royal as an act of kindness bordering on pity, thinking it near the limit of his capacity of appreciation.

That man was the new Governor of Jamaica, William O'Brien, Second Earl of Inchiquin. Appointed and sent by the new vice-regent, William of Orange, O'Brien was the first to hold the title of "Governor" as opposed to "Lieutenant Governor." O'Brien was Irish, and he had a fine taste for whiskey, but Don Diego had little concept of Irish tastes.

Don Diego looked across the table at the Governor, amazed again at how translucent the skin of people from northerly areas in Europe could be. His own skin was light when not burned by the Caribbean sun, and he himself had plenty of Celtic blood as a Galician. Nevertheless Don Diego considered pale skin unhealthy, especially when the tiny blue veins just beneath it showed through like rivers on a map. It was especially repugnant when these people were flustered and that white, white skin sprouted pink and red patches. To Don Diego's eyes there was weakness in such creatures, and he held them in contempt.

Always he had held the English in contempt (O'Brien's being Irish did not matter, as Don Diego lumped all English speakers together). Don Diego had first come to the West Indies four years ago when the new Presidente de la Real y Supremo Consejo de las Indias, Fernando Joaquín Fajardo, appointed him Consejero Especial. El Presidente carried out his administration from Spain, so he needed someone he trusted completely to impart his will in the New World. The Caribbean islands were overseen by the Viceroy of New Spain, and Don Diego accompanied the new Viceroy, Don Melchor Portocarrero y Lasso de la Vega, to the West Indies. He remained now into the new Viceroy's term as a go-between and messenger for El Presidente.

When Don Diego first arrived he had relished the opportunity to face the dreaded Captain Henry Morgan. Raised in a military family, Don Diego had lived his entire life for the opportunity to face such foes as that privateer-turned-pirate-turned Lieutenant Governor Morgan. But instead of a swashbuckler, Don Diego found an old man grown fat and tormented by dropsy. A sad excuse for a man he was, for he now spent his time and wealth drinking himself out of consciousness and vomiting it up in ghastly heaves. It had been a long time since Morgan had been Lieutenant Governor, although shortly before his death he had served in the role of advisor. He had died in the ugliest kind of way, and Don Diego had no respect for him at all.

And certainly all the other English he had encountered had done little to impress him. Not that he was disposed to be impressed by anyone or anything not Spanish. Like many of his countrymen he believed himself to be set apart, and his spirit of confidence and superiority drew deeply from the well of long-established culture and the staid power of conservatism. The roots of his family were so remote they were legendary, filled with the daring exploits of knights in desperate struggles against the Moors all the way to tales of fabulous deeds in the more recent conflicts with the Portuguese. Growing up on the family estate near Figueroa, in Galicia, he moved among the portraits of his ancestors that lined the dim halls and chambers as though they lived still, their fixed gazes urging him always to confirm the greatness they had bred him to. He had gone to the Santiago Alfeo College, but his spirited blood made him a poor student. His people had been fighters, and he would be too. He judged every man he met by his estimation of how well that man could fight. When he had engaged with pirates who held such fearful reputations he had defeated them easily. Either the great pirates lived no longer or they had never been that great in the first place. Don Diego was not sure which.

He watched O'Brien take a sip of the port and set the glass back down on the wooden tabletop. The man had a certain malleability in his face Don Diego thought he could read, but it was difficult to be sure and fatal to assume.

"El Presidente wants your assurance that you are doing everything you can to hunt down these . . . pirates," Don Diego said.

"Yes, of course," O'Brien said, his tone preemptory, as if the sentiment did not actually need to be expressed.

The man seemed uncomfortable. Don Diego thought it possible that his own presence had that effect, but, again, he knew the dangers of rigid thought.

"El Presidente believes we can work cooperatively to crush the pirates out."

"We would be most glad to cooperate," O'Brien said, his voice silvery and prim.

"Very good," Don Diego said. "Certain of these *piratas* have been making attacks on our small towns along the coast. There have been two ships we hear of: *Tetrarch* and *San Miguel*."

"*San Miguel*?" O'Brien broke in. "But that's a Spanish ship."

"Yes," Don Diego said.

"These are your own pirates?"

Don Diego looked at the man, "It is not so simple as that."

Footmen opened the door for Don Diego to pass out of the Governor's Mansion, also at times called King's House. He did not bother to look up at it as at as he walked away. The newly-built edifice lacked the grace of Spanish architecture. It was top-heavy somehow, as was the entire city, which he also ignored as he turned up High Street and began walking northwestward.

All around him the city showed signs of construction upward into the sky, which was necessary since it was built on a spit of land less than fifty acres. The Spanish, who had first settled the place, had built a fort and a small town of low wooden structures because they knew the foundation was merely sand. But the English had taken the city in 1655, naming it Port Royal. The sand foundations bothered them not at all: they blithely set about constructing buildings like the ones they knew in England, many of them heavy, made of brick. They also used brick to build new forts, a project that seemed nowhere close to ending.

There was money for it. The privateers and pirates who made this city their haven had brought plenty in. And they meant to fortify the place as heavily as possible. After all, these were wanted people, and their riches needed protecting. With them had come all the revelers, and the city boasted a stunning number of taverns, with more constantly being opened. With such little space to work with, now new stories were being added to the buildings, more brick on the already heavy layers. Here people were living and working as cobblers, goldsmiths, silversmiths, blacksmiths, tailors, haberdashers. It was almost impossible to comprehend how many strumpets lived in this city, but there were also women either of higher class or aspiring to it.

In fact, Port Royal now more than ever was striving to become respectable. In 1687, anti-piracy laws were passed, and now England was part of the Grand Alliance with its long-time enemy, Spain, not to mention the Dutch, another enemy. A respectable element had been in the city for quite awhile, and these people wanted legitimacy and to erase their city's terrible reputation. It was filled with pirates still, to be sure, and money carried its usual power. But anyone making a living in crime must now tread carefully as the politics grew more intricate and dangerous. Gone were the days when a crew of independent men could pillage a Spanish ship and carry its loot here to spend it all up in pleasure without a thought or care for consequences. Now an imposing court house stood toward the eastern end of High Street, and a prominent gallows rose in gaunt, stark, spiny anguish against the sugar blue sky ready to stretch the neck of the next jack-a-napes who took one step too far. The most telling change—wicked as the city was, it took pride in its church.

Don Diego cared little for the place. He would not even have wanted it back for the Spanish empire, and any fool could see that sooner or later the heavy buildings would sink into the sand or topple over. Typical English to build and fortify a city on a worthless piece of land. Perhaps there was something in the mentality of people who lived in island-based empires: the Venetians too had built on a worthless bit of muck, but from what he had heard at least they had approached their vain project with a process that attempted to make up for the instability of the land itself. They had driven entire trees into water with such high salt content it soon ossified the wood. Onto that they laid slabs of rare marble proven to resist the salt water. Then on top of that they built their brick. As far as he could see, the British had no such plan. They just came here and threw big heavy buildings up on the sand and walked about in their ridiculously heavy clothes and went about their vulgar way of worshipping God in their singularly unimpressive church.

It was all too much for Don Diego, as he made his way past the buildings rising in a mismatched multi-angled jumble. The stench was terrible from people sweating and tossing out bedpans and the animals everywhere—chickens and goats and cows—all baking in the heat. Don Diego would never be able to understand how people could live without grandeur. These austere people, with their whiny voices in that nasally language, were too much, and he could not wait to get back on his ship and retreat to sanity.

Although a short walk, it seemed an eternity to him to reach the docks and his ship, the *Santiago*, a three-masted galleon whose aft decks rose in resplendent beauty. It was a ship full of authority. The perfect ship for such a man as Don Diego.

He came aboard and made his way to his quarters, the wooden door of which bore a carving of his family's coat of arms. He opened it and stepped inside.

A man sat on a wooden chair with a high back covered in dark tooled leather.

"Buenos," Don Diego said.

"Buenos días, Señor Don."

II

Nick could not tell when he was conscious and when he was not. At times he seemed to see Leesh's broad grin just above him and could feel hands binding cloth around his stomach and shoulder. He sensed strange smells and the feel of both cold and warm applications against his skin. He felt pain and then would slip away into profound unfeelingness. He could not tell how time was passing, nor could he be sure exactly where he was. At times he seemed to be aboard ship, feeling the rocking of the ocean. But then at other times he seemed to be in other places.

In this state he seemed again to be in the Falstaff Tavern in Port Royal, hearing the same conversation, how many times now he could not tell . . .

. . . *he was a Frenchman," Leesh said, the yellow light from the lanterns gilding his features out of the brown dark.*

"Aye," the Captain said. "L'Olonnais."

"L'Olonnais," Nick heard Edward say quietly in a tone that gave Nick a chill.

Leesh turned up a tankard of rum, the sound of it glotting in his throat.

the sound of older people swallowing, *Nick thought, and momentarily he was back in cold England, in the tiny village of Naunton he had come from, in another time and with other people: his mother, his father, his sister and brother, Harry.*

Sarah

He shut the door on those thoughts.

"Aye," Leesh said, setting the tankard back down. He was *not looking at Nick or at anyone else, but Nick clearly was the only one who did not know about L'Olonnais.*

"He was a man to get . . . results . . . ." Leesh's grin *broadened as he went on. "You see, lads," this despite Nick being the sole addressee, "He despised the Spaniards. Literally hated them. When he was a young man. Oh, this was about thirty years ago. He was sailing about with his French amies and perhaps working. At any rate he and his compatriots shipwrecked there on the Main, and the Spanish attacked them, quite naturally. And the bloody Spaniards meant to kill them all. The way he survived—he plunged his hands into his own mates' blood and threw it all over himself and lay down for dead. Fooled the Spanish."*

Leesh laughed and looked around, the dim light *accentuating the squareness of his face and the long chasms framing his smile, making him look more a handsome man of twenty-five or thirty than the charming one of no-one-knew exactly what age but certainly over sixty.*

No one else laughed. Leesh's smile remained always on his *face, and he seemed to find humor in everything, so none of the men felt any reason or duty to respond to him.*

"Well, L'Olonnais escaped then," Leesh went on. "And he *swore he would harass the Spanish the rest of his life." Here again Leesh laughed. "One time he and his new crew he got up ran into a band of Spaniards and they killed and beheaded them all except*

15

one. That one he sent back with rather an ominous message. 'I shall never henceforward give quarter to any Spaniard whatsoever,' or some such bit of formal declaration. Except spoken in that blasted trade-wind language of theirs."

He paused to take another draught of rum from the tankard. A noise sounded back in the shadows, a door squeaking open, then faint light from a candle and the sound of the door closing again.

"Aye, love," Leesh said to the shadowy form that passed them by. It was Hannah, the owner of this tavern.

"What are ye all talkin?" she said in her thick accent, the word "talking" sounding more like "toewkun."

"Are you well, darling?" Leesh asked.

"Aye, love. But old Martin and Barbara were up there in a melting moment, I tell you, when the old man flashed his hash."

The men guffawed at the awful image.

"Tis true," she went on. "Must be cleaned up right away."

"Ach, you do it, my lady. And I'll be up to bed directly."

"Ooh-go away with you!" Hannah snapped. "You loitering ne'er do well, you . . . "

Her curses faded as she let the door to a little harder than before, almost a slam. She was too savvy about business to cause too much of a disturbance.

"You'll not be visiting Eve's Custom House tonight, I dare say," whispered Judson.

"Aye, we'll see, lad," Leesh said and took another draught, this time smacking his lips after. "Old L'Olonnais . . . Well then he and his mates began going about the same business we are these days, visiting towns along the coast. When they struck a village, the people there grew recalcitrant. That is to say they weren't inclined to tell where they kept their gold hidden. So L'Olonnais came up with some creative ways to convince them to talk. He was the one who came up with the idea of woolding."

"Woolding?" Nick asked.

"Aye, lad," Leesh said. "It's when you tie a string around a bloke's eyes and then tighten it more and more until the eyeballs pop out of the sockets."

Nick swallowed his response.

"It wasn't L'Olannais who invented woolding, Archie," the Captain said from the shadows. No one spoke.

"Aye, Captain," Leesh said. "I misremembered that. At any rate," he went on as before. "His best one was one time actually cutting a man's chest open and reaching in and pulling the man's heart out and eating it right in front of him and all the rest of God's creations watching. . .

. . . and now back to another place. Nick no longer seemed to be moving. He thought he could smell food cooking. Bacon, it seemed. He even thought he could hear it hissing in a skillet. The aroma overpowered him. Made him hungry, then sick, then hungry again.

He opened his eyes, blinking and trying to focus. He was lying on a bed. A window rose to his right, and sunlight poured in. He looked around the room; nothing familiar to him.

He tried to stretch and yawn, but as he did so pain punched through his shoulder and stomach.

The sound of voices came to his ears. They seemed to be far away in this building. He could not make them out, but he felt he must go to them and find out what was going on.

When he moved to sit up and get out of bed, the pain clinched him, and with it came his memory. Every detail—the feel of the heat, the sunlight, the look of the Spaniard's eyes, the cold way the man stepped in a circle—all of it rushed into Nick's consciousness, and he knew why he was in bed. He lay back down and said a prayer of thankfulness. He did not know how could still be alive.

Then he heard the sound of a latch uncatching and watched as the door to the room opened.

III

The man in the chair in Don Diego's quarters was small. His face was indistinguishable, as though the features could not quite come into focus. The only thing remarkable about the face was the very peculiar looking nose. It seemed a little too large for his face somehow, and its surface was strangely waxy. The waxy consistency spread to his cheeks where it faded unevenly and at certain points seemed to have a strange wrinkle that looked almost like a cut.

It was the only remarkable thing about the man's face. There was a marked coldness in his eyes that under certain circumstances might strike someone. And at times he would grow a short, triangular goatee, but then many Spanish men did so, including Don Diego. The man had shaved it off only a few days ago, so that except for the nose he would have been indistinguishable and probably forgettable. Also, because he was very short he could often infiltrate a crowd without anyone being the wiser.

Don Diego pointed to his nose, "How can you be of any use to me anymore?"

The man smiled slightly but not enough to change the set of his face. "Don Diego, my talents are many in number."

The man's rather dramatic statement underwhelmed Don Diego, who passed by him to the ornately carved desk by the window and sat down in the chair behind it.

"It is true I will stand out now. But I can turn that to my advantage. Where before I was invisible, now I will be most visible. People now will say, there goes Hector, the man with the false nose. They may even devise some new name for me. 'Ah, there he comes, the man they call . . .'"

Hector struggled to think of a name that would have a positive and hopefully intimidating sound.

"Señor Wax Nose?" Don Diego suggested.

Hector shrugged, "This game is only just begun."

Don Diego regarded him, unimpressed. But then he had seen this small man show great resourcefulness. He pondered briefly, playing scenarios out in his mind.

"You know what I need," Don Diego said at last.

Hector smiled in that slight way again, "When have I ever failed you, Don Diego? Even when," he waved his hand over his nose, "it has cost me dearly."

Don Diego was too shrewd to be fooled by such a professing of loyalty. Hector had not wanted to lose his nose or anything else for Don Diego.

"But," Hector said, and Don Diego knew what was coming. "Because I am now incapacitated so," again the dramatic gesture over his nose, "I will need more help."

Don Diego nodded, "Yes, I expected so."

Hector shrugged again, a move somehow dramatically undramatic. Indeed, all his dramatic moves seemed at odds with the coldness in his eyes, as though he were an actor in one of the Italian pantomimes.

I don't know why I bother to protect the Crown's treasures from pirates only to give it to this little man, Don Diego thought. But he knew there was a cost to carrying out his larger plans, and if this man got rich off his part in it what was it to Don Diego? After all, he could always come along later and convict the man of some crime. It took little effort for someone in his position. While Don Diego may not have had the position of the Viceroy, he arguably had more real power. And if he ever were to secure that Viceroy power along with all the know-how he had gained with that position . . .?

"Here," he said, and pulled out a desk drawer to remove a bag. He had far safer places to keep money, but he did not want the likes of Hector to know about them. He set the bag on top of the desk with a metallic clank.

"Gracias, Señor Don," Hector said, reaching his hand forward like a claw and grasping the bag.

"I want results as always," Don Diego said, catching Hector's gaze in a steady glare.

Hector conveyed his trustworthiness in his eyes as he pulled the heavy bag toward him and stood up.

"May God shower blessings on the rest of your day, Don Diego."

Don Diego nodded, and Hector left the room, leaving the Don to his thoughts.

Hector walked down the gangway onto the north dock. In the distance behind him, across a swath of sparkling water, mountains ranged in hazy blue from the Jamaican mainland. Seagulls wheeled above, their soft white bodies catching on the hot breeze until they would swoop among the forest of ships' masts.

When he exited the dock, he turned right and headed south along Fishers Row. It was late morning, and soon the heat would slow the activity here to a standstill. Already workers were leaving the wet planks along the wharf to pelicans to gulp fish parts in their long beaks, with their large pouches of veined flesh glowing pinkish in the sunlight. The smell of fish was strong, mixing with that of emptied chamberpots and vomit from those who had imbibed beyond their capacity to hold liquor.

The wharf was really many smaller wooden boardwalks constructed over the sand. Hector cast his shrewd cold eyes over the scene, taking in the level of activity, calculating in his mind the capital flowing there. One of his many talents was his ability to perceive the monetary or trade value of any item, any transaction, any industry. It was as though he had a special kind of vision.

He was sweating when he turned left at Broad Street across Lime Street into the heart of a triangle of buildings, which he turned away from, heading south along an alley so narrow even his small and trim form could barely pass through. The alley stood in complete shade, strangely dark on such a bright day. The voices of people arguing somewhere in the one of the buildings around him stabbed the air.

He paused at a door that was deeply scratched and scraped and knocked twice, paused, and knocked twice again.

Nothing happened for a moment. Then with no indication from within of anyone approaching the door it lurched open. Hector stepped through.

The inside smelled ranker still, like the old sweating rotted flesh of the elderly. The smell flooded Hector with the darkness as the door closed behind him. He felt disoriented and could not quite locate where might be the person who had opened and closed the door.

"Señor Sah," a ratchety voice whispered. "Vamos."

The latter word betrayed an accent not Spanish. Hector could neither hear nor sense the other person moving. Presently, though, Hector's eyes adjusted to the darkness that was far deeper even than the shadows outside in the alley. As they did, he saw what seemed to be a very dim candle burning.

"Come," the voice whispered again, and this time Hector saw the slow movement of a dark bulk he understood to be a person. "Come," the voice said again.

Hector followed the shadowy shape toward the burning light that drew his gaze. As he looked at the light, Hector could not say for sure that it was a candle or that there was even a flame of any kind there at all making the light. Perhaps this was some kind of unusual lantern? Perhaps it was made of cowhorn so milky it spread the light in a mysterious way? But he could not see any frame or shape that suggested it was a lantern. Rather it seemed simply to be light, and that light, he now realized, did not stay the color of a typical fire but somehow shifted into a bluish hue and then into a shade almost pink.

"Por favor, Sah" the voice said again. "Sit."

Hector did so and waited. There was silence for a long enough time that most people would have become uncomfortable. But Hector had been here plenty of times before and knew it was best to wait. Also, Hector was not one to be uncomfortable. His mind rattled along through figures and schemes at all times, so he was never bored. If he found himself in a quiet moment of inactivity, he simply withdrew into his mind and went to work there until such time as he should be called to action again.

"Now, Sah," the voice said, finally. It was as if the form had settled itself to talk in English, although Hector could not tell whether this entity was facing toward or away from him. "Would you like something to drink?"

"Yes, please," Hector replied.

"Aye, Sah," the voice said, the form not moving, no sign even that breath gathered to make the sounds. There came the sound of a clink, and a tarnished but fine silver cup appeared before Hector. It did not bother Hector that he could not explain how it reached him.

"Thank you," Hector said, lifting the cup and taking a sip. It was a strange concoction along the lines of *sangaree*, but with its fruity alcoholic flavor it blended what tasted like coffee bean with something vinegary. Hector was accustomed to it and allowed it to flow coldly down his throat and into his chest. He cooled down immediately.

"A ki dupe are eni," the shape said in a voice that sounded slightly different than before. Hector had heard this before and understood it to mean "you are welcome."

Again silence, and again Hector worked through one of the many things humming in his mind. Then again the shape spoke in a voice like its original one.

"I have, you Sah, what you want, sí."

The last syllable was accompanied by another clanging sound on the table, and Hector looked down to see in the dim light an object, which he lifted. It was a piece of brass finely shaped into a nose.

Hector looked at the shape and smiled.

"Muchas gracias," he said.

"De nada," the voice replied in a broken, almost bored way.

Hector inspected the nose, turning it over. It was beautifully shaped, far better than the nose he had been born with. Its contours shone in the dim light in its rich reddish hues. He noticed it was thin and light, the inside with a large

24

pocket that would help him breath much better than his current wax nose did since it pressed against the empty cavity. The edges were flanged, and along them were strips of wax.

Hector looked up at the shape, watching a moment, and then shrugged as if to say it did not matter if the shape watched him do what he was going to do. Then he reached up and peeled his current wax nose off his face, feeling air rush into his open nose cavities in a way that almost hurt. Now the stench of this place seemed far stronger.

He lifted the brass nose to his face and, using his left hand to help him position it, pressed it on, the wax holding firm.

"Sah," the voice hissed in what might have been approval.

"Sí," Hector said, and he felt the nose vibrate on his face, realizing he was speaking through it and that in so doing his own voice took on a metallic nasal quality.

"Owo," the voice hissed again. "Money."

"Yes," Hector said. "But this wax. Will it last? Do I not need more in case it should go bad."

"Money."

"Yes, yes, I know. But can I buy more wax?"

The voice delayed a moment in responding. "Es bueno."

"Sí, entiendo," Hector said. "Here."

He reached into the pocket of his waistcoat and brought out a pouch (not the one he had received from Don Diego) and set it down.

"One hundred doubloons," Hector said.

It was no small sum—a wooden leg could be had in Port Royal for forty-five and a lot less if you had the right connections. Even at highest prices, a glass eye did not approach that price. But Hector knew this prosthetic would be extraordinary, and he was not disappointed.

He also knew better than to try and cheat this entity.

"Empty," the voice said and Hector obeyed, pouring the gold coins gleaming into dim light.

"Do you want me to count them out here?"

The shape did not answer, and Hector could sense its eyes grazing over the coinage. It was all in a pile, and he did not know how the shape could count the individual coins. But he waited.

"Pa gen okenn bezwen," the voice said finally. "There is no need."

"We are done, then?" Hector started to rise.

"No," the voice said with authority but without urgency. "Sit."

Hector settled back down and waited.

"Give me your hand."

Hector's eyes became alert. He had not been told he would need to do anything else. Something arose in him; he did not want to extend his hand and did not understand why he should have to. In any other situation he would have asked questions with the idea of bargaining. But something about the shape did not invite negotiation.

Slowly Hector stretched his arm out, the hand face down.

"Turn over," the voice said, now in that different tone and with a cracking sound.

He turned his palm up.

"Closer."

Hector leaned forward, and as soon as his hand was in shadow, he felt a powerful grip around his wrist that he could never have broken. It did not hurt, even as it yanked him forward. But he felt the strength, which seemed not human.

Then he felt something indescribable, without form or dimension but rather a cold wet presence glide over his palm. It chilled him, and he shook once all over, violently. Then the grip loosened, and Hector eased back, bringing his palm back and looking at it. It was dry, and there was no sign of anything having happened to it.

"What was that?" He knew he probably was not supposed to ask but could not help himself.

The voice waited again. This time Hector thought he would not get an answer. But then it came.

"I just, Sah, took a year of your life, sí."

IV

U nsure who exactly would be coming through the door, Nick pretended to close his eyes, peering at it through his eyelashes.

In stepped a young woman.

She closed the door behind her quietly and moved noiselessly across the room toward the window. She did not look in his direction, concentrating as she stepped, holding up her skirts so as not to trip and make any noise.

With a smooth and silent movement she opened the curtains, and Nick closed his eyes against the bright sunlight that poured in. He could not hear the young woman at all and had no idea where she was in the room.

When he was able to open his eyes slightly again, he looked around and saw her walking toward the window again, apparently having gone to another part of the room in the meantime. As she came into the full sunlight he could make out her appearance better.

She looked to be about his age, around twenty. Her eyes were of a green that flashed in an arresting way even at a distance, and contrasted with her white skin. The features were delicate, with a small nose that spread into lovely wings at the nostrils to form an aquiline just between proud and weak. She wore no bonnet, and the sunlight brought out the full richness of hair full of liquid strands of honey through which the light filtered in candied translucence. Nick could tell there was strength in the muscles of her forearms as she raised the window and used a cloth to dust off the sill.

Watching her work, a comforted feeling came over Nick. She was so completely absorbed in her task and obviously meant to do it as well as it could possibly be done even if it was really of no consequence and no one would ever inspect the work or even know she had done it. He saw her clench her lower lip over the upper one as she concentrated, and it gave him a feeling he could not quite describe.

He did not realize his eyes were completely open until she turned and happened to see him watching her. She stopped and stepped back with a soft, "oh!"

"I—" Nick started to say, but his voice broke with disuse, so he swallowed and started again. "I'm sorry. I didn't mean to scare you."

She put her hand to her chest and let out a breath, "Oh, it's all right. I just didn't expect . . . you to be awake."

Awkwardness filled the room. She looked as if she had been caught committing a crime, and he was not sure exactly what to say next.

"I'm Nick," he said, finally, holding out his hand.

Again she let out a breath as if she had been holding it. She stepped forward, and took his hand.

"Oh, I know, Master Nick," she said, a smile appearing as she stepped forward and took his hand. "I'm Abigail."

She curtsied. Her words and actions all embarrassed Nick. They were far too formal.

"Please, you can call me just Nick."

She bowed her head slightly, her green eyes gliding upward and then back down as she did so—a timid motion that showed a desire to please but also a need to keep things in their proper places.

"Can I ask," he began, and watched as she raised her head again. Her eyes were big, and something about their sharp green hue burned in a way that arrested him. Again it struck him that her eyes created confusion, making it difficult to tell if she was mad or just intently listening. After a pause he went on, "I was wondering, where am I?"

Her eyebrows sharpened a little, making her look madder still. Strange that she should be at once so timid and yet also so harsh. Her voice when she spoke was soft, nothing like her expression, "Do you really not know?"

He looked around the room again and shook his head.

"You're at the Falstaff."

The surprise on his face registered on her own.

"They told me you're here all the time," she said in a hurried way, as if in apology. "But . . maybe . . ."

He looked at her, trying to understand what she was thinking. She looked away and then back at him.

"Maybe you don't so much come upstairs," she said finally.

He smiled at her and tried to make sense of the situation. He did not recognize her, but then he never took much note of the young women Hannah kept here. The other men of his crew teased him and tried to goad him into patronizing the services of the Falstaff Tavern prostitutes, but that had worked no better than trying to get him to drink rum with them. He figured he lived in enough wickedness, being in a line of work that required stealing and murder, although in truth he had not succeeded in doing so much even of that since arriving here in the West Indies.

Besides, there was something else: the woman he had loved for a very long time. She was far away, yes. He would never see her again probably. But . . . it was difficult to think about. For now it was easier to be alone.

Not that the sight of ankles and bosoms and slender necks and lovely hair had not caught his eye. But this was the first time he had actually encountered one of the young women here as an actual complete person.

And this actual complete person surprised him. She seemed so innocent.

"You're new here?" he asked her.

"Oh, yes," she replied. "Just arrived a week ago."

"From England?"

"No, sir. From the Virginia Colony."

"Oh," he said and furrowed his brow in question. "Why did you come here?"

"Oh," she said and turned her head away, obviously weighing how to answer. She looked back at him, "I'm afraid I shouldn't talk about that."

"Oh, ok."

"Yes," she said and looked away again.

He looked at the sun catching the irises of her eyes, glowing as if through green water. Her soft, delicate nose with its flared nostrils looked earnest somehow, in the way a child would be earnestly and wholeheartedly overwhelmed by a problem that seems unsolvable but in fact is very small to an adult. Yet melancholy hung about her like a silk veil, and it seemed real and grown-up enough. He felt a strange mix of emotions toward her.

"Well," he said, and then whatever thought he seemed about to express went out of his head.

"Yes?"

They sat in silence for a moment as he tried to think what he was going to say. But it was not coming to him at all. Then another thought occurred to him.

"Abigail."

"Um-hm?"

"Do you . . . I mean, I am part of a crew on a ship. Do you know that?"

"Yes. The *Tetrarch*."

He felt a little taken aback that she knew that. "Right. Well, I was wondering, do you know if they are here in Port Royal?"

"Oh yes," she said. "That is, some of them at least."

"Some of them?"

"Yes, sir. The one little man."

An amused smile played across her mouth, and Nick knew of whom she spoke.

"His name is Leesh."

"Yes, sir. That one."

"Is he here now?"

"I should think so. He's forever drinking, and . . . he stays with my Lady."

"Ah yes, I know."

She looked strangely worried. Nick could not tell if she was worried about Leesh's and Hannah's souls or if there was something else on her mind.

"Right," Nick said. "Well, I would like to go downstairs and see if he's here."

"Oh no," she said and stood over him as if to keep him in the bed. "You cannot be walking about. Strict orders from Mr. Leesh and my Lady both."

Nick had not moved, and he remembered the pain he had felt in his stomach when he first tried to stand up.

"Well, then, can you do me a favor, Abigail, and see if he can come to me?"

"I'll try, sir. Although I never know what he will do."

Nick smiled, "Does he sometimes give you a little pinch?"

32

Her face colored, the pink setting off the green of her eyes, "Oh, yes sir, and more besides." He watched that amused smile appear again. Nick could never imagine himself taking the kinds of liberties with women that Leesh did on a regular basis. He was sure he would have been slapped. But for some reason Leesh could always get away with it.

"Well, I appreciate your calling for him," Nick said.

"Yes, Master Pearson."

"Please, just Nick."

She bowed her head slightly and walked in her swift way to and out the door, closing it still with that deftness that made no noise at all.

V

Governor O'Brien reflected on the conversation he had just had with the Consejero Especial, Don Diego. As his mind worked over what they had discussed, his eyes wandered to the window, gazing across the bay at the blue hills of the mainland.

They might have been the hills of his family's barony in Inchiquin in County Clare, Ireland; perhaps those surrounding Lough Inchiquin. But then they could have been hills in Spain, France, Algeria, or Tangiers. He had been in all those places fighting. And all that service only to be attainted by King James II over a year ago for his services to the English, although so far as he knew no real action had been taken formally to remove his title and lands.

Ireland, his home, his first wife, Margaret—they were all far from him in time and space. These hills were not blue from chilly mornings but from tropical heat. And he, William O'Brien, Governor of this place, considered the situation on his hands, his own words from the just-concluded conversation sounding in his mind again . . .

... San Miguel?" O'Brien broke in, not in haste or anger. "But that's a Spanish ship."

"Yes," the Consejero Especial said.

"These are your own pirates?"

"It is not so simple as that."

O'Brien waited. He took another sip of the port, which he liked. He had a fondness for Operto and for Portugal, generally, because it had fought off Spanish dominance. After a lifetime of fighting Spain as an enemy it was very difficult here in his fiftieth year of life to rid himself of his dislike and distrust of the Spanish. Portugal's defiance of Spain always filled him with a quiet glee.

"This San Miguel," O'Brien said after waiting and receiving no more information. "It is a Spanish galleon, no?"

"No," the word came out graceful but slightly curt, not being followed by a "sir" or "Governor." "It is a schooner."

This news surprised O'Brien even more. The schooner was a sleek, smaller, two-masted ship with a very shallow draft. It was a Dutch style of vessel, and it made sense that pirates would like its great speed, which could be used to dart out of hiding, attack a ship, and then retreat. But with that shallow draft, it was difficult to arm a schooner adequately. Surely it had been stolen from one of the Dutch islands, perhaps Sint Maarten. Or it may have been captured. But why the Spanish name? Not that it was inconceivable that a self-serving pirate might attack his own kingdom's treasure for personal gain.

"Who captains this ship?" he asked.

Again the Spaniard's dark eyes peered at him.

"Well, Governor," this time with the title, which rolled off the man's tongue with studied precision. "That may surprise you . . .

And indeed it did. What to do with such information?

The pirate situation was difficult enough for an administrator. A vocal and growing segment of the population opposed every kind of piratical act and was especially appalled by all the drunkenness, gambling, whoring, stealing, and violence in the city. When there had been war with Spain it made sense to keep these cut-throats around to protect the city, which they valued so highly. But that wartime had passed, and now these pirates had become simply a nuisance at best and were a dangerous blight on future civic development at worst.

O'Brien understood their viewpoint, of course, but he also saw the need to keep the pirates happy. First, it was hardly practical to round up every single person known or thought to be a pirate. Not only were there simply too many, but a number of them had spent years as privateers and had their own political pull.

Second, like it or not, the pirates were good for the economy. Most of them were quick to spend their loot, and the gold and silver from them coursing through the city kept business in full swing. Their activities might now be illegal, but money always maintains a disturbing connection with the unethical, whether in the form of outright crime or in more nebulous dealings. O'Brien well knew that wealth was rarely created without some kind of inequity or exploitation and that second and third generations of the rich may either have never known or chosen to forget about how the fortunes they enjoyed were actually secured.

A third reason to keep the pirates around, O'Brien reasoned, was that one never knew when Spain would become an enemy again. It was very important to remain vigilant in peacetime as well in war. Certainly, he had more soldiers at his disposal now than ever in Jamaica, and more

English were coming every day. But he knew the role the privateers had played in attacking the Spanish, and he knew that many of the men now considered pirates were simply doing the work they had always done, and that one little shift in the political situation could turn them into legitimate English fighters instead of illegitimate thieves—privateers "working" for the crown instead of pirates "stealing" for their own.

And the reality was that O'Brien enjoyed the idea that the Spanish were vulnerable now, their numbers and their military strength now depleted. His life had been one of warfare, and he liked having his boot on Spain's West Indian throat. When he envisioned tough crews attacking ships, villages, and even cities of the Spanish he felt a certain joy. Indeed, that the Special Counselor Don Diego should be forced to ask his help in protecting against the pirates gave O'Brien a certain thrill.

Still, he faced the question of how to balance these two opposing groups—the pirates and the respectable people. The values of these two could not differ more. The pirates believed in living large with a certain democratic equality. They had no respect for the social hierarchies that the respectable citizens clung to. Those respectable people practically fainted at the everyday acts and attitudes of the pirates, their rough talk, their sense of freedom to do and act as they pleased. It was an outrage not to act in the way of normal society.

Bridging this deep civil divide was not easy for O'Brien, especially because even though he himself came of the peerage, as a man of war he tended to side, in his heart, more with the pirates. Still, he understood his directives from above as well as those from Port Royal's aristocracy: clean up this mess. His mind whirred constantly, trying to find the best solutions to this situation.

The tall door that connected the study he now sat in to the sitting room opened, and a servant appeared.

"My Lord, Lady O'Brien requests your presence at tea."

A smile bent O'Brien's lips at this call. Best to store the problems away to the back chambers of his mind for now. There they would continue to work on themselves.

He rose.

VI

Nick looked up at the ceiling, thinking about where he was. If his mother had known he was in a place of sin, where women gave their bodies for men's base tastes and pleasures, it would have been awful. He remembered the dirty hovel he had found her and the rest of his family living in when he returned to Bristol after his first voyage on the *Tetrarch*. He remembered his mother's last days and her questions to him about how he had come by all his money.

He had lied to her.

He squeezed his eyes, feeling the pain of his guilt not just in his awful deeds but in misleading his mother as her life ebbed away. And now here he was in this place. He may not yet have sinned in his body, but he was here where such sin happened. He tried to say a prayer but found that difficult.

He thought about Abigail. She seemed so delicate and innocent in this place. Surely she did not actually work for Hannah in the way the other women here did. He suspected maybe she was simply a house-cleaner and helper, not a . . . he hated even to say the word, felt wrong in even thinking he should apply it to so sweet a young woman as Abigail.

The image of her green eyes stayed in his mind. He found himself endeared somehow to her, and he wondered what her story was. Something had happened to cause her to leave Virginia and come here. She did not feel comfortable talking about it—did that mean it was something bad? Or was she not at liberty to say?

That feeling of endearment, of immediate attachment, although not necessarily strong, immediately filled him with guilt, and again his mind roamed back to England. He thought of Sarah in that awful place. Bedlam. Where the mad and lunatic stayed. He thought of the last time he saw her, sick, deranged, unaware even of who he was. She was no longer the girl and woman he had known and loved in their hamlet of Naunton in the Cotswalds. But love must not end when people fall to illness, he believed, and he loved her still, in the deepest parts of his body and soul. No day passed when he did not think about her and pray for her.

But these days it seemed difficult to pray. Praying seemed distant from him just as did Naunton and Bristol and Sarah and his friend Harry and his family. He had made the voyage over to the West Indies, playing his part in attacking and looting ships along the way. The *Tetrarch* sailed now under a solid black flag that whipped in the wind like an evil shadow.

He had resisted many of the temptations Port Royal had flung his way. It had not always been easy, but he had kept his eyes off the alluring women all over the city who were offering pleasure. Alcohol still held no temptation for him— when he was around the rum the other men drank smelled to him like poison, and he had no desire to put it in his body.

But after several months here this place was beginning to take hold of him. He had come to know more and more people, not only the pirates but some of the respectable people too. He had fallen in love with the palm trees that rose into the sun on their smooth, slender trunks and cast their small, shifting splotches of shade from fronds whose delicate spikes clattered in the breezes. The water here glowed in colors he never could have imagined heretofore, and his world had now become a place of eternal summer, filled with yellow and blue and the fresh sparkle of the sea, broken at this time of the year daily by afternoon downpours that ended after a short burst, giving way to the rising of steam into the sun that stored up all that water and energy in building heat until the next afternoon.

Into Nick's life had come all kinds of new foods, brought by Africans free and enslaved. He had now discovered little brown peas with black spots, and he ate the strangely shaped okra. Pork, particularly, reigned as a meat of choice here, and at any time of the day or night Nick could smell it cooking, the smoke of the sizzling meat wafting out from a hundred kitchens.

Even as these good things stole into his heart, he also felt the insidious creep of evil, so subtle he did not even realize its effect until quiet moments such as this one. He was a . . . he did not even want to say what he was. Could there ever be any hope for him to have anything good and right in his life given where it was headed now?

For a moment his mind went blank, and pain wrenched his heart. But then he thought of Abigail again, of how sweet she seemed here, and hope rustled back up again like a fallen calf staggering awkwardly to a standing position. He remembered that in the big world innocence still existed.

The sound of slow footsteps interrupted his thoughts. He shifted his gaze to the door as it opened.

Leesh's face appeared, his brown eyes catching the sun in two focused pinpoints that strengthened his amused gaze at Nick. He smiled as usual, his teeth so white they almost did not look real (and perhaps they were not, for all Nick knew, although he had never heard Leesh suggest otherwise). His face was tanned very dark, and two deep furrows cut downward from his cheeks—the topography of constant smiling. Although his hair was sharp, virile silver, somehow he always looked younger than he was, except one had the feeling he was probably handsomer now than when he was young.

He kept his gaze on Nick as he closed the door. Then he walked toward Nick in slow uncertain steps. He brought with him the smell of rum.

"I understand you're better now, lad," he said, drawing up a chair from the corner and sitting down beside the bed.

"Yes," Nick said. "And I expect I need to thank you for sewing me up."

Leesh laughed softly. The laugh gave nothing away, told Nick nothing, did not seem to mean anything—just a laugh as if Nick had told a joke.

"What I don't know," Nick went on, "is how I got out of that village alive."

Leesh laughed louder now. When the laugh subsided, he said, "Tis true, my boy. I am afraid you were a bit outmatched."

Nick felt his face redden with embarrassment. His swordsmanship was very important to him: not only did he take pride in it, it was also the thing that made him most valuable to the crew.

"I'm not sure what happened," Nick said.

"Aye," Leesh smiled still. "The Spaniard was dangerous, a cold-blooded son of a whore."

"Did you all attack him together?"

Leesh shrugged. Nick was not sure why the old man would withhold such information from him. Leesh carried secrets about him at all times. He knew and saw everything in ways others did not. Best just to file this moment away, especially because there were other things to ask about.

"Did we get any treasure at all?" he asked Leesh.

Leesh laughed harder, his chin drawn in so that he looked like a little boy who just told a dirty joke, "By the powers, no. No gold to be had there."

"Did the Captain torture them?"

"No," Leesh said and fell into more hilarity. Nick waited for him to catch his breath. "I—I—I say, I do wish I had brought a draught of rum up here with me. When that little new bawd told me—"

"Abigail," Nick said before he thought, and he felt himself redden again. Leesh looked at him, and this time his eyes gazed, prodding.

"Aye, that one. She told me, 'Oh, the lad's awakened. And he wants to talk to you, Stinky.' Of course, I was not altogether disposed, you know lad. For you see, there's a certain churl about who's forever wanting to fleece me in Noddy."

Nick knew the card game, although he had never played. He was not sure it was altogether a good thing to do.

"The poor fellow," Leesh continued. "I do think he is likely touched, which makes me feel just a little bit poorly to beat him so all the time. But it is good practice to keep myself limber chopping cards, and then we all must make a living when our regular occupations lag."

Nick's lips twisted in a smile. "Chopping cards" meant manipulating where cards went in the deck.

"Did you finish the game on out?"

"Of course, lad. But it doesn't do to have a little tart come up aft and break a man's concentration."

"Well, it *is* nice to gain a bit of coin."

"Ha, two pieces of eight. A couple of crumbs from a varlet. About the only kind of funds to be had in a stews such as this. Zwounds."

"We're all soon broke," Nick said, trying to get the old man back on topic.

Leesh looked at him in his knowing way again and laughed softly, "Aye, lad. It's dark times in this bright city."

Nick understood exactly what he meant. This was not just a matter of money, although it was always about money. But there was more now too.

"Do you have any idea who the spy in the crew is?" Nick asked

Leesh looked at him, still smiling, as though nothing in the world were wrong or in danger of any kind.

"Every whoreson man of the crew has scattered out," he said. "I stay here, of course, where I belong among the ladies. And there are others in such houses about. But we are scarce to one another these many weeks."

"Weeks?"

"Aye, lad. A Spanish rapier opening your guts to the blessed sun and rain doesn't heal in a day. I don't doubt you may have spent an hour or two in hell before we brought you back."

Nick processed the comment, but pressed on with his line of questioning, "No one speaks to you? To each other?"

Leesh shrugged, "It is hard to know much. When we got out of that blasted village from Hades, at first we sailed off tending to you. But once we got you treated and we went about the sailing, the closer we got back here the quieter everyone became. We had no meeting when we returned. The Captain said nothing to anyone. Everyone just scattered."

Nick waited.

"That's all? No one is trying to find the spy?"

Again Leesh shrugged, "Who can a fellow even know who to talk to? Who to trust enough to figure out who *not* to trust? The whole situation is so bazaar. *You* know."

Nick did. It had been bad enough the first time they had sailed to a village they had learned of only to encounter the strange pre-arranged drama. The crew had picked the village from a list stolen from a Spaniard they had captured in a foray near Hispaniola. The list identified villages where treasure was kept out of the way, hidden where pirates would not expect. Stuart had managed to get that information out of the Spaniard before he gave up the ghost and the crew sent his body down to Davy Jones. Dead and buried, there was no way the Spaniard could have tipped off the villages.

The crew had planned out the attack, so they were shocked when they encountered the prearranged routine. Meeting about it afterward several mates had acknowledge being mightily drunk or caught in the passions of a whore and having perhaps unknowingly let out such information. Captain Stockett was plenty incensed but chose not to assume the worst. Instead, he brought together only Leesh and Stuart, his most trusted mates whom he had known the longest, and they had planned out the next attack without making the crew privy to the where and when.

But encountering the same greeting in the next village provoked deadly suspicion. Had there simply been no treasure, the crew would have assumed the Spaniard's list was just false. But the drama played out in each village made no sense. Something strange was happening, but for what purpose? Was this some kind of bizarre prank? And was it the

45

work of a traitor? If so, what was such a traitor about? The villagers played out their scenario with such disturbing precision. They knew exactly where to go when attacked, as if they had rehearsed it a hundred times. And then there were the swordsmen who showed up to challenge Nick.

Had the ghost of Hobbs returned to wreak vengeance? Hobbs—the man who worked for Mr. Berry back in Bristol and who had been Nick's antagonist. Hobbs—who disappeared mysteriously from the *Tetrarch* one night on the way back to port after attacking a Dutch ship that had given itself up under a white flag?

It seemed that only someone with a grudge would set up such a strange situation, for what was there to be gained? Was the treasure being protected from the *Tetrarch* in order to be given to someone else? Or was there some other force at work? And why should Nick be singled out?

"Well," Nick said. "What is to be done next?"

Instead of shrugging, this time Leesh tossed his hand in the air, "We'll see what the Almighty next has for us." He stood, "But for now you must rest, lad. It is good to see you back among the living, but uh," he laughed now, again as though at a marvelous joke, "don't overdo it here in the bed while little Nursey is bringing you around."

Nick colored, "I'm not!" He pulled the pillow from behind him and hurled it at Leesh, which brought immediate pain.

Leesh parried the pillow, tossed it back on the bed, and walked out, shaking his head and laughing.

VII

"C ome along, Abigail," Hannah said.

Abigail slipped the strap of a small bag over her shoulder in a move that could have been awkward and unbecoming but, when *she* did it, had a certain grace. She followed Hannah outside where the carriage sat waiting. Even covered over with a veil of dust from the trip to town, the carriage gleamed in its black lacquer and painted gold leaf filigree. The mare hitched to it was tall, and her healthy coat gleamed just as black.

Hannah looked nothing like her everyday self. Her dress, cut of the finest material, gave her a stately appearance. Her hair she had arranged in a regal fashion, and her face she had powdered to a fine look. If she never spoke—indeed, if an artist had captured her in this attire—she would have seemed the ideal lady. But she was cursing as sharply as any of the seamen who frequented her tavern.

"Hurry up there, blast ye," she was saying now to a stunning beauty named Vivian, although she pronounced it closer to "Vivienne"; she was French, and her accent conveyed a vulnerability that clashed with her Amazonian build. She had a naturally ruddy complexion, dark, rich chestnut hair, and big eyes of soft brown. Her yellow dress set off the color of her skin and the voluptuous curves of a body that to many a male eye seemed to have been constructed according to an ancient blueprint for providing pleasure. She was above average height, and lifts in her shoes elevated her to a size that fell just short of intimidating for most men and turned her into a kind of goddess. In a time when delicacy and fair skin and hair dominated fashion, this woman should not have been beautiful, but something about her appealed to the deepest wells of a person's physicality, as though she were a paragon of nature to remind people of what they were and always would be.

Vivian was considered the most beautiful woman at the Falstaff, and as the carriage driver helped her up into the vehicle he could not keep from looking over the way her climb set off different parts of her. He knew he was not supposed to look, for he had been brought here from Africa as a slave and had quickly learned that he must not interact with the light-skinned women of this place. But there was something so raw and earthy about this woman, and she was so different from the ideal pale creature of the moment, that he could not help himself.

Best to get the looking done now before we get home to the man, he thought to himself in his native African language.

He also helped Hannah and Abigail up into the carriage. He looked both of them over too and was struck by Abigail's brand of sweet prettiness, but Vivian's presence was so powerful it overwhelmed him.

"What is all this!" a man's voice called, and out stumbled Leesh.

"We're heading off on business, you rogue," Hannah roared.

"Ayou!" Leesh uttered a sound not quite a word. "What shall I do for supper? You'll not be back til late, I'm bound."

48

"Lout! Rum will do for you tonight as it does every other, I should think. Now, off with you! I've work to do. Driver, carry on!"

Even though the driver could tell from this lady's voice that she was accustomed to being obeyed, he was not much impressed. He liked neither the sound nor meaning of the word "driver." His African name was Izegbe, and that was who he understood himself to be. He hated the name the man who now owned him called him by—Caesar. It was the name the slave trader had given him at the auction in Port Royal. Even if Izegbe's grasp of language had been strong enough for him to set people straight about what he should be called, there was no allowance for him to do so as a slave. He showed his hatred of his situation and of being called these different ways by always delaying slightly in following whatever orders they barked at him.

He delayed so now, and as he did he saw the little man in the doorway stumble toward him and look up at where he sat, his eyes squinting against the sun nearing its zenith.

"Aye, lad. You've a hard job today."

He looked down at Leesh, and something in the man's smile made Izegbe smile.

"Leave the driver alone, for heaven's sake, you knave!" Hannah snapped.

"Ashiwere," Leesh said quietly.

The word struck Izegbe. It was not a word from his own language, but he recognized it as meaning "crazy." Why would this man know such a word? Izegbe grew immediately suspicious. Maybe this man was or had been a slave trader. He tried to read the man's eyes—they did not look threatening. If anything, he seemed to be trying to communicate, to approach Izegbe in his own language. Something about the man Izegbe liked, but he was one of

49

them, the people of this place, and you could never tell what kinds of tricks they were up to. Izegbe quickly decided it was best not respond or let on that he understood what the man had said.

"What gibberish are saying!" Hannah said, rising up from her seat.

"Nothing at all, love," Leesh said, not backing away, still squinting into the sun, his smile as broad as ever.

"Well go on now, for the love of God—driver let's go!"

Again Izegbe delayed before he finally snapped the reins and clicked the horse into action. Leesh doffed his hat as the carriage wheeled away.

They left the city behind and now were making their way along the narrow spit that led to the mainland. The sea stretched out to the south in a turquois sparkle, the waves rolling onto the beach in a lazy slow insistent rhythm.

Abigail shaded her eyes as she peered at the ocean, taking in the white foam where the waves curled against the earth, flattened into glimmering sheets, and then withdrew. A breeze kept the air from being completely dead, but even that stirring of air was overwhelmingly hot. It had put both Vivian and Hannah to sleep.

Abigail was not one to sleep. Life was too precious for that. But that was not all—her mind was too occupied for rest. And it was not just her mind.

She had arrived in Port Royal just before the crew of the *Tetrarch* returned with Nick. She had watched them bring him in on a stretcher and lay him on the bed. She had helped Leesh treat the awful wounds, holding the medicine, the wraps. She had looked long at Nick's handsome face and thought about what his voice might sound like when and if he ever awoke and said something.

Today he had done so, and she was glad to be confirmed that his voice had the kind of pleasant strength she had expected. And he had spoken to her very kindly, not in the rough way of so many of the men that came into the Falstaff. Just as she had suspected, this young man was different.

How strange life was? That she should go through such an ordeal in Virginia only to arrive here, so far away from anything and anyone she knew and here to find such as him. Nick.

Nick

The name sounded strong and kind at the same time just as his face and voice conveyed a mix of strength and kindness.

Ah, can this happen so soon?

Yes, it could. Surely it could. Her heart had fled to him within moments of first seeing him.

She told herself she needed to be on guard, that she had no idea how he would feel about her. And, for all she knew, he had his own sweetheart somewhere. But another part of her knew it did not matter if he never cared for her. In a very strong sense, she *needed* to be in love. If nothing ever came of it at all it was all right. She would hurt, but something in her said it was worth it. And who knew anyway?

It was approaching mid-afternoon now, and looking ahead she saw the lower hills rising just beyond where the land spread out, signifying the mainland. The path forked there, and she wondered which direction they would take. Surely not the left one that led west, since otherwise they probably would have taken a boat across the bay to the mainland north of the city.

She also saw dark clouds over the hills. These would likely bring a storm within the hour, the heat and energy having built all day until the pressure was too great and the skies broke in a crack of thunder, lighting, and torrential rain. She hoped they would reach their destination before the storm struck.

And perhaps they would, for they were passing by a field of sugarcane, the stalks spiking upward in their anxious green, emanating a lazy aroma of earth and plant life in the hot sun. She knew the look of a plantation, having lived on one her entire life in the Virginia colony. Sure enough, she saw slaves moving among the stalks, their backs bending in the sun that soon would vanish behind the encroaching clouds.

She thought about Vivian going to a new life. The owner of this plantation had recently become a widower and was wanting a wife. He had sent to town to try and find someone, and Hannah had caught wind of the search. She had sent word back that she knew (in other contexts she might have said she "had") a young woman who would make him a splendid wife and that she would personally escort the lady to the plantation. No need for the man to come to town at all.

The carriage began to turn slowly at a break in the cane field, and as it started down this new lane, Abigail caught a glimpse of a white mansion behind a line of palms. The house sent a quiver through her as she remembered the last time she had been at such a place. She had worked to force all those memories out of her consciousness, and she applied herself to keeping them there now. Her best way to do so was to summon the face and remember the voice of the young man who lay recovering back in town.

VIII

Images of yellow roses festooned the wallpaper, creating a pleasing brightness that set off Elizabeth O'Brien's charms splendidly. Not that she needed any help, for she was beautiful almost beyond imagination, like a perfectly-conceived doll. She existed in a soft haze of dimples, sparkling eyes, hair that fell perfectly of its own accord, exquisite proportions, and always the most fashionable clothes. One of her earliest suitors had described her as "a great beauty of over £10,000."

And she was indeed worth every bit of that as a co-heir and youngest daughter of George Brydges, 6th Baron Chandos. Streams of young men felt the torment of loving her only to see her slip away at her father's bidding into marriage with a man eighteen years her senior. The man's name was Richard Herbert: he had distinguished himself during the Civil War but was by the time of his marriage morbidly obese. He died in their fifth year of marriage.

After that she had entered into a secret affair with a certain Sir John, who had in fact been her lover before (and it was rumored during) her married years. Sir John died mysteriously after a few years of their consorting, and a few years later she married William.

And William now felt overwhelmed by her beauty all over again as he entered the room and saw her backlit by the afternoon sun yellowed by the wallpaper. Pride filled him as always that he should possess such a woman, and he bent over her.

"Darling," he said.

"Willie," she replied in a cultivated voice as she lifted her face and he planted a kiss on her lips with a loud smack. He felt his own clumsiness before her but consoled himself that at least she was his.

As he sat down a new painting of the O'Brien coat of arms over the yellow roses caught his eye. He had mandated that the heraldry be displayed in every room of the mansion, and he looked in admiration at the arm holding the sword rising above the helm over the center of the shield. If he really was going to be stripped of his arms and title, then he would make sure it would be everywhere visible here.

"Thank you, Rachel," he said to the woman who poured his tea.

"Yes, my lord," she said. Then setting the tea pot down, "Shall I do anything else?"

"No, thank you," he replied, and she curtsied and left the room.

"How was your siesta, my dear?" he asked Elizabeth.

She smiled, her dimples showing as if it were their duty, her eyes however betraying a kind of labor, as if he had spoken in a language she did not know and was trying to translate it. Finally, she answered, "It was really so very nice."

At once the illusion vanished, and O'Brien came back to reality. She was, to his thinking, a classic case of the cruel inequities of nature, or perhaps its way of balancing things. She was, in the end, all beauty, and nothing else. She was not the kind of woman he could confide in or who had any grasp of anything interesting. She was simply beauty incarnate, and even that of an inaccessible kind.

Strange that someone so beautiful should have practically no physical appeal. It was difficult to explain because when in the hunt to possess her he had wild ideas about what it would be like to be wrapped in her arms. But once he had her she fulfilled none of those promises. She was not resistant to amorous advances in any way; she simply did not seem to know anything about them or to respond to them, as if physical love just was not part of her. O'Brien had assumed it was Herbert's fault her first marriage had produced no children. But when he married her he immediately realized that, odd as it may seem, the very beauty that had so enraptured him suddenly deterred him.

In fact, he could not understand how the dashing Sir John had managed to have an affair with her for so long unless perhaps she acted very differently around him. Or maybe he was like her in that way, both of them lending their beauty to the earth the way two comets might do, flying across the sky together. O'Brien pitied him that he likely lost his life over her, for he could not imagine that the man ever had any pleasure with her.

Indeed, between being no kind of lover and no conversationalist, she was, to O'Brien's thinking, simply another beautiful possession, like a perfect sculpture.

Nevertheless, he attempted to chat, "Have you plans for later?"

Again the delay and smile. Again beauty lifeless as marble.

"Oh, I thought I should read."

His heart turned within him.

"And what today?" he asked, knowing the answer.

Again after a delay, "Oh, that poem of Mr. Dryden's."

"Very well," he said before she had completed the final syllable. She had been trying to read through Dryden's *The Hind and the Panther* for two years now. Given how assiduously she worked at it every single day she should have read the thing at least a hundred times by now. He actually marveled that any human could be so inept.

He resigned himself to having the remainder of the tea in silence, so he turned his mind again to the problems he faced.

The fact was that O'Brien did not care to spend his time as Governor simply reacting. He had enough experience in administration to know that reacting was a regular part of the experience. Even when you had everything set up ahead of time, inevitably a call or missive came with a question or clarification or something out of left field to be addressed. But aside from those things, O'Brien well understood that it was important to have vision. You must know exactly what you want to accomplish when governing. And it had been clear from the beginning the two things concerning Port Royal and Jamaica, generally, that were paramount in the minds of William and Mary: protection and wealth.

Neither of these things were strangers to the city, but both were tricky. The protection part might look simple enough—ever increasing numbers of soldiers were arriving as construction continued on the forts. But protection had grown more complex and shadowy since the various players in the Caribbean had quit warring. No longer were the enemies simply the Dutch, Spanish, or French. No longer were privateers the simple friends of the Crown. Now the line between friend and foe had grown blurry, and very often people switched back and forth according to situation.

This problem fed into the problem of wealth. The one-time privateers now turned pirates still brought the greatest riches into the city. But also powerful were the planters whose sugarcane was exported along with the cotton and tobacco also grown throughout the island. Not a few planters had, like Morgan, once been pirates, and some were not above taking off on a romp again. But many were also part of a long-established plantocracy, and they populated the House of Assembly, which was a complete mess. These men had owned land for a very long time and in their long-established power were convinced they knew far more than the Governor and certainly more than the Crown. They resented any form of tax, and whenever word of a new law came from London they exploded. How dare people in England presume to understand what happened here on this island! And the nerve of the Crown grabbing money!

To make matters even more complicated, these plantation owners hardly spoke with one voice but were always fighting with each other, usually over the smallest and most ridiculous things. They studied each bill intently, ready to fly off at the least perceived slight. Very often they would become mired in endless debate over the wording of even the most insignificant proposals.

Furthermore, these Assembly members often had fraught relations with pirates, forming and breaking alliances with head-spinning speed. They shared with the pirate population a frantic desire for greater and greater wealth and could be just as ruthless in obtaining it.

Into this mix came the more and more vocal respectable citizens of Port Royal, who appreciated wealth also but who did not care for the messy ways to gain it. These people were far more pious as a rule, and they brought with them from England certain ideas about society and behavior that did not easily fit into this wild, harsh setting.

And now here came this Spaniard, who, if he was to be believed, stood near the top of the chain of command. Indeed, if O'Brien understood correctly, this Don Diego may even have been *the* de facto authority here, since he was clearly the mobile figure who negotiated the bidding of Spain, which effectively positioned him even over the Viceroyal. It was obvious that the Special Counsel was concerned about the fact that two ships were engaging in the same tactics because that suggested to him that they were working together. He did not care to have a banding-together of pirates in the manner Morgan had done in the not so distant past. Especially when one of the captains was so peculiarly remarkable.

O'Brien tried again to get his head around what Don Diego had said about that personage—the captain of the *San Miguel*. He found it hard to believe such a person existed.

But such a person did, and now O'Brien had been enlisted in thwarting that person. O'Brien would need information. Don Diego obviously had an informant, probably a network of them, and that put O'Brien at a disadvantage. He was still very new here and did not truly know whom he could trust. It took time to get the feel of a place. Here again he was forced to react. He would have to move quickly to get that feel for this island and especially its rough and tumble city.

And was he really prepared to help a Spaniard? From all he could tell, this Don Diego had succeeded in anticipating each attack that had been made on the villages along the coast of the mainland. He would not say how he had done so, and O'Brien speculated again that his network of informants must be enormous. But if it were so effective, then why had Don Diego come to him for aid? It felt like a trap of some kind.

Perhaps Spain was trying to lure England into attacking. It seemed inconceivable since the Spanish fighting forces in the West Indies had been reduced so dramatically. But it may be that Spain was building her forces without his knowledge. The Spanish ship attacking the Spanish Main was especially suspicious—was this information even true?

More importantly, a poorer Spain meant a richer Jamaica. He well knew that the island's government could not be understood to condone any acts of piracy, but if that island were to grow wealthier and Spain were to be damaged, English interests would be served. The trick then was to allow the pirates to take treasure but show that the government hated piracy. One way would be to punish the pirates, taking their gain in the process. But that carried many risks, for a war with pirates would be dangerous indeed. And, in his heart, he could not bring himself to dislike or even disagree with them since they had learned a certain set of skills by serving the Crown, only to have the crown no longer sanction those skills. What were they to do? Warriors without a war. His own situation was not that different.

Well, again, he would need more information. And for that he would need contacts. That must be his next move. He would summon his military leaders, especially the ones who had been here for a long time. They were likely to know their way around the pirate networks.

He stood abruptly, and without saying a word to his wife, exited the room.

IX

O pen up," Abigail said, advancing the fork with a piece of pork stuck on the end. "Come on," she coaxed, smiling.

Nick smiled too but kept his lips shut tight. Abigail waved the fork around in circles. Then she put her other hand toward his mouth and tried to pry his lips apart with her fingers. He exploded with laughter and she laughed with him. He took her wrists in his hands.

"Come on," she laughed, but he made no response as he tried to keep his mouth closed while he laughed, which seemed the most difficult thing in the world. She pulled her hands behind her back and pressed her body toward his, and he felt himself wanting the contact and knowing she wanted it too.

Then pain ripped through his stomach and shoulder.

"Ah," he winced. A week had passed since he had finally recovered his consciousness, and he felt fine most of the time when just lying in bed. He had discovered certain ways he could turn that helped him. But movement usually brought that awful pain.

Her smile collapsed into a frown, "Oh no! I'm sorry, Nick."

She pulled back and stood by the bed, watching him with a worried expression. He hated that the pain had hit him because he was having a great time wrestling with her and did not want her to stop. He also did not want her to be shy about playing with him.

"It's ok. I'm just not quite well yet. But I'm better."

She made a noise and looked away, clearly blaming herself for bringing him pain. "I'm very sorry."

"Please, it's ok," he smiled. She searched his eyes and, convinced he was telling the truth, smiled back. "You really should eat. It will help you heal."

"Ok," he said, his voice docile.

She offered the pork, and this time he ate it. As he chewed, she sat back down in the chair she had pulled up beside the bed to feed him. She had set the plate on the floor, and she lifted it back to her lap.

"Um," he said as he chewed. "You were telling me about . . . the . . plantation."

"Yes," she shrugged. It did not seem to interest her much, but he had been fascinated with it. The idea of a great deal of land and people working it appealed to him. It seemed both the same and different from the manor of Lord Furth where he had spent many days as a child. Lord Furth had been his real father, but it had ended badly, and part of Nick hated the manor, with its big house.

But part of him also had always wanted it, as if somehow the blood of the aristocrats that ran in his veins called out for a proper estate. He well knew the importance of being atop the food chain, and he remembered returning to England with more money than he ever could have imagined. It had opened doors for him there. But he had not been there long enough to see just how far his new money could go.

Here, however, there was land for the taking on the island. Men of any station could start anew here. The big house could be theirs, with servants, and a . . .wife.

The image of Sarah's face came into his mind again. It seemed far away, and he felt guilty for playing around with this young woman here on the other side of the world. He could not bear to betray Sarah. But Abigail was so very sweet, a gentle soul who seemed to want nothing more than for him to be healthy and whole again. His feeling for her was different than what he had felt for Sarah. It was softer, somehow, and strangely on the line between that of a brother and that of a . . .

He looked at her eyes as she asked, "What else do you want to know?"

Those eyes—they were so green, earnest, innocent.

"Well," he thought about it. "How big did you say it was again?"

Again she shrugged, "I heard Mr. Dunne say seven hundred acres. Not all that terribly big, really. It's all mashed up against the side of the mountain, stretched out in front of the beach."

He envisioned the fields of sugarcane standing tall and green and the waves rolling in beyond them.

"Do the curtains blow from the seabreezes?"

She looked at him, her green eyes searching, "It's queer thoughts you have, Nicky."

Now Nick shrugged, "Better give me another bite."

As she stabbed more pork onto the fork he went on, "I would like to see that place sometime. You say he just called up a woman and Hannah sent her along? The most beautiful one here?"

Immediately the air in the room changed, but he could not tell how or why. Sarah lifted the fork to his mouth again

62

but made no effort to make eye contact when he took the bite. Instead she looked back down and stabbed another piece of meat fiercely.

Heat filled him with the sense that he had said or done something wrong, but he did not know what. It occurred to him that maybe Abigail wished *she* had been called to marry the rich man, and the thought gave him a funny feeling. He was not sure what it meant.

He wanted desperately to get her talking again, to recapture that good feeling and time they were having only a few minutes ago. But he had no idea what to say, and something told him that if he asked her what was wrong he would regret that even more. Silence loomed so strong it seemed it would burst the room.

A knock came at the door.

The door opened and in walked Captain Stockett with Leesh following.

"We need to have a word with this man in private, Miss," the Captain said. His tone was harsh, but not intentionally so. He had spent so many years in the company of rough men he had forgotten how to modulate around women. He simply did not talk to them except when he absolutely had to.

"Yes, sir," Abigail responded, setting the plate on the small table beside Nick's bed and standing up. As he watched her walk out of the room, Nick hated that he could not deal with whatever the problem was right now.

When she closed the door, the Captain sat down in the chair she had occupied, and Leesh sat on the edge of the bed.

"I hear you are healing," the Captain said.

"Aye, sir."

"Very good. Leesh, you're quite sure we can speak here?"

"Aye, Captain," Leesh said, his smile as brilliant as ever in the afternoon light that poured through the window. "I've checked this house through and through, and there is no place one can listen in on this room."

The Captain nodded, then looked to Nick, "Leesh has told you the situation."

"Aye, sir."

"It's a bad business, lad. A bad business."

"Still no idea who told the Spaniards we were coming?"

The Captain shook his head, "No. It may not be that anyone is actually talking to them. All the men have been running about with all these whores. They could have talked without even knowing. Maybe when they were drunk.

"It makes no sense that one of our own crew should talk. Never did make sense. We were so very careful after that first time. But it is all so strange, of course. With the strange little drama they had planned for us. And that Spaniard with the sword who challenged you."

It was quiet for a moment.

"But there is something at last."

Nick waited for the Captain to explain.

"We've heard there's a schooner sailing about called the *San Miguel*. It seems they have been in the same business we have. Attacking these smaller villages along coast of the Main."

Nick watched the Captain, "Have they met with the same reception?"

"Aye. The very same. Although it seems the very swordsman you fought fared not so well later. It seems he had his nose cut off."

Nick flinched, his chin drawing in at that news, "Really?"

64

The Captain nodded, and suddenly a smile played across his lips, "An interesting story, actually. I'm not sure I believe it, but we shall see soon."

"Why do you say that?"

"We have reason to believe the *San Miguel* will come to Port Royal."

"*San Miguel*," Nick thought about the name. "A Spanish ship?"

"Aye, a Spanish name. That's a new one for us. We're not sure what to make of it all."

New questions flowed into Nick's mind, but he had one he had wanted to ask for awhile, "Captain, that list of villages we got from that Spaniard. Has it . . . ?"

The Captain regarded him, "Has it what, son?"

"I'm sure you've thought about it already."

"What?"

"Maybe the Spanish planted that list for us just to draw us to those places."

The Captain smiled, "Aye, lad. That is indeed a possibility we considered. And it could be true. Maybe it *is* true. But there are things about it that don't make much sense. If the Spaniards did plant it, why not just give us one place with a big juicy reward and then send a fleet of ships to intercept and destroy us? Instead they give us a list and then train everyone in the town to greet us in that bizarre way. And then they knew about you and your skills with the rapier. Passing strange."

The Captain looked down in thought. Leesh watched him a moment and then spoke, "Aye, strange indeed. But as the Captain was saying, Nick, we expect maybe to have some answers soon. This *San Miguel*, well . . ."

Leesh's smile grew broader than usual, and his eyes took on a sparkle and gleam full of mischief. Nick knew the look—

it meant that the little man had some knowledge that was sure to surprise but that he was withholding.

"Well?" Nick asked finally.

"Well, we'll say it this way, lad. When that ship rolls in, *she* is liable to tell all the meaning of the cursed world or hand us a gowpenful of nothing."

Nick sensed a riddle in Leesh's words, that they meant far more, but he could not figure out what. He knew well enough that a surprise of some kind was on its way.

"Aye," the Captain said, softly, still looking at the floor.

"You must be up soon, lad," Leesh went on. "Or has that bonny lass taken the wind from your sails?"

He laughed and Nick felt himself go red. The Captain looked up and smiled at him. Somehow his smile was so rough it looked worse on him than his harshest frown.

"You *do* need to make yourself whole, lad," the Captain said. "We must soon be at it again. Who knows how quickly things may move once that schooner arrives."

"Aye, aye, sir."

The Captain put his big heavy hand on Nick's shoulder, and Nick looked up to see the rough man's eyes looking at him with a strange mistiness. That look quickly faded, replaced by his typical glare.

"Come along, Stinky."

"Enjoy yourself, lad," Leesh said, laughing and following the Captain out.

When the door closed Nick lay back, trying to puzzle out what Leesh had said. That was too much to think about in the face of the strangely pleasant feeling he got out of Leesh and the Captain associating him with Abigail. But then that pleasant feeling fled before one of uncertainty at how quiet she had been when she left. He tried again to think what he had said wrong, remembering how nice a time they had been having scuffling and carrying on.

And then in the midst of all that came another feeling about Sarah in Bedlam. It was the usual guilt, but this time, for the first time, it had another feeling added to it. A feeling that she was chained to him and weighed him down.

He fought that feeling away.

X

Having always been a small man, Hector had never known what it was like to see people pull back agog with fear when he entered a room or walked down the street. He had always wanted to be one of those monstrous bear-like fellows whose great strength intimidated everyone so much that no one would think of speaking or raising a hand against him. Hector had spent many years eating as heartily as he could in hopes that if he could not grow taller then at least he could bulk up to the point that he would strike fear and inspire respect.

But it never worked. Somehow his metabolism was too high. He ate and ate and never grew any bigger. When he finally accepted that he would never find success that way, he began to develop a kind of mental projection of himself as someone of strength, authority, and terror. He was cold by nature, and it was not difficult to project that. He also worked in earnest to learn the arts of defense, and in his cold, surgical way became a deadly swordsman. He had never met someone better than himself until recently, but that was not because of his opponent's superiority. It was a misstep there, a break in concentration, a . . .

He put that out of his mind. He remained the best. Even the greatest at anything occasionally makes mistakes. This mistake he had paid for, but he had turned that to his advantage. For his brass nose had the very impact he had hoped for. It immediately transformed him into a strange, disturbing, horrifying creature. He saw it the moment he hit the streets with it affixed to his face the first time. People who would never have noticed him before suddenly could not take their eyes off his nose and him.

And he did what he could to encourage the terror of his new look, paying an entire troop of minions to whisper in the pubs and back alleys about the dreaded man with the brass nose. Not only did they tell of him, he encouraged them to spread many different rumors about how he came by that nose. He even instructed them to write on walls in the alleys and draw crude sketches of him with the "Beware the Man With the Brass Nose" written beneath in Spanish, English, French, and Dutch. Already his name was circulating among the Spanish throughout the Caribbean as Señor Nariz de Latón: Mr. Nose of Brass.

For many people it was if he had come from nowhere. They had no knowledge of him or memory of seeing him even when they had passed him on the streets of Port Royal hundreds of times. Now they could not help but notice him. For the people who did know who he was because of various business dealings, they did not know which rumor to believe: the true story of how he lost his nose circulated along with the false ones, but they were all so incredible it was difficult to know which one was really true.

He felt his power now as he wound through the tiny booths of the meat market that were hung with red, raw beef, tremendous cured hams as well as pink fresh pork, and chickens both plucked and feathered hanging on hooks while their still-living siblings made their shiftless nodding walks all over the city streets, crying out the final days of their lives in the early mornings.

The thick crowd parted as he made his way swiftly through them. Even the many people who did not actually see him but felt his presence instinctively drew out of his path as he made his silent way. Finally, he stopped at a booth where a huge and powerful man was working. The man's blonde hair contrasted strangely the parchment color of his skin and features that betrayed his mixed heritage. His father had been an African slave and his mother a Dutch prostitute.

This man handled a side of beef with massive, powerful hands. Hector watched him maneuver the meat, whet his knife, and carve. Hector had wanted to be like this man, but now he realized he had found a way to even greater power. The fact was that this man would lose his physical strength as he aged, while Hector—if he made the right moves— would grow more and more powerful. It took age and experience to learn this reality, and Hector, who was only just thirty, was glad he had learned about it early enough to use it to his advantage.

After carving and wrapping the meat, the man handed it to the customer. When he held out his hand to take the payment, his eye caught Hector standing there. The man's blue eyes seemed to go white, and Hector felt a tremor of thrill at seeing his fear.

When the customer walked away Hector drew closer.

"Señor Matheeus," Hector said in an understated way, as if nothing in the world were wrong. He noticed the man twitch, and he felt his own power surge.

"Aye," Matheeus replied.

Hector waited.

"Come around," Matheeus said finally.

Hector stepped around the edge of the booth and came inside as another customer stopped to ask for a cut of beef.

"Cordelia is not well," Matheeus said, referring to his woman, who normally helped him. "I must tend to the customer."

"Yes, of course," Hector said in a tone that an observer might have thought friendly.

He watched Matheeus work, again seeing the ripples of the man's powerful muscles. Truth be told, there was part of Hector who was in a way in love with such muscles. It was the closest thing to the kind of love and excitement other men seemed to feel toward women and their bodies. Such things had no impact on Matheeus. He felt no real attraction to either men or women. The only things that truly excited him were money, control, and planning ways to gain both and seeing those plans come to fruition. But when he did respond to other humans it was to men with these powerful bodies.

When Matheeus finished with that customer and another who came right behind, he turned to Hector again. He could not keep himself from looking at Hector's nose, but Hector pretended that there was nothing unusual about his appearance now.

Hector could see in Matheeus's eyes that while tending to the customers a thought had occurred to him. The fear was still there, but Hector sensed a plan.

"You—" Matheeus started, and then fear filled his eyes again. He continued on anyway, "You want meat. I can . . . . for free you can have the very best cuts."

Hector looked at him as if he had said nothing. He did not make his eyes look colder than usual, did not alter his expression at all. He simply stood there, waiting. He had no time to play games. There was much more that needed to be done.

Matheeus's courage drained quickly. He hung his head.

"I do not have the money," he said so quietly Hector almost could not hear him.

"The month is nearly passed," Hector said, his tone neutral.

"I know," Matheeus said, and looked up. "Cordelia . . . a woman . . . money goes. They . . . need . . . . they need things . . . . women."

Matheeus's eyes searched Hector's as he tried to come up with something that Hector might understand and that might break him. He continued, "Children . . they need . . . . it is very hard . . . ."

None of these things mattered to Hector. This was simply business. He needed his payment on his loan. That was all. He had not filled his own life up with dependents who drained money away, and he had no sympathy for anyone who had.

"You do have money, señor," Hector said quietly.

Comprehension lit Matheeus's eyes, "You mean . . . what I have from this morning?"

Hector's silent response showed what a stupid question it was.

Another customer appeared, and Matheeus turned slowly to take the order. He cut the meat mechanically. His inventory for the day was dwindling.

Hector waited patiently. He had other places to be, other things to do, including an appointment later this afternoon. But he did not mean to show any sign of humanity to this lowly butcher. For he was the man with the brass nose. He was not even completely human but part metal.

Hector watched Matheeus take his payment and put it in a leather pouch behind the counter, which he took up as he turned to Hector.

"How much do I owe?" he asked, the meekness of his voice almost incredible compared to his mountainous physicality.

Hector knew exactly how much he was owed, but he also felt his leverage. Matheeus should not have asked that question that way.

"How much do you have there?"

Perhaps Matheeus realized his mistake, but he did not show it as he poured the money out. As was typical here in the West Indies, the coins were of various nations: guilders, pieces of eight, sovereigns. Hector had a gift for glancing at such a pile and instantly recognizing its value. He knew it was far more than Matheeus actually owed him this month. But he needed to teach this man a lesson, to show him that he must stay in line.

"This doesn't quite cover it, but it will do for now," he said, scraping the money into his leather pouch.

Matheeus's eyes clouded, "This is my living."

"And you won't have it if you cannot pay your loan."

"You—"

Hector cut the next word off with a swift movement that pinned Matheeus's free hand to his side as Hector laid the sharp side of a dagger against his stomach. The move was swift and put Hector behind the bigger man so that passersby would not have noticed him or that anything was wrong.

"I'll open you up," Hector said quietly. "And be gone out of here before anyone knows. Think of Cordelia, señor. Of your children."

The wonderful thing about this new brass nose was that it did not impede his ability to smell, and he had a fine

73

olfactory sense that could actually smell fear. He caught the whiff of it now.

"Don't be late again," he said in succinct, separate syllables. Twisting around behind Matheeus he snatched the pouch from his hand as he allowed the blade to cut through Matheeus's shirt and into the skin, just enough to draw blood. Then he swept out of the booth into the crowd and back out onto High Street.

Hector passed the old church, then a line of buildings, and then turned right heading southward toward the ocean. About half-way down the street, he entered a building and mounted dark stairs lit only by a small dirty window on each landing. He climbed to the third and top floor and there unlocked and passed through another door, which he closed behind him and locked back.

The room was as dark as the stairs had been, even after Hector lit two candles on the desk at the room's far end. A large window looked out over the city's cemetery, but Hector had put a shelf in front of it so that only a sliver of pale daylight made its way inside.

The desk, a hard wooden chair behind it, and a second chair in front of it comprised the room's furnishings. All of the walls save one were lined with shelves. The one unshelved was partitioned off by shelves to form a kind of bedroom where Hector kept a pallet on the floor. On the shelves sat stacks of wooden boxes and cases of varying sizes.

Hector took down three of the boxes and set them on the desk. Then he opened his leather pouch and poured the money from Matheeus out on the desktop, the metal clanging in hollow hardness on the wooden surface. He regarded the coins for a moment. Seeing them brought him a sense of satisfaction, joy even, that nothing else could do in exactly the same way. He loved power, but it was often something that moved invisibly. It needed ways to show itself. Money was one of those ways it could do so.

Also, whenever he encountered coins of any kind he had a way of thinking about where all they might have been. He had himself seen some of the mines that had produced these precious metals. He knew what they looked like in the raw and that certain kinds of lesser metals could fool people who searched for them. He understood the process of refining those metals and then casting them in bars and stamping them into coins. He imagined them passing from one hand to another in payment, then stored away until eventually passing from hand to hand again. It was awesome to think of how coins were so handled, with people of all different kinds taking possession of them. But only for a little while, and for so many different reasons. He thought about the people who had worked so hard to own this coin or that one. He also thought about how quickly that coin could leave them and never remember them. He wondered if anyone had killed or died for any of these coins. In this part of the world, such a scenario was highly likely. But then maybe it was in any part of the world.

After allowing himself these thoughts he shut them out and went to the equally satisfying work of separating the coins out according to their nationality. Once he had divided them into heaps he counted the coins in each heap, patiently and carefully creating stacks, feeling the coins' smooth hardness as he placed one on top of the other and evened the little tower of coins. When he finished the first group he opened a drawer and took out a ledger book, which he opened, turned to the appropriate page, wrote the amount at the end of a column of figures, and then added them up. Then he opened one of the wooden boxes, which was filled with dividers, and set each stack in a divider. Then he went to work on the next pile and then the next one.

When he finished he put the boxes back in their places. He had all the boxes placed deliberately according to his own intricate system. Someone unfamiliar with it would have been completely bewildered by the all the boxes, which was his design. Most were empty, some held counterfeits, and a few held real money, but there was no easily discernable pattern to know which was which so that a burglar would have faced big challenges to get away with a sure catch.

His mind was already working in other directions when a knock came at his door. He grasped one of the rapiers he kept hung on the edge of the shelf behind the desk and made his way to the door. He had fixed up a rude peep window with a wooden swingdoor, which he opened.

Outside stood one of the young boys he paid as an informer. He was thin and dirty, his hair dark and stringy.

Hector opened the door and let the boy in.

"¿Qué es, Juan?" he asked the boy.

"Por favor, Señor Nariz de Latón."

"Sí," he said and brought a coin out of another purse he carried. He dropped it in the boy's hand and again asked what he knew.

"Sí, señor. La *San Miguel*."

Hector showed no emotion, asking him in Spanish, "Where?"

"On her way. They say in two day's time."

XI

Don Diego watched the two iguanas eating the fresh green leaves he had brought for them. The reptiles' jaws snapped as they chewed, their green scales undulating over their muscles.

He was sitting in the open courtyard of his mansion, and he kept these two as his pets, visiting them each evening at dusk when he was home. This was his time to let go of all thought as he lay back on his low couch beneath the towering elephant ear plants and watched the lizards, focusing on the rhythm of their eating while the fountain in the center of the courtyard plashed. Four skinny-trunked date palms created a square around the fountain. Out of the fountain's basin rose a marble sculpture of a woman who looked straight up, her left arm extended to the sky, while water flowed out in swan necks around her feet.

The servants as well as his own personal guard of thirty all knew to leave him be during this time. Only attack justified their disturbing him in this hour and sometimes more that he lay here alone while the day made its transition. Every day the sky was just a little different, and Don Diego attended the nuances of those difference, peering at the play of light around the courtyard itself as the walls of his mansion towered over him, summitted by the heavy baroque cupolas and intricate designs of stone and marble that danced along the top.

When he first emerged this evening the sky had already retreated into a quiet, soft blue such as may be found in a quiet lagoon. A few coral colored clouds smeared across and a couple of birds had skittered in, circled away and back to each other, then darted out of view. The adobe walls themselves had already lost their daytime white heat, cooling now into a sleepy cream. Don Diego brought the lettuce out with him and laid it out for the iguanas. Then he lay back.

Discipline had taught him well how to clear his mind, and he had no trouble focusing on the sound of the fountain and the feeding of the iguanas. The trick was to focus on what happened all around him in this particular moment, as if he had no past and no future. His father, who had been a far more curious person than he, had spent time among the monks in the monastery of San Salvadore de Celanova, and they had taught him techniques of meditation. Don Diego had learned them, analyzed them, and then used them for his own purposes. He considered himself very religious, but monasteries held no interest for him, and he tended to view monks as being weak because, in his view, they could not cope with the real world and maintain their religious zeal. His father had always held monks in the highest esteem and at times claimed he wished he had been one, arguing that they were the strongest of mortals precisely because they shut themselves off from the world. Whatever his disagreements, Don Diego did believe in the power of such meditation and understood that achieving true focus required labor and concentration.

He allowed his eyes to rove around the plants and walls, noting how they took on a rich purple as the shadows deepened. Outside, the sun was setting in an orchestra of reds and oranges, which he could tell from the clouds as they turned to a fierce rose color. The moment would not last long, and he drank it in, knowing how delicious a thing it was. A thought invaded—he realized how quickly another day had passed he would never get back, that he was one day closer to death. The thought had begun to occur to him quite often now and had done so since he had entered his mid-forties. He was now fifty-two, although except for the graying at his temples no one would have believed it.

No such thought of rushing toward death was welcome now, and he stomped it out as he would a glowing cinder sparked out from a fire. He focused on the sound of the water and turned his eyes again to the iguanas, allowing his mind to latch onto the changing color of their scales here in the new shadows. Then he shut his eyes and listened only to the sound. And for a moment it was as if he went away altogether into another realm. Now he seemed to have something in his lap. What was it? He kept his eyes shut but focused more on what he saw in his mind. It was a sheaf of documents. They seem to have come from Madrid. Orders of some kind? No, that was not likely. What did they mean? What did it matter?

Keeping his eyes shut he allowed his mind to drift out of engagement, and now the water plashed along and his consciousness went away so that he existed between sleep and waking. His mind held nothing at all except the ability to hear the sound, and he stayed that way for he knew not how long.

At length he blinked his eyes open again, and now everything had paled to varying shades of the achingly soothing blue of the gloaming. The fronds of the plants all around now melded into shadows with no definable shapes, and the trunks of the palms seemed not so much to rise but to depend from the sky like the burnt-out tails of darkened falling stars. Looking to the sky itself, he saw a single glimmering star.

His mind now emptied and his pulse under control, Don Diego reentered the house, passing through a massive wooden door carved with the same baroque excess as the tops of the walls. Juan, his most trusted servant, stood waiting for him.

"Don Diego," he started, but Don Diego raised his hand to stop him and then beckoned him to follow. They passed down the dimly lit hall and to his main study, which was a massive room whose ceiling rose far above the lighting, vanishing into depths of darkness. The walls were papered with gold-burnished scarlet leather.

Don Diego poured himself a glass of wine and sat in the great leather chair behind his desk, motioning Juan to sit also. Once settled he nodded, "What is it?"

"Don Diego, a messenger has arrived."

That was not unusual. For a man of Don Diego's importance messengers were constantly coming and going. Information—whether gaining it or dispensing it—was the main currency of his position.

"Yes?"

"He informs of two things, Excellency. Both from a Señor Hector of Port Royal."

Don Diego showed no emotion as he listened.

"First, he says goods have been shuffled."

Juan looked at him quizzically, but Don Diego simply nodded, "Go on."

"Second, he says that the *San Miguel* is on its way to Port Royal."

"How did you receive this information? Was it written down? Is the messenger here?"

"It was not written, Excellency. And the messenger is staying here."

"Bring him here to me."

"As you wish."

Juan stood, bowed, and made his way out of the study. Don Diego pondered the information and thought again about the trap he was setting up. It was intricate, the work of a great deal of planning. It required finesse and that required timing. And timing required perfect knowledge. Rooms were kept ready in the buildings of the estate for messengers who made their way to and from this island doing the bidding of Don Diego and for Spain herself. Indeed, the entire island was Don Diego's domain as Special Counselor. He would have expected a messenger from Hector to want to speak to Don Diego alone, however. The message was sufficiently vague, so there was no need to think that any sensitive information could be derived from it (he thought of Juan's bewildered look). But Don Diego would like to talk to this man.

He grew impatient waiting. Perhaps the messenger was sleeping after a brisk sail from Port Royal. But surely he had simply caught a ride on a vessel bringing goods and had likely not done any of the actually work of sailing. Hector typically sent mere waifs who lived on the streets of Port Royal. Don Diego shuddered to think of a creature from such a filthy place staying anywhere in his vicinity.

He was about to call for someone when a knock came and Juan entered alone.

"Well?" Don Diego asked.

Juan's face was composed but troubled.

"Excellency, the messenger is not in his room."

"Did you look for him?"

"Yes."

Don Diego waited, his eyes narrowed, "What do you mean?"

"He seems to have vanished into thin air."

XII

A lthough he still dealt with pain, Nick was quickly healing. The first efforts to get out of bed were difficult, as were his first steps. But he was ready to be moving again, and being young and strong helped him.

Also, his mind was lighter than it had been in a long time. The dull ache of his bad memories remained in the shadows of his brain. But more and more he thought only of the present moment, and the past seemed to recede.

Now he sat on the beach, watching Abigail as she stood in the waves. The ride in the carriage out here had been rough, but it was worth it, for the sun was low, casting the beach entirely in purple shadow. The ocean itself displayed shifting hues of copper, green, and blue, all highlighted by the white foam of the waves that turned to cool blue as they reached the shadows of the beach. Fronds of palm trees clattered and mixed in the breeze that thankfully blew the unseeable bugs about enough to keep them from biting too much. The breeze could not quite conquer the heat, but Nick did not mind.

He watched Abigail as she waded, her long skirts held up, her pale legs blue-exposed. Her hair fell in fabulous loose curls, and when she stepped into the sunlight it shone in burnished brilliance. Her figure was sensibly balanced, substantial in a way that matched her personality, with curves that would stand for decades.

She is so sweet, Nick thought and allowed his mind to roam over the past weeks. He never tired of her presence. She was always laughing, smiling, playing. They never ran out of things to talk about. And she had that sweetness, a kind of innocence that seemed untouchable. It was easy to forget the hint about her that her life had not been completely one to preserve innocence. But she kept that innocence somehow. She would throw her head back and laugh, her sharp green eyes dancing. And when she did, it was as if they were the only two people in the world. He would go to any length to get her to laugh that way, and just thinking about it now made him smile.

She made her way out of the water toward him, still holding up her skirts. When she reached him he looked at her feet now covered with sand. They were the very strong feet of a very solid woman. Seeing them produced a strange set of feelings in him—before he could stop himself, he thought of Sarah's feet, which were so delicate. And indeed Sarah had always had a delicate, fine kind of beauty. She had an innocence too, but it had something else mixed with it that lifted her to a higher level somehow. There was something about Abigail that was . . . . he did not know exactly how to explain it. It was as if she were maybe just a little too sweet, a little too loyal and predictable. She was very pretty, but her personality lacked some indefinable thing that would have made her truly intriguing.

"Do you want to come into the water?" she asked him.

Part of him did. But that part of him wanted . . . if he were being truthful, that part of him wanted to go into the water and play, not with Abigail but Sarah. An image of them frolicking in these tropical waters flashed across his mind.

But she's gone mad. Sarah's mad. Gone. And this girl is here. And I am here. And it is very beautiful. She is so pretty. And sweet. And . . .

He needed to let Sarah go. Had not the Bedlam doctor said she would never recover? It was time to move on. He could sense that Abigail's emotions were running high for him.

He looked at her. Her eyes were soft, the pupils larger here in the shadows, although they were never very large.

The thing for you to do is live your life. She would want that.

That is what the doctor had told him. Had he been correct? He dealt with the mad all the time. Perhaps he knew best.

And Nick was so far from England, and it was so very beautiful here. Is this not what so many on that cold island dreamed of? To be here in the tropics, the sun setting, and here a pretty girl with him? How many people would have loved to be in his place now? Surely Harry would . . . .

His mind snapped into a decision, pushing away further debate.

"Yes," he said.

She smiled and stood up, holding out her hand to help him up. When he took her hand he felt her strength, and again a hesitance arose in him. Something told him this was not the right girl for him. Suddenly he remembered his own hesitance with Sarah. She had wanted to marry him when his family had to move to Bristol, but he had hesitated then. Why had he done so? Not because he did not love her. That had nothing to do with it. He knew she *was* the right girl for him. The hesitancy *then* had to do with his family and the kind of life he wanted to build. He felt a shame in not being able to take care of her and had been determined to make a fortune with which both to claim and support her.

85

But he had shown hesitancy then as he did now. What did that mean?

Again he fought those thoughts away.

Live in this moment.

Standing now, he did not let go of Abigail's hand. He could sense a surge of pleasure and excitement in her. He felt like running and diving into the water, but he knew he was not well enough for that, so he started walking, still holding her hand. Part of him felt guilty knowing this was not really the hand he wanted to be holding. But he had been given this moment from God himself. It was a just reward for the many hardships he had been through. And maybe God meant this girl to be his. Maybe . . .

The water washed warm on his feet, and the beach seemed to melt beneath him as a wave rolled in and then slid away, a swath of velvety wet sand receding from it. Sandpipers darted along where the wave had been, their tiny legs dancing in flurries the eye could not follow, their beaks pecking. When the next wave rolled in they scurried away just beyond its reach and then went back to work as it too retreated.

An impulse seized Nick. Bending over, ignoring the pain of the motion, he reached down with his free hand and splashed water up over Abigail. She squealed and laughed, and he did it again, releasing her hand and using both his hands to splash water over her. She braced her shoulders and shut her eyes, laughing. He did it again, watching her dress plaster to her body, its curves suddenly revealed in luscious fullness.

He stopped, laughing. Before he realized it she had come close to him, and he could feel her body against his. He folded her to him. Her eyes were still closed, but her face lifted, her

86

lips parted. It struck him how completely she gave herself up to this moment.

He pressed his lips to hers.

It was dark when he and Abigail reached the Falstaff tavern. Nick felt better than he had in a long time. He still dealt with physical pain, but hope flowed through his body and mind, and he felt a comfort that now he had someone in his life who would stay there and who would make him happy.

He helped her down from the carriage, feeling her strong hand as it took his. It was not exactly the kind of delicate hand he liked, but he could get used to it. He knew it was the hand of someone who loved him.

Port Royal was not a city to sleep, in fact it lived much more in the night than it did in the daylight. The noise of taverns all along the street sounded in the hot air, and the Falstaff contributed its own raucous clatter.

Nick looked into Abigail's eyes, which the light from within just caught, exposing their brilliant green dimly. The warmth of his closeness to her filled him and, feeling their intimate agreement, he led her inside.

Laughter erupted as they entered, and Nick noticed everyone gathered around, evidently with someone in the center. He and Abigail slipped along the edge of the crowd that did not notice them. She stopped before passing through the door that led upstairs, turning and smiling at him. He smiled back and squeezed her hand. She turned and headed up the steps.

He watched her disappear and then turned back within. The hot night, the excitement of being with her, all made him thirsty for fresh water. He took a tankard from the shelves behind the bar and walked over to the barrel of fresh water, scooping it up and tasting its metallic tang as he took large gulps. He emptied it quickly and then dipped it again.

"Aye, lad, it's thirsty business with a lady."

It was Leesh's voice, and Nick felt himself redden as he turned to look at the older man.

"We have some visitors, my boy," he continued, his smile fixed and gleaming. "Come along."

Nick followed him, sensing the high spirits of the room. He was not sure if people really *were* feeling better—which was quite a change from the way things had been lately—or if his own happiness just made it feel so.

Another eruption of laughter told him it was everyone else in the room as well as himself. He and Leesh shouldered their way forward. Finally he was able to see who everyone was gathered around.

There stood a short man with a very red face. His legs bowed and his little round stomach protruded in his white shirt, wrapped in a red sash. The shirt itself was undone far down his hairy chest. His nose was bulbous, the nostrils curved over, his eyes squinty. He wore a cap common among seaman; indeed it resembled the one Leesh wore.

He was talking with an accent that Nick recognized as Mediterranean, probably Italian. And Nick could tell he was acting out a scenario.

"He was standing there," the man said. "This man, this Spaniard. He was a little man."

"You're a little man!" someone yelled and everyone laughed.

"Sì, sì, certo," the little man nodded. "But there he stood like so, eh?"

The man stood straight now as though he held a sword. And then he raised his arm in a way Nick recognized as the manner the Spaniard had done he had fought. Seeing him do so triggered Nick in his stomach, bringing back the image of that man and the feeling of not knowing how to fight and the bitter defeat he suffered.

He looked away as the man started to step in that circular way now emblazoned in Nick's memory. As he did, his eye alighted on someone he had not noticed at first.

On a bench facing away from him sat someone whose appearance momentarily confused him. The person had long black hair that fell in loose waves that shined in dim ribbons. It was common for men to wear their hair long, but this hair was different, full of spring and brilliance, and Nick realized this was no man as he followed the lines of the black coat that clung tightly to the person's body. This was the narrow torso of a woman, and he could tell the coat had been skillfully tailored to accentuate her exquisite shape, as he was able to catch the bulge of breasts along the lines of her back the tapering downward to a tiny waste which then spread into perfectly proportioned hips. His eyes grazed back upward to the woman's shoulders, which she held straight, in a commanding posture. She wore a tall black hat, lined with white lace and decorated with a massive plume.

He felt himself wanting desperately to see her face, and before he realized it, he was angling his way among the gathered men to try and get a view. He paid no attention to the story the man told nor to their laughter. Just as he positioned himself to get a glimpse of her profile, however, she turned her head away to a man who sat beside her. Nick looked at him and instantly felt a strange sensation that he

89

wished *he* were the man she was talking to. Something about the way they sat so close and the angle of her head as she turned it made it seem the most wonderful thing in the world to be in her confidence. From Nick's angle he could tell she tucked her chin inward against a lifted shoulder.

Nick looked at the man she spoke to, unable to make out much about him except that he was evidently very tall and extremely thin. Nick could see his long shins in the woolen stockings and his feet clad in shining shoes and brass buckles gleaming in the lamplight.

Nick waited for her to turn her head back, but she still looked away, listening to whatever the man was saying. Nick could feel impatience burning in him. He could also feel himself being watched, and turning he saw Leesh standing beside him, looking up and smiling, his eyes twinkling. Again Nick felt himself caught, and he felt guilty trying to peer at this woman when he had just enjoyed such a wonderful time with Abigail. What was he doing?

He turned his attention back to the Italian who continued to act out the scenario.

"Eh! And then the Spaniard stepped this way, so. And then the Lady Evernia stepped so, and then," the man swung his arm in a slashing motion. "Off came the nose!"

All the men roared and clapped and shouted "bravo!" Someone called for drinks and then the men all broke and migrated toward the bar. Nick did not know many of these men, but he did recognize his own crew among them, and then he saw Edward Corbyn stop in front of the woman and the tall man. Nick could not will himself to move, waiting with a strange anxiousness for her finally to turn her head. It was as if she knew he watched her and refused to let him see her face.

"Lady Evernia," Edward said, and Nick looked at his eyes and saw them filled with a mix of awe and helpless wonder. "Can I get you a drink?"

Finally she turned her face, but her abundant hair still hid all but the tip of a delicate nose.

"No, thank you," she said in a voice that struck Nick as being almost that of a child's. "I don't drink."

"I could get you water," Edward said, his voice as strange as the look in his eyes, as if he wanted more than anything to be granted the opportunity to do something for her.

She delayed a moment. Nick watched her, then looked back to Edward.

"That would be well, thank you," she said at last.

Edward bowed slightly, a move Nick had never seen him make, and then he hurried toward the bar to get a tankard of water for her.

Nick realized he stood there alone, staring. That would not do. He felt he must see her face, but standing here this way would just embarrass him. He forced himself to turn and walk back behind her and the man sitting with her. He sat down on a bench and took a gulp of water, watching the men milling about and feeling awkward and unsure what to do. Everything in him wanted to turn back and look at the woman, but he made himself not do so. Some of the men made their way back now and nodded at him.

Edward did not see Nick as he walked by with the tankard of water, which he took to the woman. Nick felt it was all right to watch him do so and turned back. He watched her take the tankard and sip from it, her head inclining backward gently. Then she handed it back to Edward, stood up, and turned around facing Nick.

It was impossible to tell the age of that face, framed in the raven locks. It could have been that of someone Nick's

91

age, yet it had a certain knowing quality about it, as of someone much older. It was beautiful, the skin perfect, the cheekbones high, the nose delicate, the chin small, the lips curved into a voluptuous bow. Her eyes were large and blue, shadowed by long curving lashes. Her thin neck plunged long into the fragile meeting of collarbones and the skin there curved outward from a cleft deeply displayed by her open blouse. There against her pale skin lay a gold cross on a gold chain.

"Well, gentleman, I'm—" here she yawned, lifting her hand to her mouth in a way that might have been that of a little girl. Nick looked at her small arms and then allowed his eyes to graze down her body to her hips and thin legs in tight britches. Her tiny feet were clad in boots that slouched in large flaps and looked to be made of the finest leather.

"Whoo," she said, finishing her yawn. "Goodness. I'm very tired. I bid you all good night."

The men erupted in their own statements of good night as she walked right by Nick without noticing him. Nick saw that the man beside her stood when she did and that he was very tall indeed, with a long face that wore a foolish grin. He followed her closely as she walked out, stepping awkwardly in front of her to open the door for her to pass through and then hurrying in a fussy way to keep up with her.

"A fine wench indeed!" George Larson, one of the *Tetrarch*'s crew, yelled and all assented with a loud roar while Nick stood watching as the door closed behind her.

XIII

Captain Stockett, Excellency," the footman announced and stood aside for the man to enter.

O'Brien watched the Captain walk in. He was a burly man with wiry, white hair O'Brien guessed had been red at one point. In fact, there was something familiar in the man's eyes, which looked out with a frank and almost soft expression at odds with the hard features and deeply-etched lines of his face. He was physically powerful, it was obvious, his neck thick, his hands large, his body barrel-shaped. The man had more of a loyalist whiff about him—more of a fidelity to privateering in the service of the state than to pirating in the service of himself. His clothes were humble, old even, the edges of his coat frayed here and there, where most pirate captains would have dressed in finery for such a meeting. The man had surely come by his share of treasure but had not spent it on clothes. What *did* he spend it on?

And why did he look familiar? O'Brien reached back into his memory, trying to think through all the thousands of soldiers he had known and commanded. Had this man been one of them? He could not quite place him, but he felt he had met him before.

He rose, "Good afternoon, Captain."

"Good afternoon, sir," Captain Stockett replied, inclining his head with proper decorum.

"Please be seated."

"Thank you," the Captain said and eased himself down in the seat on the other side of the desk with labored breath. It occurred to O'Brien that this man may not have been altogether well.

"Would you like a drink, sir?"

"Thank you, sir."

O'Brien ordered the footman to provide refreshment and a glass of sherry soon appeared. The Captain took it in his big hand as though it were an egg in the paw of a bear.

O'Brien was not sure how best to start as he watched the Captain. He thought of how wary this man must be.

"Are you quite well, Captain?" he asked finally.

"Yes, sir. Middlin."

"Very good."

An awkward beat of silence. O'Brien continued to think, to link that face with a memory, but he was not succeeding.

"Well, sir," O'Brien began. "I want to thank you for agreeing to meet with me."

The Captain watched him, still holding the glass. His eyes betrayed no thought or impression.

"I want to discuss something with you. It has been brought to our attention that your ship, the *Tetrarch*, has been attacking certain locations along the coast of the Spanish Main. These attacks have been reported to have . . . piratical intentions."

The Captain made no reply or even response, as though he had merely heard an unremarkable weather report.

"You are, I am sure, well aware of the Crown's current relationship with Spain. And I am sure you also are aware of our own view of pirate activity."

Again the Captain made no response.

"I will not ask you," O'Brien continued, "whether these reports are true. But I must warn you that as the tides now have turned, such attacks, if they are found to be true, would be punishable even to the point of hanging. The Crown does not wish to reinitiate hostilities with Spain, nor do we wish to sew discord and unrest in our area. You are . . . aware of that?"

Still the Captain remained silent and still.

"Very well," O'Brien went on, unsurprised at the Captain's response. The man was, after all, the leader of pirates. He *should* know when to respond and when not to. "I would make you aware of the likely not surprising news that Spain itself has brought these claims to bear. But what is most distressing to that entity is that reports claim that the *Tetrarch* has confederated itself with another vessel, one *San Miguel*."

Again no response.

"We and Spain have both found such an alliance . . . unusual. We wonder if it is true or simply hearsay. We understand that the ship is captained by a . . . woman. A woman of unusual birth and affiliation. Because of this, the situation stands to have an impact larger than simple isolated criminal activity. Indeed, its political ramifications could be far reaching, which means that we might well be forced to take drastic action to prevent further mischief."

O'Brien paused not for a response but simply to catch his own breath.

"This *San Miguel* we know now to be in our own harbor and that its captain has already been found to be consorting with your own crew and perhaps even yourself."

He paused this time to gauge any reaction but again saw none.

"As yet, we have no proof of anything, but the situation being as it is we will monitor the situation. I give you fair warning because you are a subject of the Crown. Do not think that, if you are indeed in league with this other crew, we can protect you or that we will make allowance for you as a result. It is our hope that neither you nor any other Englishman will ally with such disruptors of the peace. We hope that the rumors are not true. But if they are, be warned."

Still the Captain sat still, rigid as a stone statue.

"Do you understand, man?" O'Brien asked.

Still no response.

"Very well. I hope your lack of response does not bode ill. You may leave."

The Captain stood up slowly and set the glass down. O'Brien noticed he had not taken a sip. He was clever, distrustful. O'Brien wanted to break through that. As the Captain turned to go, O'Brien spoke up, "Captain Stockett."

The Captain stopped and turned back to him.

"Stockett . . . . did you ever in your life serve in the Crown's military?"

O'Brien thought he saw something. A flicker in the eyes, maybe just the slightest dilation of the pupils. Maybe not.

"You'll find no George Stockett in the rolls, sir."

"Thank you," O'Brien said. "You may go."

XIV

Hector stood in the crowd, back straight to make himself as tall as possible, his nose jutting in menacing aggression. He stood across the way from the Governor's Mansion because one of his informants had spied the captain of the *Tetrarch* going into the mansion, and Hector wanted to see what was happening for himself. He trusted himself better than anyone else.

It did not surprise him that the captain should go to the Governor. What Hector really wanted to know was whether the Governor had summoned the captain or the captain was going to the Governor.

He waited patiently. Patience was, in fact, one of his great strengths.

The crowd was bigger than usual, gathered for a carnival being held in the old churchyard. It included jugglers, sword swallowers, and other such performers.

Hector milled around, stopping to watch a man walking a tightwire. The man stood in a tight colorful outfit that showed off the powerful muscles in his legs so wonderfully that a number of ladies were giggling.

"Ladies and gentleman," he cried. "You have seen me walk across this wire with the greatest of ease! You have watched me walk both forward and backward! As you can see below, I have a cart. If I could have my assistants hand this cart up to me, does anyone believe I can roll this cart forward on this wire, balancing myself and the cart the entire time?"

The crowd spat a mix of cheers and jeers. The man bowed, the muscles of his thighs bulging.

"Let us see!" he said and the assistants handed the wooden cart up to him. He grasped both handles and positioned the cart on the wire. Its wheel was grooved to fit the wire. At first he seemed to struggle, but it became obvious that he was only playing with the audience and that he could perform this feat with ease.

"Ah! He's a blighter!" a man yelled, and Hector turned to look at him. The man was short and reeked of rum, a bottle of which he held. He wore a red cap and a broad smile that Hector could tell might normally be dazzling but that somehow seemed dimmed by the man's drunkenness as he stood there weaving.

Hector recognized him. He was a member of the *Tetrarch*'s crew, a known drunk. He had heard his informants refer to him by a nickname. What was it?

Ah yes, Stinky

"He's a whoreson jack-a-napes!" the little man yelled again and looked all around, his eyes bleary and unable to focus.

"And now everyone!" the tight-wire walker said after reaching the end, ignoring the man. "Does anyone doubt I can walk backwards with this cart?"

The crowd cheered, and the man bowed. Clearly he had won them over. But as the cheer died down, suddenly the little man beside Hector bellowed:

"You're a beetle-headed knavish fustilarian!"

"Ah, thank you sir!" the tight-wire walker called. "Very nobly said!"

The crowd laughed, looking back up to him. Hector peered back at the little man and saw him gazing up at the wire-walker, his grin broad, his eyes still unfocused as he stood there weaving. He tried to take another sip from his bottle of rum but missed his mouth.

Hmph, stupid sloppy Englishman.

Hector looked across at the Governor's Mansion. He hoped he had not missed the captain leaving. He would need to be more alert and not allow distractions.

"A pox on you!" the little man shouted, bringing hisses from the audience as the tight-wire walker made his way backwards easily, which produced applause and shouts from the audience.

"Ah, you shlou—" the little man seemed beyond reason in his drunkenness now, and Hector watched as people began to hiss and yell at him.

"Please, everyone! Please!" the tightwire walker called. "Save your jibes! I have one last feat to perform."

The crowd cheered, and Hector watched the little man weaving, his smile broad but steadily dimming more with drink.

As the cheering died down the tightwire walker went on, "You have seen me push this cart up and down the wire. Now, I ask you this? Is anyone willing to get in the cart and let me push you?"

The crowd broke out into laughter. It was a long way up that wire, and it was one thing to cheer the man and quite a different thing to take that risk themselves.

When no volunteers stepped forward the tightwire walker began to scan the crowd. Hector looked away, not wishing to be called out. He also took that moment to look to the Governor's Mansion again. He saw no sign of the captain.

"You, my friend!" the tightwire walker said, followed by laughter. "You have so much to say. Why don't you come up here with me?"

Hector turned and looked as the crowd drew back from the little man who stood, smiling and weaving, his eyes unfocused. The crowd was laughing.

"Come on up, man!" the tightwire walker called and the crowd laughed more.

Hector glanced back at the Mansion and then back at the man just as someone pushed him toward the ladder up to wire. The little man stumbled from the push and nearly fell to the ground. He used the bottle to keep him from going all the way down, and the crowd roared with laughter.

The little man stood up unsteadily and again the tightwire walker beckoned. The little man's smile widened slightly and he started weaving toward the ladder to more laughter.

"Sir," the little man said, stopping at the bottom of the ladder. "May I . . . bring my . . . bottle?"

The crowd laughed, and Hector noticed in it a mix of good nature and derision.

"If it will help you get up here!" the tightwire walker called below.

Again Hector looked to the Mansion and saw no movement of any kind in the hazy, hot sunlight.

The sound of more laughter brought his attention back to the little man as he struggled up the ladder, his foot missing a rung here, his hand slipping there. Somehow he had managed to get up about a third of the way. And here he stopped and took a drink, which brought more laughter.

In fact, it seemed now that the little man was unwittingly stealing the show, and Hector looked above as the tightwire walker skipped over to the top of the ladder and began

100

encouraging his volunteer. He did not want to be shut out of his own act.

Again Hector looked back at the Mansion. This was taking quite a long time. Perhaps the captain was waiting in line with others to talk to the governor. If not, then what did this span of time mean?

He looked back to the little man's slow ascent—he was now two-thirds of the way up, and the tight wire walker was descending to help him the rest of the way. Hector looked to the Mansion and then back as the little man finally made it to the top of the ladder where the tightwire walker helped him, bottle and all, into the cart that stood on the wooden platform at the end. Despite it taking so long, everyone watched, smiling. Once the little man was positioned, the tightwire walker made a sweeping gesture and began the walk across the wire.

There seemed nothing left to see of this performance, so Hector turned to reposition himself. Just as he did the crowd gasped, and Hector looked back in time to see that the little man was tilting out of the cart while the tightwire walker struggled to hold it steady. Hector could see the look of terror in the tightwire walker's face as the two figures and the cart teetered immobile for a moment.

Then the cart turned all the way and hurtled to the ground, the crowd scattering below as it crashed to pieces.

But no bodies fell with it, and again the crowd gasped. For there holding to the wire by one hand was not the tightwire walker but the little man! His left hand held to the wire while his right hand held to the neck of the bottle. The tightwire walker was holding tightly to the little man's right wrist, dangling from above. The crowd was breathless, and Hector himself watched, his heart lurched to a standstill.

Both men were swinging in the air, but now the little man snapped his body into a stronger swing and after a few swings back and forth lifted his arm, throwing the man upward to catch the wire, which he did. Then, still swinging, the little man swung *himself* up onto the wire, bottle still in hand, the other hand held out to catch his balance.

The tightwire walker dangled there watching, utterly astonished, as the little man took a sip from his bottle, perfectly balanced, and then took a step toward him, bent over as if he were standing on a plank ten feet wide, and held his hand out for the tightwire walker to grasp. The little man then helped the performer up, the wire pitching all around, which sent the tightwire walker struggling while the little man stood steady and took another draught of his rum.

Then, still holding the bottle, the little man stood on one foot, stretched his leg in a graceful pose, bent his leg back in, and hopped onto his other foot.

And now Hector and the rest of the audience realized that the drunkenness had been an act the entire time and that this little man was a tightwire walker as well. The crowd cheered triumphantly. Even the tightwire walker bowed to the little man and clapped.

Hector was so caught up in the drama himself he almost missed the motion at the Mansion, just catching the captain leaving. He hurried along to follow.

Hector's mind was divided—a strange sensation for him—as he followed the captain. Even as he tried to focus on the man he was following, his mind tried to make sense of what he had just seen.

What kind of man was this Stinky fellow? Clearly he was not one to be underestimated, and that was worrisome information to have. But Hector was glad he knew it. Now he would know to be on guard. He was grateful to have been in the right place at the right time.

He was not sure exactly what he hoped to find out by following the captain. The man seemed to be heading to the Falstaff, where Hector knew he stayed. But it was best to make sure nothing unusual happened.

Hector turned a corner and there stopped, turning as smoothly as he could. It was as though he walked into a nest of snakes. For there in the street in front of the Falstaff, with a crowd watching, stood the woman who had cut off his nose.

XV

Good morning . . dear."

Her hesitation in adding the "dear" made Nick feel drawn to Abigail. Somehow she seemed strangely animal-like to him, an endearing creature that, blended with her femininity, made him feel sure of her, himself, and the world as a whole. After the heartache he had been through, this was the kind of stability and affection anyone and everyone hopes for, and he knew how fortunate he was to have it in his grasp.

But it was not Abigail who glided into his dreams and woke him at three in the morning short of breath, sweating, and fully and completely alive. In that dark hour when the room he slept in was full of shadows that took on a mystery full of unimagined promise, a very different vision filled his senses. It was the woman with the long black tresses. The woman with the proud narrow shoulders. The woman whose body curved into her black clothes like the fulfillment of an eternal dream. The woman who wore tight pants that revealed the graceful tight length of her legs. The woman whose mouth made a perfect bow and whose blue eyes gleamed with a tantalizing combination of innocence and naughtiness.

In his dreams she appeared silent and beautiful, as though she were a treasure like a gold piece or silver ingot. In his dreams she carried with her an aromatic aura, perfume incarnate. In his dreams he held her, and she was otherworldly in his arms.

She was the kind of woman he had never known he would probably never know.

A deep instinct in him arose to tell him that no good would come from ever trying to possess her. Indeed, his instinct told him he would do well never to interact with her at all. He did not know exactly what trouble she would bring, but his instinct was powerful enough that he resolved not to interact with her except in the most innocent and disinterested way.

And why should he bother with her? Here was Abigail, true, loyal, and loving. She could not replace Sarah, but she was wonderful in so many, many ways. She was the kind of person with whom he could go through life laughing and loving. She would always be there with him. Surely God Himself had sent her his way. Everything about her and about being with her was sensible, and his instinct told him happiness lay that way.

But some other part of him took hold while he slept, stirring and rousing him into the spiraling depths of night until, like clockwork, he arose in that early hour with his body and mind alive. No—more than alive, super alive. This was far more than the surging of desires he had known throughout his teenage years. This was something more powerful.

By morning that would fade, though its energy lingered in him through the daylight hours. He could go about his day just fine, and now he was almost at full strength. And he spent that energy on Abigail.

For now they were riding out together often, finding shelter for the rains that struck almost every afternoon after which the sun would lift the moisture back up into its glaring rays in tattered clouds of steam.

He and Abigail had an ongoing conversation of their own no one else was privy to. It was a laughing conversation, full of jokes just between the two of them. And it was really wonderful to see Abigail laugh, throwing her head back, her strong jaw and neck beautiful in their solid, athletic way, her green eyes full of light, her teeth strong and white. She found the humor in what he said quickly, and her laugh emanated innocent trust of him.

The crew teased him quite a bit, and they were forever asking after her. Nick found he liked it when they did so. He liked the sense of Abigail's being his. He had even mentioned that to her, and she had confessed that she had the same experiences with the other women of the Falstaff. He and Abigail had laughed about that.

And with their every touch he felt a soft energy, a melting engagement that brought him excitement and a soothing sense of stability. They kissed now regularly, and he felt he wanted more involvement. But he still had the memory of his mother and her religion, and he really did live such a wicked life in so many ways that he did not want to dishonor her memory even more. Still, his body urged him onward, and he began to wonder if they should get married.

His mother . . . . what would she have thought about this bonny girl? She would have liked her. But she also would have reminded Nick to mind himself, and Nick thought of that often just as he still managed to avoid the rum all these men drank. He would find himself around those bottles and tankards, and he could smell that alcohol, which to him smelled like poison. He could not imagine that liquid in his body, burning his insides, clouding his judgment.

And yet there was another side even to that drink. Here in this hot place so far from the civilization he had always known his mates would sit in the evening drinking that rum without a care, focused completely on their treasure for a day. Much of the tension over betrayal had subsided, and as trust grew among the crew of the *Tetrarch* so did their focus on their enjoying the pleasures of this city. To be sure, no one truly trusted anyone here in the West Indies. But crewmates must find some way to get along, and Nick noticed that somehow the rum helped with that.

That way of drinking and enjoying the moment appealed to Nick. It must be the Caribbean getting into his system. Sometimes he would look out at the beautiful teal ocean and the palm trees all about the city, and he thought of what a great paradise this was. And there was something really very nice about being far away from civilization. Certainly many in this city worked hard to import that civilization here, but they were far from dispelling the true raw nature of the island and of the area round about. This New World had its own rules, or lack thereof. The burdens of morality did not weigh one down here. Nor did the oppression of class. Here you could be what you made of yourself. And Nick found that very appealing.

And here Nick could do what he pleased, including marrying this fair lady who bade him good morning.

"Good morning," he replied. And then thinking on it he added, "Darling."

She smiled, and he believed he knew the warmth that spread through her chest when she heard the endearment because that was how he felt about it.

But somehow his saying the word had not come naturally. There was something in him that held back.

Still, he encircled her waist, drew his face toward hers, watching her glad green eyes watching his. He kissed her solidly, and he felt her collapse a little in his embrace and knew that this was exactly what she wanted as much and maybe even more than anything in the world at this moment.

She kept her eyes closed as he broke his lips from hers, and he relished the look of contentment on her face. Then she opened her eyes.

"I do love you," she said.

It was the first time she had said those words, and they filled him with a mix of emotions. The foremost was triumph. He was already convinced she did love him, but hearing it made it real in an entirely new way as Sarah's face resolved itself in his mind. He felt a hot sense of betrayal. And then something else, deep in his spine, brought the sense of another betrayal . . . to the nightly visitor of his imagination.

"I . . ." he started and looked into her expectant eyes. He tried to shut out the presence of the other two women, but it was difficult. Then he peered harder into Abigail's eyes, feeling the power of their green glow and the innocence embedded in their limpid, marbled, sea-like depths. Then the other women fell back in his mind, and a pure emotion surged through to his lips. "I love you, too."

She smiled and took his face in her hands and kissed him, smart and clean and final. That was that.

"I'm off to help Miss Hannah," she announced and whisked out of the room.

He stood there, his mind and heart tossing emotions about like a juggler with gaudy pins. Out of the tumult of this silent roar a sound came to his ears from outside. It was a familiar one, and it drove him out the room and down the stairs.

It was the sound of swords clashing, and Nick stepped out of the Falstaff to see a crowd gathered round, and in the center stood the lady in black and the tall man Nick had seen with her.

Not only had Nick seen her only in his nightly dreams since he first encountered her a week ago but each day she and the tall man did a fencing practice demonstration. Nick had tried to watch for technique but usually could not take his eyes off her. Now again there she stood, rapier in hand, her long black locks springy, shining blue in the light. Her white blouse plunged deep, revealing soft bulges tanned, smooth, and flawless. Dust had formed on her black boots. She wore dainty black gloves.

Nick noticed that the two seemed to have come to a halt. Now they saluted one another, and each raised the point at the other again, standing upright, just as the Spaniard had done in that village on the Main. The tall man brought his blade smoothly to the inside of hers, and as he did so he took a step to his left, moving in that circular way Nick remembered the Spaniard doing. It was important to Nick to watch how she responded, and he watched as she circled her blade underneath his and also stepped to her left, moving in the same circular way.

But then the man reversed course and stepped back in the other direction, still in the circle, the blade transporting hers, and then he stepped smoothly forward, the blade aimed at her throat. This move she parried, and he stepped not exactly backward, as Nick would have done, but in a different relation to her along the route of that invisible circle.

On and on the moves went, Nick trying to follow and analyze them. It was difficult enough to grasp what they were doing, being such a different way of fighting. It seemed hardly a fight at all but a kind of cold-blooded dance.

What made it even more difficult to follow was the lady in black, herself, whose movements somehow lent her even greater allure. Standing there unlike any woman he had ever seen, her legs in their tight black pants, she seemed like a creature out of fantasy. And her movements were lithe and sure, graceful and full of intent.

Nick felt his mouth going dry, his senses overwhelmed even as his brain struggled to understand. At last her point connected just below the tall man's right armpit, a thrust that would have penetrated straight through his ribs to his heart had the point not been covered with a button. He cried, "Touch!" and they stopped, saluted, disarmed, and shook hands.

After a moment of quiet, applause erupted from those gathered there. Nick shook his head and blinked himself out of the trance he had fallen into.

XVI

Abigail drew the line in and took the dried clothes off it, holding the fresh laundry to her nose and smelling its air-dried aroma. That smell was glorious. This day was glorious. The world was glorious. She could hear the clash of the swords outside, but they seemed mere punctuations to the day rather than the sounds of battle.

To think she could love again . . . . how glorious and wonderful life really could be. She would never have imagined it . . . .

. . . the smell of ham invites the promise of closeness on cold mornings, and it drew Abigail out of bed like the song of sirens she had read about in Homer. She could not tell if she really smelled the ham when she awoke or if it was simply in her imagination, her . . . desire.

She drew the heavy curtains of the bed back. It was the bed she had slept in ever since she could remember. Everything here was familiar to her. The furniture, the wallpaper, the morning light slanting in trapezoidal shapes through the wavy-glassed panes.

That light was dull this morning in early March, and it would likely be a sloppy day of rain and low clouds, a necessary watering that had already brought the jonquils sprouting amid strong, fresh, dark wild onions. In the wooded area nearby sprays of white and violet had begun to appear indicating the dogwoods and redwoods coming into bloom. Already the tobacco had been planted and the tiny seedlings were beginning to push up out of the soil in their beds, growing toward the height when they would be transplanted into the proper fields.

She got out of her bed, put on her heavy robe and slippers. Then she made her way quietly out of her room. She saw across the hall that her brother's door was open and he seemed to be out already; George was the one who would go on to oversee the plantation in the next generation, and he worked alongside their father to administer the operation. He delved into the intricacies of ledgers, deeds, political negotiations, and the thousand other things involved in running a great plantation such as this one. For this was one of the greatest of all: Wanderway Plantation. George was like someone from a different family altogether, far more serious even than their father.

Her other brother, Jack, could never be serious, and glancing down the hall she was not surprised to see his door closed. He would sleep late into the morning, and when he awoke he would be irritable until he had had his tea. Then he would come alive and dash about, telling jokes and playing pranks in his boyish way before heading out to the stables where Coriolanus would already be saddled, stamping and pulsing for action. He and the horse would form their own terrific burst of energy, exploding out of the paddock. Jack had at least a thousand girlfriends, and he spent most of his time embroiled in the drama of courting them all at once.

And she, Abigail, could never be serious either. Her great loves were reading, flowers, and the sea. If she could interact with all three at once she would, taking herself into a certain spot in the garden where the roses clumped all around. Through their twining thorny vines could be seen the sea moving in its various hues as the day accomplished. There she would set a nest for herself and read through long hours, falling asleep and waking as the lazy quiet hours drew along. It was as though she entered a fairy realm of her own, and in her imagination as she read she could pass through far away worlds. She had an easy way with learning languages from the tutors her mother and father brought in, and she had read and reread Boccaccio and Cervantes. She had read Chaucer's tales. But what really excited her were the tales of Arthur and Lancelot as told by Geoffrey of Monmouth in English and Chrétien de Troyes in French. She especially loved Chrétien's stories, for she never knew when a troll or dwarf would appear in that beguiling landscape to thwart the efforts of a brave knight. Perhaps best of all she loved the Red Cross Knight himself in Spencer's Faerie Queen, which she read over and over again.

And she had read Homer over and over again in the sonorous Greek. How often she had wished she could sail off to the Mediterranean and one day encounter brave and handsome Odysseus battered and worn on an island strand so that she, like Kirke, might imprison him forever for herself.

Here she was nearing her twenties and had never known a single man that fired in her any passion. There were young men of nearby plantations, but all of them were more like George than Jack. If only Jack had not been her brother, what a splendid man he could be for her!

No, not one man had she known throughout her life. But now . . . this had changed.

About a month and a half ago, in the dead of winter, a new man had shown up at Wanderway. Abigail had noted his strong, fine features and powerful build. But she had no reason to pay attention to him for one simple reason. He was a slave.

Her father had purchased him at a cut rate from a friend of his who owned a plantation down in the Carolina colony. It seems this slave did not know his place. And there was more hinted at—the possibility that he may have been the child of his owner.

It was his name that gave Abigail pause: Ulysses. This was the Latin version of the name Odysseus. It was common to name slaves for figures out of classical literature, but the irony of his bearing the name of her foremost hero struck her. At first she responded only with bitterness that God had finally sent her a hero but made him a slave.

But then came the day when she encountered him in the dining room. She had been passing through long before supper was to be served but stopped, noticing this new young man directing the butler. He had been assigned to the butler as a kind of understudy, for he was clearly not meant to work in the fields. But he was actually telling the butler what to do.

It was not what he told the butler but how he said it that stopped her dead, for he spoke in a beautiful rich voice with perfect elocution. He had clearly been trained to speak so.

When he and the butler had finished he turned and saw her. He did not go into the routine other slaves did of hanging his head and acting startled or embarrassed. Instead of looked at her frankly,

"Can I be of service, Madam?"

It was not the obsequious statement of an inferior but rather the reasonable demand of someone who saw himself as being at least equal. And she believed in equality and had always felt deeply uncomfortable with her superior position as a member of a slave-holding family. She was meek by nature and would have much preferred to be in a subservient role herself, strange as it may seem. The fact was she had a romantic view of the poor. Now she was encountering someone who did not acknowledge her so-called superiority, and she grew immediately intrigued.

"I—" she started, looking into his eyes, which were an unusual greenish-yellowish color.

"Yes?" he said, and she could detect a hint of impatience.

"I—" she said again.

He turned away, muttering. He was speaking French. She caught it and responded to him in French.

He looked at her. She smiled. He smiled.

The weeks since had opened life in such new ways. She knew she was going against the grain of the ways things should be done. This man was a slave, but he had such a marvelous intellect! His Mistress had taught him to read and to do arithmetic, all with the blessing of the Master, or so it seemed. Throughout Ulysses's life his Master had looked so favorably upon him.

But Ulysses had gone a step too far. Fiercely proud of his mother, he had asked for better lodgings for her. He had been quickly rebuffed. Then he came up with an idea to make money for himself with an eye toward buying his mother's freedom and eventually his own. He had proposed that he be a tutor—the novel idea of a slave teacher. As he reasoned, slaveowners would see that they could pay him less than white teachers.

The Master was having none of it, and conflict ensued, the Master's brow darkening daily. Then, like snapping your fingers, men came and took Ulysses away. Tied him up and brought him here.

He seemed happy enough now, though, it seemed to Abigail. They would talk through the afternoon and laugh. No matter what book she would mention about he had already read it, and that tickled her mightily, for it seemed that he shared in that imaginative world she loved so much. And, most importantly, she felt she could be herself and not part of some hierarchy.

But she was spending too much time with him. Whether she liked it or not, he was a slave, and she knew she should keep a careful distance. So at first she when she interacted she was very watchful. She waited for her father or mother to admonish her. But no one did, so she became bolder.

Then she decided they were not going to say anything. She could not understand that, having been taught all her life that whites must always maintain control and a sharp divide between themselves and slaves. Maybe she had misunderstood? Or maybe it was all right to interact with a slave if he was in the house? She was not sure, but her instinct also told her not to bring the matter up. It may just be that her parents really did not notice, and she did not want to ask a question that would lead to trouble for her.

This morning she made her way down the central staircase. The mansion here at Wanderway was built of brick in an H shape. One square-built dwelling had been built first, and then the second beside it. Then the two were connected with an enclosed center section.

She made her way down to the kitchen area where she expected Ulysses to be. As she got closer she could smell the ham, and it warmed her. It was great to be alive.

When she walked into the kitchen she could already tell something was wrong. George was standing there, a whip under his arm. She looked to him, seeing the sternness on his young features, and then she looked at Ulysses.

"Good morning, sister," George said in his cold voice.

"Good morning," she stammered.

"This slave," he pointed to Ulysses. "Has he . . . touched you?"

She looked at Ulysses, trying to search his eyes for some clue as to what was going on but received only a blank stare in return. Panic flowed through her.

"What do you mean?"

"This creature," George said, raising his voice. "Has he touched you in an . . . inappropriate way?"

"Wha—" she said, again looking at Ulysses, who now was staring at the floor. "What are you talking about?"

"We have been watching him. He has been trouble from the start. And we have reason to believe—"

"Who is 'we'?" she asked, courage filling her. "What are you talking about, George?"

George looked at her coldly, "Simply let me know if he has touched you. If he has attempted to .. mount you."

The word "mount" shocked her. It was not like George to say such a thing. She could not understand what was going on.

"George, that's .. that's awful!"

"Yes, or no," he said, quietly and coldly.

She shook her head, "I don't believe this—I—"

"That'll do," he said, and snapped his fingers, bringing other men into the room. Abigail knew them all to be friends of George's from neighboring plantations, and even one from Williamsburg.

"George! He has done nothing!"

"We'll be the judge of that," he snapped. Petulance filled his voice, betraying a kind of fear.

"No!" she screamed.

They marched Ulysses away unresisting. She tried to follow, but two men remained behind to prevent her. She went about the rest of the day a nervous wreck, wondering where Ulysses was and what they were doing to him. Guilt flooded her. She felt she had done this to him. If she had only been more careful..

Later in the day she left her room, expecting someone to stop her. But no one did. She made her way into the slave quarters. It was eerily quiet there. Where could everyone be?

She knocked on door after door, but no one would answer. Finally she saw that the door of the smokehouse, where the ham hung to be cured, was open. Her nerves braced. Something in her told her Ulysses was in there.

When she went in, the smell of ham mixed with that of blood and something else. It was awful, sickening.

As her eyes adjusted to the dark she saw him lying on the floor. He had on no shirt, and his pants had been ripped to shreds. He smelled of urine, and all around were piles of manure that had evidently been dumped on him.

She realized something did not look right about his skin. It was shredded, as though someone had skinned him. Dried blood had caked on him, but the outer layer of his skin was gone in many places.

Then she saw his eyes. She could not tell what was wrong at first, but then she did. The eyelids had been cut off. Big white balls stared at her.

"Ulysses," she whispered, her throat and lips dry, horror and guilt filling her. "Ulysses! Ulysses! No!!"

She threw herself on him and realized he was not breathing. Feeling his body, she realized she had wanted to embrace him, to . . . yes . . . to kiss him.

But now he was gone.

It's my fault

She tried to stand, but her legs were weak. She bent over and threw up, just missing his body. Her head burned; she thought she might die.

It took her a long time to recover. And when she did she sat back and looked at Ulysses's corpse. Then, as if it were the most natural thing in the world to do, she started talking to him. Talking about books as they would usually did. She imagined what kinds of answers he would have given.

Eventually she finished talking, stood up, and walked out. She walked right past the mansion she had grown up in and kept walking right off the grounds. She kept on until she came to Jamestown.

Moving in the cold darkness on the docks she overheard some men saying that a certain ship was heading out for the West Indies in the morning. She found that ship, slipped aboard, and hid.

That awful smell came back to her now, and she thought about the trip to here. She loved the adventure of it. And as she left her old life farther and farther behind she focused on who she wanted to become—a respectful, quiet person no longer in that uncomfortable and even cruel role of the superior social position. She wondered if perhaps she would do well to convert to Catholicism and become a nun.

But she was glad she had not gotten herself to a nunnery now that she had Nick. Her nose filled with a new pleasant smell—that of new hope—that banished that awful old one of Ulysses's death. She smelled that new aroma as she plunged her nose back into that fresh laundry and thanked God she had come to this place. Funny she should fall in love with Nick. He had none of the sophistication of Ulysses. But he was very handsome, and he could read quite well and had responded when she had brought him books while he was convalescing.

She was far from her old life now, and here she was filled with hope and excitement. This may not have been an island in the Mediterranean, but it *was* an island. She may have lost Ulysses, but she had found Odysseus.

Dropping the laundry in her basket she made her way downstairs. She could hear raucous noise coming from the pub, and she thought she might peek in to get a glimpse of her man.

She saw him coming the doorway, and she paused hoping to catch his eye. But he was watching something or someone else. She looked to see.

Immediately she saw the woman in black. Immediately her heart gripped.

He's not necessarily watching . . . .

She looked quickly back at Nick and saw the slightly foolish look on his face.

XVII

Hector could not tear himself away from watching the woman in black, even though he did not wish to be recognized as her most famous victim. After weeks of making himself visible, today he was reverting back to his old covert ways. Yet that nose could so quickly give him away, so he put his hand over it as he watched.

He was not mesmerized by her beauty: he understood that she was universally thought to be so, but that did not move him in the least. It was her swordsmanship that he wanted to watch, to analyze, so he could understand what had happened.

She raised her rapier at shoulder height, pointing it at the tall man. Her form was perfect, there was no denying. Her movements were deceptive—smooth and really very slow, she fought with controlled grace. Too many people who wielded the sword depended on their speed, but this woman understood that quickness rarely helped. Hector himself had learned at an early age that a perfectly executed combination made too quickly often failed because it did not give the opponent a chance to react. About nine out of ten times the original position of that person's sword was sufficient to make the parry because few could actually match great speed and so could not displace the sword in the way a feint dictated.

So you had to slow down, make the movements demonstrative, give the person time to react. It was the reaction that gave the opportunity. If you could get the other person to react, then you could make your move while he (or she, in this case) reacted. Then you beat the opponent's time. Time . . . timing was everything in swordplay. It was much easier to mix up the timing of your own moves if the other person was moving slowly.

This woman understood that, and part of Hector grudgingly had to admire her as she changed the angles against the tall man. Clearly this was some kind of public demonstration, for while she was serious, this bout lacked the urgency of a real conflict, and the gathered crowd was obviously more drunk than tense, clearly there for entertainment.

As he slipped away, his mind had gone back to his own conflict with the woman. He had thought her victory over him simply a fluke at the time. But now he found himself respecting her more. It was a bitter thing to lose to a woman, but as his respect for her increased he began to wonder if this permanent loss of his nose might not actually work as a kind of badge—something he could turn to his advantage.

He had not thought of that before. Already he had found plenty of advantages in this brass nose of his, but he had not known how to face people who actually knew how he had come by the injury. Really, it was silly ever to have thought no one would ever find out how it had happened. He was not sure he had ever really thought to keep it a secret; he simply did not know how to work the situation to his own good when actually brought face to face with the person who had done the deed.

But he should have thought of that. And he should have thought about the particular kind of honor in the action. After all (he realized with some embarrassment about not having done so before), this woman actually captained a ship. A woman! It stood to reason she would be resourceful and talented and . . . deadly.

And also a worthy opponent to defeat. He stopped in the street and started to turn back in order to observe her style so that he might find a way to be foil her in the future.

But no . . . . wait . . . . .

The beginning of a plan dawned in his mind. It was not so much a revenge plan. Not that he was above revenge, but revenge was always short-sighted, driven by emotion, and not dependably profitable. And profitability always reigned supreme for Hector. If he could achieve profit *and* avenge himself then he would succeed wonderfully, but he would be greatly pleased with profit alone.

Now his mind went to work on his new plan, and he allowed it to do so in the back of his mind. He knew his best thoughts came with patience, allowing information to sift unconsciously and produce something viable and powerful.

Meanwhile he had other things to think about—schemes and processes here in this city, around Jamaica, on other islands, and even on the Main itself. What a wonderful place this New World was! Here a peasant such as himself could rise to great power. And the beauty of it was that no one even knew as he worked away in his dingy cell. He did not need the ostentatious show the royals and the nobles demanded. He also did not go in for the swashbuckling of the pirates: he regarded them as fools, exerting so much energy into gaining gold and silver and other treasures only to spend it all on women, rum, and finery.

No, Hector wanted the boring, nonglorified ways of wheedling money out of the world. It was quiet and invisible but terribly, terribly powerful. And there was something more: when you became a target for your wealth you must defend yourself. Always it had been that way. For a noble, there were always people to fight for you. But for a poor person such as he wanted people to think him (at least for now), facing the whole world alone with no governmental structures, no army of his own, he must take extreme care.

Not that he intended to work alone forever. He dreamed of one day hiring his own guard, maybe even his own army. The thought made him giddy.

He felt that giddiness as he made his way again to that deeply scarred and scratched door. Again, after delay, the door opened into even more profound darkness, and again he made his way inside.

The dark form moved seemingly without steps but rather as a ghost might, gliding across the floor, sometimes seeming even to be hovering far above it and never in one spot for long. Hector did not bother to try and understand why the form did the way it did or why it said what it said. He never bothered to try and figure out what gender the form was and certainly not its age or the strange ways of talking it had. As far as Hector could see, the form was motivated by the same thing that mattered most to himself—gain. And so Hector found communication easy.

The strange drink was already waiting for him. This time a kind of vapor or smoke curled out of it, and Hector was not sure if that came about because the drink was so cold, so hot, or for some other reason. He sat down, looking at the silver cup.

"Drink, Sí . . Sah . . ." the form said out of the darkness. A strange earthy smell insinuated itself, or so it seemed to Hector, and he felt a kind of humidity in here, as though an invisible garden had sprung up in the darkness and breathed its fetid, heavy, plant essence upon him. He knew there was no point in resisting the form's demand, so he lifted the cup, feeling a slight dread he fought back.

As soon as this liquid touched his lips he realized it differed from the usual, being bitter instead of fruity sweet. He winced as he swallowed it, and as he did so he heard low laughter sound from the darkness.

"What is this?" Hector asked, choking.

"Ah Señor Sah, esto es . . . this is . . ."

The voice trailed off. Hector sat waiting for more explanation. But none came. In fact, Hector sensed that the form had somehow gone away altogether, perhaps left the room. The silence went too long, uncomfortable.

Then, in his right ear, "Ssssss," the breath fluttering. Hector lurched but held himself back from an outright leap out of the chair as he heard the form laughing again in a low way behind him.

"El Consejero Especial . . ." the voice whispered, now in Hector's left ear.

Hector grew more alert still.

What of Don Diego?

"Ogunnnnnn," the voice seemed to zoom away.

Ogun? A gun? Gun?

Hector struggled to understand.

"A gun? Someone has killed him?"

"Una . ." the voice zoomed back toward him, but more slowly this time.

"Sí?"

"Una . . . ."

"Sí, sí. Una?"

"Guerra . . . ."

War

What kind of war? With whom? Between whom?

"Si. Puedes explicar, por favor?

Silence again. Hector's mind spun. Then he heard breathing, and finally words,

"Make ready."

XVIII

Ahoy, lad, may I join you?" Leesh asked Nick.

"Of course," Nick said, distractedly. He had sat here for over half an hour since the woman in black had ended her fencing demonstration. Nick came in with the rest of the crowd after and had simply sat here watching her talking, hoping she would make eye contact. But she had not noticed him when he walked past her. He, on the other hand, could smell the perfume she wore, and it invaded his nostrils with a teeming array of insisting promises. He tried to fight them, but both his mind and his body thrilled at the aroma.

Nick did not know when Leesh came in. But now the older man sat down beside him with the tankard he always carried about and took a long draught from it, his Adam's apple lurching up and down beneath his thin, tan, loose-hung, wrinkled skin. Finally he set it down and belched. Nick could smell the rum.

"Nick, my boy," Leesh said, and then belched again and tapped the middle of his chest with his fist. "Whew, that rum is fine, so it is."

"Yes," Nick said, still distracted.

"Ah, I've been about performing my old tight-wire act," Leesh said. "But really I was keeping my eye on a certain churl with a false nose. Followed him to an odd place in this city. There's knavery afoot."

Hearing Leesh pause, Nick grunted assent. None of the words had actually registered. Leesh followed Nick's gaze and his constant smile broadened.

"Ah, lad. I knew you would find that one interesting."

Nick knew he was talking about the raven-haired lady. He started to object but knew it would do no good to deny anything to this man, so he listened.

"Let me tell you all about her. Perhaps I should start with . . . her name? Do you know it already, lad?"

"I've heard her called 'Lady' something?"

"Indeed, lad. As I hear it, her full name is Lady Damiana Teresa Floriana Evernia."

Leesh rared back in his chair and put his hands up as Nick struggled to get his name around such a florid and foreign name.

"What do you think?" Leesh asked.

"I . . ." Nick thought. "I . . . . is she . . . ?"

"Yes, yes, you want to ask, should you call her Señora? Or perhaps . . Señorita? You see, many of us around here call her 'The Lady Evernia.' But she could just as easily be called 'La Doña Evernia.' Do you know that Spanish way? No? Well, it is the same as saying 'The Lady Evernia.'"

"So . . . she is . . or is not?" Nick reddened as he asked, but he felt as if something bigger than himself now carried him along beyond his control. Also, talking about the woman brought him pleasure.

"That is a very good question. So far as anyone knows she is not married and never has been. But then again she may *have* been married and widowed. Maybe she's married now. Who knows?"

Leesh lifted the tankard again, taking a sip but finding very little rum left in it. "Blast it, I say," he waved over the new tavern keeper. Somehow none could stay employed here for long—it was no easy thing to deal with Hannah. "More rum!"

As the man came and took the tankard away to be filled, Leesh continued, "So, no one knows, lad. In fact, no one knows that much at all about her. For example, her age."

Nick had wondered at this too. She looked young enough. And yet there was something about the way she carried herself that was unimaginable in a young woman. She bore herself with a self-assuredness that Nick did not see in . . .

Abigail . . . Nick looked around the room to see if she was around. He suddenly felt he had betrayed her, even though he had not even so much as spoken with this . . this Lady . .

"What did you say her name was again?"

The left corner of Leesh's mouth twisted in a smile, "The Lady Evernia is how we call her."

"Evernia," Nick repeated softly, confirming it was as he thought he had heard. The new man returned with the tankard full.

"Bless you, my boy," Leesh said, giving him a coin and quickly taking a deep draught of the newly replenished rum, smacking his lips.

"This is how the story goes," Leesh said, leaning toward Nick confidentially. "At least this is how I heard it. It seems her father was a Spaniard, although Lord love them I've never heard the name 'Evernia' among any of the Spaniards. Perhaps that name came from somewhere else. Or maybe it came down from the Romans, since they say they were once in Spain."

Nick wondered at Leesh's knowledge. It was easy to think him the smartest man in the world, yet Nick often viewed what he said skeptically.

"At any rate, this man was a royal, it seems. Evidently, there was some connection far back to Queen Isabella. It seems maybe that one of old John of Gaunt's bastards somehow made her way to the Spanish court and married someone or other. And then the generations made their way down, the whole time this family maintaining its ties to the English royalty.

"It seems this man, Evernia, or Don Evernia as he was known in Madrid or Barcelona or wherever he lived. It seems that this man during one of his trips to England courted a young lady of the Bavarian House of Wittelsbach."

Nick's head spun with all this royalty. As a Protestant whose parents were shaped by the English Civil War he had always had a deeply ingrained idea that there was nothing intrinsically special about royalty. As far as he had ever known or believed they were no different from any other human being. But now that he was possibly up close to one, doubt crept into his mind. Some kind of aura surrounded this woman. She seemed to be another kind of being altogether. And whatever this aura was riveted him.

He could not help himself from turning and looking at her. As usual, she was facing away, and his eyes traced the lines of her proud shoulders and the narrow slanting of her back into a v-shape that then spread heart-shaped into her perfectly proportioned hips. He roved his gaze back up to her luxuriant black locks. Yes, there seemed to be something different about her. And it gave him a strange feeling he could not describe. It carried a certain pleasure, but it was also . . . what?

Terrifying

"Aye, look her over, son," Leesh said, and Nick turned his head back to him. "Royalty."

The sensation of being caught between Leesh's watching and his own watching the Lady Evernia made Nick almost lightheaded. He tried to keep himself sailing aright in such waters.

"So, sometime, the date being unknown to anyone save the Lady herself, she was born to such high parentage. And then the stories abound. Stories of a child so bewitchingly beautiful that grown men pledged to keep themselves unmarried until such time as they could claim her. Tales of a beautiful black-haired little girl stopping entire crowds in streets. And wild tales of her coming of age. Tales not to be told of any lady . . ."

Leesh seemed to lapse into reverie, and in that silence Nick's head filled with imaginings far beyond anything he had ever thought of before. He felt as if he were under a spell.

"As I have heard it," Leesh said at last, "this girl so devastated everyone in Madrid or whichever Moorish city in Spain harbored her that at last her mother took her from there to Munich to live with those cousins. I can only assume they thought perhaps a nice bland Germanic influence would tone the child down. Or maybe they thought even *she* could not move such men as Germans."

"And did it work?" Nick asked.

Leesh shook his head, "How can anyone know? All I know is that she learned that gibberish confounding language they speak there just as well as the Spanish she speaks—the pure Catalan, they say, although they say too she can speak just as well the language of any gutter in that kingdom. Who am I to know?"

"And English," Nick said.

"Aye, lad. And English as well as any and better than most."

Nick sat in silence, thinking.

"And you can see her. Aye, what a vessel, lad. The kind of hull that could cut through the heaviest chop. And with a fine pair of cannon. And masts that will do for a day. And—"

"And," Nick broke in, "she captains a ship."

"Aye. Captain of a ship. Splendid, no, lad?"

Yes. Splendid. Almost not believable

"Many a man has attempted to navigate those waters," Leesh's voice turned to something like a warning, and Nick looked at him, attending the shift to seafaring terms. "She's a strong breakwater about her, though. Few survive throwing themselves about it."

"There's a man with her."

Leesh snorted, a single hard laugh of disdain, "That man. The tall one?"

Nick shrugged.

"A wheedling Manchester poppet. A ne're-do-well."

"Who is he?"

"A dalcop. A fop. Look at his rubbish clothes!"

"Leesh, does he have a name?"

"Aye, Pew it is. I believe his Christian name is David or Dick or some such. But everyone calls him Pew."

Nick looked at the man fussing around the Lady Evernia. Pew. What a strange name . . .

Like something that stinks

"Look at him carry on like an old grandmother," Leesh said. "What an everlasting stinking knave, huh!"

Leesh took another slug from the tankard and wiped his mouth. Nick watched Pew, taking in his fancy clothes that glittered just enough they reminded Nick a little of a man he had seen long ago in a moment when his life changed. That

Frenchmen, dressed all in gold in a gold carriage. He had dueled and defeated Lord Furth. Had that man been royalty too? Pew was hardly like that elegant fellow, but this Lady Evernia was. She had won in their little fencing display here just as the man in gold had won. Did being royalty mean always winning? He did not know. But there was one thing he did realize from watching this woman bout with the tall man.

It was time for Nick to pick up the sword again.

XIX

"Oh, Willie, you must hold a ball for my birthday!" Elizabeth exclaimed, perched in her bed in a silken fluff of perfume.

O'Brien looked down at her. It was impossible to ignore her beauty. Her dimples, the radiance of her face, her hair, everything about her was perfect. So strange that she should hold no allure.

Perhaps she is not the problem but I am. Have I reached an age when I am no longer stirred? Have I learned too much of this world?

The thoughts disturbed him. Age had disturbed him from the time he first became aware that his life no longer moved toward a crescendo but in fact, without his even realizing it, had passed a fairly low high point and had started sliding down toward its end. And it had not been that much of a crescendo, really. He had a lofty position and a distinguished career to show for, to be sure. But he had hardly attained immortality.

But, then, how valuable was immortality in the end, really?

"You shall have it," he told her.

"Oh, thank you!"

She seemed such a child. To be so excited about such an inconsequential thing as a birthday party when there were so many complicated problems to be solved. Part of him envied her, wishing he could be someone who could retreat into a life of recreation and frivolity.

He wondered if she had ever seen anyone killed as he had. Many times. Not a few of those times *he* had been the one doing the killing. And the killing made no sense. He had watched great warriors giving their all fall before fighters with only a fraction of their ability but with the great advantage of timing on their side.

Timing . . .

That was what he needed to be keenly aware of now. He had learned a lot in the past weeks. Much of it remained puzzling, however. According to his sources, the crew of the *Tetrarch* now seemed to be in accord again, as if by magic. This after deep distrust had grown from bizarre failed efforts to raid those seaside locations along the Spanish Main. O'Brien had heard how mercurial pirates here could be, but he wondered what had brought them back together. It seemed to have something to do with their involvement with the crew of the *San Miguel*, but what?

Could it have been the captain? This *woman*?

She went by the name of the Lady Evernia. O'Brien had grown suspicious from the time Don Diego had first told him about her. He doubted such a person could exist. English? Spanish? Bavarian? Might she be an angel too?

Certainly the reports had come to him of her possibly being a heavenly body. At least she had such a body. And such a face, his sources told him. Was it her beauty alone that so charmed and controlled these rough men? His informants sounded utterly foolish talking about her in the mooning kind of way they did.

He mused again on feminine beauty and its lack of effect on him. He wondered if he should be so moved as those pirates when he encountered her. He doubted it. He possessed one of the most beautiful women in the world, and he knew what a sham beauty was. Elizabeth may have seemed a being of ethereal existence, but he well knew that in reality she was stupid, was constantly farting and belching and laughing about it, and had the physical passion of a tortoise.

It actually embittered him to know these realities. Part of him had always been something of a romantic. Always throughout his life he had wanted to believe that women really were different kinds of creatures from men, that they lacked all the grossness, selfishness, and cruelty he had seen in the dealings of men. But that was not the case. They were just human, as everyone is human.

If anything he tended to sympathize with these piratical fellows more. Many of them came from poor families in England who had been moved off their lands because of inclosure laws and other such measures of Parliament. Others had served in the royal navy but had been paid such a pittance they were forced into piracy simply for survival. Yes, there was the allure of riches, but many of them never managed to obtain that much money, and very few of them had any idea what to do with the money they did have other than to spend it right away.

There were exceptions among the pirates, but it generally held true that they came from humble origins. But not this Lady Evernia, according to the stories. If the reports were to be believed, she had everything she could ever want, had been born into royalty itself, had spent a good deal of her childhood at the royal Residenz Palace in Munich amid the finery of that ancient Wittelsbach family.

O'Brien knew something of that family. He had actually been to Munich in his travels. He remembered entering that city, feeling its heavily Catholic atmosphere draped over him like a massive mantel. He had been very young then . . .

. . . and had come here with his cousin, Sean, who had decided he would go to Univerzita Karlova in Prague. It was not something anyone else in their family understood—why should he want to go to Bohemia? Now that William was in Bohemia he realized how very barbaric Ireland was. For all about him Prague glowed and glinted with gold, and this only a few years after the terrible battle of 1648 when the Swedes looted the city and carried away much of its art. The city that had once harbored the Holy Roman Emperor and scores of artists and scientists was now in decline. Yet even in its fallen state it was far more beautiful than anything William had ever seen or known before. The city's tragical quality even added to its beauty, and during his visit he would wander over the Karlov Bridge to watch the sun descend into dusk, and see the statues in their frozen swirling poses transform into ghostly shadows while the Vltava River rolled below not in a stately slate sheet like the Thames in London but like an open-armed hug that caught the sartorial light of the dying day and flowed it over its surface like a net of fire burned quickly out.

But now Munich seemed another sort of place altogether. Sean had a Wittelsbach friend at the university, Ludwig, and he was taking Sean and himself home with him for Easter. Unbeknownst to their family, Sean had been flirting with Catholicism, and William had been shocked to find out.

But I'm here now. I must make of it what I can.

They were riding down a wide boulevard in the carriage. Clumps of snow remained here and there, not fully melted though the day was warm and the sun was still shining even as it was lowering into the sky. The days were growing longer now, and the birds were singing, and William felt the excitement of spring.

The Residenz was not the most beautiful or largest palace he had ever seen by any means, but it did rise up in stately grandeur, a little cold, secretive. William looked down the lane to see two lion statues guarding one entrance to the palace, but the carriage turned into the garden in front and drove up to the main entry.

Servants met them first and began unloading the carriage. Almost immediately, a young woman tore out of the doorway and ran to Ludwig. William was struck by her beauty—her black hair, the swarthiness of her skin, all trademark Bavarian features. The image of her and the energy of her running to see her brother froze William.

"Katarina," Sean said, patting his arm. "She has that effect on everyone."

Ludwig introduced her to William in due course, but somehow he could barely talk to her. It seemed his voice did not work anymore, and when he did manage to make a sound it came out as more of a grunt. He had dreamed of such situations in which his mouth would not work correctly and was horrified to see them come true.

The days passed in a kind of haze for him. There were balls in which beautifully-dressed ladies danced in the glittering candlelight. He accompanied them to mass in the Alter Peter cathedral with its tremendous spire that speared the sky, higher even than the Rathaus nearby. As William gazed on the gold high alter and smelled the wax of the candles burning he felt the stately grandeur of the Roman religion in a way that contrasted sharply with all he had been taught of it growing up. It had been a condition of becoming part of the peerage of England that the Irish renounce Catholicism, and successive generations made sure to maintain allegiance to the Church of England by careful indoctrination of their children from birth. William thus felt guilty for being in this place, looking askance at and yet reflecting on similarities between this mass and the ones he knew. He was not altogether sure that someone who knew no better could have told the difference very easily.

But the differences were there, and he felt them. But he felt more the radiance of Katarina. To his eyes there were no other women there. Yet he could never quite seem to get close to her. Open as she was, there was something impenetrable about the circumambience around her.

Except it was not completely impenetrable, for Sean managed to swing into her company with an intimacy William could only stand and envy. Perhaps Sean knew better how to communicate with her, for her Bavarian (she spoke only a little English) was utterly lost on William while Sean had a gift for languages, having picked up Czech quickly and finding ways to communicate with Katarina that clearly delighted her.

So the days passed in that glitter and worship, interrupted by a hunt into the enchanted forestlands and a trip to view the snowcapped mountains south of the city. Actually, it did not feel much like a city but rather a kind of large village, nestled among mountains alongside a murmuring stream where women washed their clothes, their reflections broken by the small rocks around the edges of the shallow, clear water. A sleepy charm pervaded the place, and William realized part of him would like to stay forever. He could not help but imagine himself spending his entire life day after day this way.

But it only would have worked if he could have had Katarina, and disappointment filled him because he knew he never could. He could tell every day that she was falling more and more in love with Sean.

Then came the day to leave and return to Prague. Sean had kissed Katarina dramatically as William and Ludwig waited in the carriage. William had not wanted to watch but something in him *made him do so. When the kiss finally ended, Katarina was crying, clinging to Sean. But he bowed to her in an almost jaunty way and climbed into the carriage. As they rode away, William looked back at her, but Sean did not.*

Later, when he was able to be alone with his cousin, he asked him,

"Are you not going back for her?"

"For whom?"

"Katarina."

"Ah, yes, that lady."

"Yes, that lady."

Sean looked at him, "I say, cousin, are you in love with her?"

William looked away, his face hot.

"You are!" Sean said. "I wish you had told me."

"What?" William looked back at him.

"Well, I would have set you up with her."

"You—you," William stammered.

"Ha, that would have been lovely," Sean said. "She is lovely."

"You don't love her yourself?"

"Of course not. She's a silly girl. I have places to go and things to see, and there are so many women."

There are so many women . . . .

. . . O'Brien recalled the feelings he had then, as a young man, a boy really. He doubted he could feel such disappointment now. His cousin Sean had been right. There really were so many women.

And yet, from what he had heard of this Lady Evernia's parentage, he wondered . . . . .

"I beg your pardon, my lord," a voice broke into his reverie, and he looked up to see his footman standing in the doorway of the bedroom.

"Yes?"

"A missive has arrived from the Special Counselor of Spain."

O'Brien snapped to, his attention now focused. He stood and turned from Elizabeth as if she had never been there. As a young man he would have bowed. But much had changed since then.

"Thank you," he took the letter and walked out with the footman. He could hear Elizabeth's voice as he walked away, but he paid no attention as he opened the envelope and took out the letter.

> To the Honorable Governor of Jamaica,
>
> It is my sincere hope that all is well with you in Port Royal. As we discussed in our meeting, it is my desire that we can together trap and destroy the two piratical factions working in league to plunder the Spanish Crown. To that end, I am informed that the two ships, *Tetrarch* and *San Miguel*, are at this time docked in your city. If this is true, it is my hope that you will punish these pirates accordingly. As I realize the delicate political nature of your situation, I am glad to come with troops of my own to Port Royal that we might work together to apprehend these villains, which will bolster peace between our nations and within the West Indies and bring glory to us both. If you are amenable to this plan, please let me know. I trust you to keep this information secret; you may return this letter by the messenger I have sent, who is my most trusted servant.

By the Grace of God and Our Lady
I remain gratefully yours,
Don Diego Pedro de la Figueroa

Beneath the signature was the royal seal in scarlet wax. The letter did not surprise O'Brien; if anything, he was surprised it had taken so long for it to arrive. He had delayed his own communication as he gathered more information. Also, he wanted the Special Counselor to contact him first, so that he could then set his own plan into motion.

And now he could do just that. He walked into his study and sat down to his desk, shifting a blank piece of paper before him and taking up a quill and dipping it into the ink well. Having sent out his own spies he had come by the information that gold and silver were being held in a stronghold along the coast of the Main called Nueva Lebrija. He had had this fact confirmed and reconfirmed and had formed his plan accordingly.

He began to write, the quill twittering with the tight movements of his hand.

Most Excellent Special Counsel,

I am pleased to receive your letter concerning the delicate situation of which you speak. The plan you outline runs along the lines of my own thinking. I believe a cooperative effort to snuff out the most villainous of the West Indian pirates to be a most sound approach. I therefore warmly welcome yourself and a small unarmed delegation here for the purpose of a combined show of force against piracy. You will understand, I am sure, the importance of your coming unarmed, as no one would wish to create the impression that the Spanish would be invading our city. Our own forces are sufficient here to tend to the matter, and I will see to it that our own ships do not permit the *Tetrarch* or the *San Miguel* to leave this harbor. In the interest of maintaining surprise, I recommend that you not sail here in your own ship. Instead, I propose to send one of our ships from the royal navy to bring you and your delegation here. I propose that we set the date of August 29 to arrest the parties in question. Let me know if this plan is amenable to you and we will proceed.

> With Gratitude I Remain Your Humble Servant,
>
> William O'Brien
>
> Earl of Inchiquin and Governor of Jamaica

O'Brien set down the quill, blotted the page, read over it, and reached for his own sealing wax, which he lit and allowed to drip onto the paper. When the pool of blue wax had formed, he pressed the seal in it, folded the paper, and sealed it again.

"Dawson," he called to the footman who was waiting outside the door. The man entered, and O'Brien handed him the letter. "Take this to the messenger."

Dawson bowed and left with the letter. O'Brien waited a moment and rang the bell for the kitchen. After a few minutes a small boy appeared. He was ragged and his bare feet were dirty to the point that O'Brien hated to have him walking through the Mansion. But he needed someone inconspicuous through whom to send messages to the piratical element. It was true he had summoned Captain Stockett to the Mansion, but that was in order to set things up for the future, to make a show of the Captain's cooperating with the Crown. But this communication needed to be more secret, and he had devised certain secret terms to use between them. His name for Stockett was Molly.

"Hallo Tom," he said, handing him a shilling. "Tell Molly to prepare for an August 29 visit to grandmother."

"Yes, sir," the boy replied, bowed, and ran out of the room.

XX

Sunday mornings depressed Nick. They were as sunny and bright as other mornings in this place, but it did not matter because they brought so many emotions. He never felt lonelier than on these days. The weekdays blended into each other, and, as he was feeling stronger every day, he found it easy to get caught up in the flow of being in this tropical place. He lived among pirates now, and while he abstained from certain practices of his crewmates, he nevertheless indulged in the lifestyle of taking things as they come.

But when Sundays came a whole set of feelings assaulted him. His first thoughts were of his mother. Different images of her presented themselves to him, from when she was young and beautiful through the time when she was in the full bloom of her matronly years until the end when she was so sick and wasted away. He could hear her voice in his ear as if she were still alive, and he thought of all of her cherished beliefs. She had converted so completely to the Baptist faith and had taught her children to do the same. He had learned and internalized it.

He was accustomed to having no place to worship, but in the tiny village of Naunton where he had been born and grown up he had always had his family and other faithful people to worship with on these Sundays. They had no beautiful building, but then they believed the building was not important but rather what was in your heart. Also, they did not believe that you did works to gain salvation; instead you must be part of the Elect. Always in the back of his mind Nick wondered if he was for sure in the Elect. Certain signs had told him he was. If it was true and his soul would be saved, then it seemed to him it did not matter what he did.

But then there was the teaching that you should not do certain things. He should be careful of his speech, avoid lying with women, avoid drunkenness. The drunkenness he had resisted. The speech . . . well, the truth was that when you were on a ship the language of the crew had a way of creeping into your language, and his language had grown quite a bit saltier than he would ever have wanted his mother to know. As for women . . . .

As if on cue, Abigail knocked and entered his room.

"Good morning," she said in her soft voice, her green eyes catching the morning light and seeming to make them bigger than usual. "I'm off to the church now. Are you sure you won't come with me?"

Part of him wanted to go, very badly. He had seen the people gather in the new church, and at times when services were not being held he had himself slipped in when no one was watching. He had in fact gone to the Anglican church in Naunton before his conversion, and this building inspired warm feelings in him. Part of him felt how easy it would be to go back into the practicing of that religion. After all, his mother was dead now, and he was far away from England. He could start a new life here and live whatever way he wanted. And here was this lovely woman wanting him to go with her. He could see the possibilities of domesticity with her, of settling in here among the respectable people, perhaps actually working some kind of job.

Yet against all that he recoiled, and for a strange combination of reasons. First, he felt he would be betraying everything his mother was about and stood for, a thought he just could not abide at all. The second reason was one that had interfered with his life with Sarah, that same rising feeling in his throat that he could not stand the thought of an ordinary existence, that he was meant to do other things. Well, here he was in the West Indies, was that not enough?

No, it's not . . . .

There was something else too. He tried to fight it, but he knew exactly what it was. It was the black-haired beauty that now walked within his world. He had not so much as spoken to her, and he was pretty certain she did not know he existed. There was no reason for him to think he would ever have any involvement with her at all. But perhaps it was the fact that someone like her actually existed—someone so far beyond the normal walk of life—that now he found himself grasping toward her and whatever it was she represented. He could not say exactly what that was, but he could feel in himself that he wanted it.

Or was that really what it was? Could it be that the Lady Evernia was simply a mirage, a kind of ideal that he had formed to replace the woman he had really lost?

Sarah . . .

These thoughts rumbled through his mind now as Abigail stood before him.

"Not today," he replied finally. "Maybe. Someday soon."

"All right," she said, and he saw the innocence in her eyes as she bent over to kiss him. "Don't stay in bed the whole live-long day. You're fit now."

He laughed, "Yes, I am. I'll be up soon. Just enjoying this morning."

She laughed with him and then stopped, still smiling but searching his eyes with her own. He was not sure exactly what she was looking to find, but it made him a little uncomfortable, which he tried to hide. After a moment she kissed him again and walked out, closing the door behind her.

Watching her exit, he thought about how she so evidently trusted him, and the thought of it depressed him more. She wanted him to be something he could never be, just as Sarah had. As lovely as she was, she was not Sarah, and the thought of Sarah sent his mind far over the waves to that cold tiny island where she was locked away, and memories of her flooded his mind just as memories of his mother did on these Sundays. He thought of her smiling, of the time he had spent with her playing as children and later in the bantering of adolescence and the early stirrings of romance.

But he found he could not quite keep his mind even on her, for her face would be replaced by that of the Lady Evernia. That face thrilled him, which he hated himself for. He realized that sitting here today in this bed he was betraying Abigail, Sarah, and his mother all at the same time.

He squeezed his eyes to deal with the sting of this guilt. It was more than he could stand. He thought again that maybe life simply was such a series of betrayals.

But Mother . . . Lord Furth, and now your own son by that man . . . maybe betrayal is in my blood. Maybe it is something even the blood of Christ cannot purge

He could not sit here and deal with this any longer. He plunged out of the bed and quickly dressed. Then he headed to the door, but before he passed through he went to the corner to pick up something.

His rapier.

148

He knew he had healed enough now, and he raced down the steps feeling the power of his strengthening limbs. He was very ready for action. With healing had redoubled his great hunger for gold and everything that came with it. The fact was that his funds were running very low, and he knew that his mates who spent the money far more quickly than he did were surely down to their last farthings, ducats, reals, or whatever coins they might have. They were all ready for plunder, ready for the excitement of being back on the sea and the profits a new voyage promised.

He supposed that was enough to get them all back together again. He sensed that suspicion had not departed from their ranks, but the influx of the crew of the *San Miguel* had brought new prospects. There was still a concern about who might be spying, but now there were more people to blame if things went wrong, and those people did not have to be part of the crew of the *Tetrarch*.

Also, for reasons he could not quite understand, the Lady Evernia had somehow brought them together. He was not sure how or why or if he was even correct about this. He knew of nothing she had done to consolidate them. All he knew was that since she had arrived things had changed. And he must be ready for action, which meant that he must get back in practice with the sword.

He passed through the Falstaff quickly. It was very quiet, for his mates and Hannah and her women were all sleeping in from last night's revels. Only Abigail would have gone to the church. That was all for the best, as Nick did not want an audience for his practicing.

He walked into the alleyway. It was quiet, and the sunlight fell in a long slant across the sandy ground. Nick looked around and up and saw no one looking out of the windows.

Arming himself, he settled into his accustomed stance, knees bent, arm thrown back just as he had seen the man in gold do years ago. He went into his on-guard position in what he knew to be called "tierce," palm down, covering his outside. This stance felt natural, even comforting to him. Stepping forward he switched his guard to the first position, the sword covering his inside, his wrist held up toward his face. Both of these positions he knew to be strong ones that could disarm an opponent. He stepped forward, aware of the ground beneath him. Awareness was so important, he knew.

He went through various movements, the feel of them coming back to him effortlessly. His legs lacked their normal strength, and they rebelled a little against him, failing to achieve the smoothness of motion he knew to be so important. But he knew it would not be long until he was back in fighting shape.

Fighting shape

He stopped and stood up. He had thought much about the style of defense he had faced in that village and then he had watched the Lady Evernia perform. He needed to understand it, and this was the first time he had held his own sword in weeks.

Standing there he raised the sword to shoulder level and tried to recreate how he understood this style to work. He stepped with his right foot to his left and forward as though following a circle. That much he had figured out. But leading with his right foot twisted his body in a way he did not think quite right. So he stepped again, this time leading with his left foot. That felt more natural, but then it seemed as if he was simply stepping in a circle to be stepping in a circle. Was that all there was to it? Just moving in a circular way instead of backward and forward?

Plenty of times he had wheeled about, slashing as best he could in group fights. There was little use for technique in such moments, especially on a ship as it moved up and down on the waves, people slashing and shooting all around. It was a wonder if you survived. Luck and instinct in positioning played as big a role as anything else in such situations, and the ability to spin and slash was something simply dictated by necessity.

But in a duel, facing only one opponent, technique meant everything. Nick tried to understand what that technique was. He could feel within himself that something different was happening in this approach. It was as foreign to him as the Spanish tongue itself.

He stepped again, this time back to his right, again unsure which foot to lead with. Perhaps the purpose and advantage of this movement would come to him. Certainly he had been on the receiving end of its deadliness.

Then he heard the voice.

"That's not right."

XXI

Nick knew the voice as well as if he had heard it all his life, and he felt something inside him click into a place he could sense would stay there a long time.

He looked behind him to see her standing there at the corner of the alley, the morning light slanting across her body, her face in shadow, which brought a cool glow to her blue eyes that somehow seemed paler than normal, set off against her black hair.

He knew he should say something, but he was not quite sure what. She was leaning against the wall, but now she pushed herself away from it and stepped toward him.

"It looks like you are doing a French style," she said.

"I suppose what I've learned comes from the French," he replied, the words coming a little awkwardly.

"Yes," she said perfunctorily and then laughed in a light way that sounded like windchimes clanking softly in a breeze. "What it looks like you want to do is Destreza. Do you know that word?"

"No ma'am."

She did not acknowledge his address, "It's Spanish. The word for the Spanish style of defense."

She stepped toward him, one foot directly in front of the other, her hips swaying. She stopped in front of him, closer than men and women who did not already know each other usually stood. Her back was arched in, thrusting her chest forward, and he forced himself to resist looking down at her body. She cocked her head, looking up at him, a smile playing on her lips, her eyes narrowed slightly.

"Put your rapier down," she said.

He stood there looking at her. It was as if she wielded some kind of invisible force so powerful he could feel it taking over him. He tried to resist it, but it seemed petulant to do so.

"I want to show you something," she said, her tone a little softer, as if she were not working to wrest control over him but simply encouraging him.

He nodded and leaned his sword against the corner, point up against the wall. Then he turned back to her, his vision taking in at once the symmetry of curves that seemed beyond any possible awareness or control she could have over them. It was as if her body just happened to her, like a fabulous carriage she simply rode around in.

Then that impression gave way as she moved into a stance, feet together, chin high.

"Stand this way," she said.

He did the same, sensing that in his masculine shape he could not match the appearance she gave.

"Hands on hips," she said, and he realized he was not following her exactly, so he did so.

"Good. Now," she lifted her right arm, extending it toward him in the way he knew to be the Spanish stance. He did the same.

"I'm going to step toward you. I'll pat your shoulder and pass you. When I do you turn with me."

He felt a jolt at the thought of her touching him. Again that force she seemed to possess threw itself over him. He nodded to her to begin. She stepped forward in graceful steps, passing to his outside. When her hand contacted his shoulder, her flesh seemed to burn right through his thin shirt to his skin. He could not hold back a shudder of excitement, his whole body alive. He forced himself to turn with her so that he faced her as she turned with him.

"Move with me," she said. "You were behind."

He nodded again. Again she advanced. This time he focused to move in rhythm with her, and he did better. But when they had turned in a circle she said, "Watch my eyes this time."

He did so, peering into their blue as she stepped again, and this time he felt the soft touch on his shoulder again and felt himself turn with her.

Without delay she advanced again and they turned. Then again and again. He felt they were moving faster, but he could not be sure. All he was sure of was that a kind of momentum moved them as though they were mounted on a wheel that turned them.

On and on they whirled, everything around them starting to spin in his head as he kept his eyes locked on hers, two spheres of blue that somehow blazed with heat and chilled with cold at the same time. Again they whirled, and again, and again, and he felt himself melding with her, his very spirit merging with hers, ghost limbs entwining.

Then he became aware that their physical proximity grew so close that she no longer advanced but simply moved with him, her hand resting on his shoulder now, her thighs brushing his own, her breast sliding across his side. Her perfume invaded his nostrils, swirling up into his head, sending him into an intoxication utterly foreign to him. Still those eyes held his, their blue exquisite. And then he realized they were not looking into his own eyes any more but had drifted their focus down to his lips. And his own gaze lowered to her lips, the upper one curved in a bow, the lower one set in a pout. They parted, and he could see the small white teeth inside and the wet inner flesh, red with a small glisten fading into dark cavernous promise within. He felt some invisible part of himself press into that darkness, and as he did so he felt her body coming into fuller contact with his own, a soft pressing undulant with the twitches of the working of muscles.

Then her arms came around his neck and she pulled him down toward her, her lips meeting his, and he seemed to lift off the ground as his entire person surged, shot through with the strength of heaven and earth combined in a full surmounting power propelling him to the summit of all existence.

The very concept of seconds, minutes, hours, days, years, decades, and centuries passing from one to the next suspended. Nick was not even aware when her lips softly broke from his and she stood, her body curved into his as though she were a malleable thing formed to his own shape.

He realized his eyes were closed. He blinked them open and saw hers peering up at him in a bleary haze of that cold blue, and he felt himself completely blended with her so that if she were to step away he would collapse into the sand.

Her mouth broke into a smile, her teeth gleaming. Then she lifted her chin, her eyelids shifting downward as her head went back into that cocked position again.

"You want to learn more?" she asked quietly, her voice invading his ears like the suspiration of a dream. He was not sure exactly what she meant him to learn more of, but he no more could have refused than he could have stopped breathing and lived.

He tried to speak, but his mouth and throat were too dry, and the words "Ye-es," choked out. Her smile twisted up more as she stepped back, letting her right hand slide off his left shoulder and down his arm to his hand, which she took.

She tossed her head for him to follow, leading him to the street. As they stepped out of the alley she dropped his hand.

XXII

Abigail raised her head and looked up. She was not looking at the arches all around her, which were crude compared to the ones of Westminster and other edifices in England but were far more imposing than anything she had ever seen. She was not looking at the ceiling either, with its reflected light from the high windows.

She was looking past all that to heaven itself, to the unseen face of God, searching that invisible visage for scenes of her future. She wanted those scenes to feature herself with Nick. She imagined what their children could look like, how they might live here in this place or maybe somewhere else. Across her imagination rolled years and years of life together, mellowing into old age with grandchildren and the bounty of a life fully lived in prosperity.

Prosperity . . . . what a word. Her mind darkened and so did her vision, as though a cloud had passed over the sun outside and so dimmed the cool light herein.

She could not deny Nick's being a pirate. One of the things she loved—yes, she loved him—best was his strength. She realized he did not fully realize his strength, but she could see it in every fiber of him, whether the strength of his recovering muscles, his mind, or his heart. She could see the courage in him even though she had never seen him actually

157

put it on display. She could tell in the things he said that he was capable of vision, that once he fully healed the strength and stability would be breathtaking.

But his healing would also bring his return to his occupation, and with that she could see the other, darker side of his strength. For, as she well knew from her own family, the strong took from the weak. Her father had done this to build the great riches and plantation she lived on. Her brother had . . . .

Ulysses

She shoved the thought of Ulysses out of her mind. She loved a new man now. But this new man plundered other people and took their possessions just as her father and brother did. A pirate. No one called her father and brother and all the other planters in the colonies pirates. They enjoyed approval of the Crown and society, generally. They were simply building civilization, bringing salvation to the savages, imposing order on the wilderness, following out their own divinely-ordained duties as higher beings on the planet.

But really they just stole and killed. And Nick . . .

Yes. Nick has killed

Doing so was part of his occupation, what "licensed" him to take what he could from his victims.

But he is good

She knew he had to be good. She loved the sweetness of his eyes, his kind thrilling voice, his way of enjoying things.

She smiled as she remembered one of the things he said that had amused her, and her heart lifted with joy. Then the thought struck her again as it had before:

He can learn another occupation

Yes, she knew he could do anything he wanted. He was so smart. He could learn quickly. Whatever trade he learned may not bring him quick wealth the way piracy did. But it would give him a living, enabling him to support her and the family they would have. He would be out of danger, and she would make sure to provide him with thrills to replace those he lost by staying off the high seas.

Meanwhile, he would earn his money in sensible amounts instead of tremendous lumps. They would use that money to build their life together, and he would be grateful to her as she knew he already was. She could tell in the softness of his eyes when he looked at her how grateful he was to have her in his life and how much he appreciated her. She could feel the warmth of his love. She knew he felt comfortable to talk to her, and she never tired of his talking. She loved it when he said things to make her laugh, and she could tell he loved it when she did so.

But now it was time for *her* to talk. To reason with him. He was really too good a man to continue as a pirate. That she could feel in the deepest depths of her heart. He had been drawn into this life for reasons he could not help. But he need not stay in it. She knew he hated drunkenness. And while she knew she excited him to passion, he had refrained from showing his love in ways forbidden by God (although, truth be told, part of her wished he would one day lose control and actually ravish her). He was far sweeter than any of the other men in his line of work here she had encountered. It was sad, really, that he should have been brought into this whole sordid world of crime.

Yet it was also wonderful, for it had brought him to meet her. So, she thought, things worked out for those who love the Lord. And the Lord was forgiving of sinful ways. All Nick had to do was to repent, turn away from his sin, which should not be that difficult because she was sure he never would have done any evil had he not been forced to it. He could abandon those ways and pray for forgiveness and all would be well.

And he would be happier. Of that she was convinced. She was not sure if everyone in the world was happier striving to be good and right, but she knew Nick would be.

She needed to get him here to the church. He seemed as if he might go soon; she did not understand why he had not already. It seemed that he had a different idea about God, but as far as she could see as long as you were not Catholic you were generally in the right. But somehow he believed he should not worship with the Anglican faith either. Surely she could show him that he could and that then he could come here and God would forgive him and bless him. Nick, in turn, would be happier and would, with her, attain completion.

She bowed her head again as the vicar began to speak.

When she returned to the Falstaff, Abigail noticed some of the men who stayed there sitting around, their heads down on the tables, trying to stir their blood after the late night of carousing. Some of the women who worked there were cleaning up the mess from those revels, and they said hello to Abigail as she passed through and headed up the stairs.

She hoped to see Nick, but now that he was almost completely well she knew he was not likely to be in his room, and she was sure he would not still be in bed. Part of her did not like that he was well; there was something very nice about knowing where he would be and being able to go in and spend time with him. But she was also very happy he was feeling better.

Stopping at his door she knocked twice and was unsurprised not to receive an answer. She opened the door and walked in. As she expected, he had left the bed unmade, so she went about taking care of that, humming to herself as she worked. There really was something very lovely about a Sunday. Whether here or on the plantation the day was quiet and still. She imagined it was probably this way in London itself at this very moment.

London . . . she had never been, but her mother and father had spoken many times of it, and it seemed to be the most splendid place on earth. Thinking of her mother and father saddened her. She did miss them. She missed George, cruel as he was. And Jack—oh, dear Jack! How she missed him. How . . .

Something occurred to her:

Nick is like Jack

She had not realized it before. They were not exactly alike. Jack was far more of a daredevil than Nick seemed to be, although she might find out he was too, now that he was up and about. But there was something the two of them shared, like two different expressions of a similar core.

Surely that was why she always felt a familiarity with Nick and even a certain comfort—a sense that she was somehow at home. He was the Jack she could have, which flooded her heart with a good feeling. She could not imagine feeling better, for many times she had wished Jack were not her brother so that she could spend her life with him.

As she fluffed the pillows on the bed her mind wandered to Jack's girlfriends. He had many. There was Polly, who was a blonde with pale, weak eyes. Abigail had never been able to figure out how he could be interested in her. And maybe he was not that interested, for there was also Barbara, who was a buxom brunette, whose energy came closer to matching his.

161

Then again, often he showed a certain favor toward another brunette, this one a bit thinner but vivacious, even a little pugnacious, named Mary. Then there was Grace and Fanny and Ellen.

Also Rosamund had captured his fancy. Indeed, she was the one who seemed to hold his heart when Abigail had run away. She had been truly beautiful, black-haired, with dark smoldering eyes.

An uneasy feeling came over Abigail as she thought about home. The image of Ulysses dead came to her and she worked to shut it out by thinking of Jack. But then it made her sad to think she had left without even saying goodbye to her dear brother. And then there was Rosamund with her black hair.

The uneasiness grew, and suddenly Abigail realized she was pacing back and forth across the room. Why was she feeling so anxious and bad when she had been in such a wonderful mood only a few moments ago?

Rosamund

The image of Rosamund's black hair insinuated itself in Abigail's mind, growing significant and even immense. Why would that be?

Then that black hair morphed in her mind, the smoldering eyes turned blue.

That woman

She spun and walked out the room and down the hall, glad to find her friend Susanna in her room. Susanna was her closest friend among the working women of the Falstaff. She was still lying in bed in a soft heap, one long leg outside the sheet. She had spent the night with the man Abigail had learned was called only Stuart. Moody, powerful, a force of nature, he seemed to prefer to spend most of his time aboard the *Tetrarch* except when he came into the city wound tight and snorting like a bull, searching for Susanna. From the moment Susanna first saw him she had gone all to water, she had told Abigail, and she knew she was his forever if he wanted her. Whenever he appeared she left off whatever she was doing and went to him, even if she were entertaining a high paying client. If William the Co-Regent himself had been here to pay the top price for her services she would have forgotten he existed when Stuart appeared in the doorway. And that Stuart came tearing after her, dragging her up the stairs silently, followed by a terrible commotion that sent everyone into convulsions of laughter.

Normally Susanna was up early like Abigail no matter how much she had worked the night before, but whenever Stuart came she always slept in and in fact was almost impossible to rouse. And she generally spent the next few days in a happy haze.

Abigail shook her awake.

"Whu—wha?" Susanna said, rolling over on her back, the sheet falling away from her lovely body.

"Sue."

"Wha," she swallowed, wetting her throat, dry from hard sleep. "What?"

"Sue, I'm sorry to waken you, but I need to talk."

Susanna opened one eye, "What, Abby?"

"Nick . . ."

"Yes."

"Do you think . . ."

Susanna waited, "Do I think what?"

"Do you think he fancies me?"

"Of—" Susanna rolled yawned and stretched, "of course."

Abigail looked away. Susanna had answered a little too quickly, as if she just wanted to say what would make Abigail happy and get her to go away.

"You look worried, love," Susanna said, watching her. "I'm sure he does. I've seen him with you."

"You really think so?"

"Yes."

"Thanks, Sue."

"Of course," she said and rolled back over on her stomach.

Abigail stood up and walked out. She felt a little better but not completely so. Nick had not changed in any way. Nothing had happened. Why should she be worried?

Hannah was passing her, and Abigail hailed her, "Miss Hannah, have you seen Nick this morning?"

"No," Hannah replied, her voice rough with her usual morning phlegm. "He's probably off with Stinky and the Captain. They seem to be cooking up some kind of rubbish. I suspect they'll be off soon."

"Really?" the prospect jabbed Abigail's heart.

"I would imagine. A pack of rogues such as that won't stay put for long. They must be off to plunder and pillage." She noted Abigail's worried look and tried to approximate a reassuring tone, "It's good for business."

"Yes," Abigail said.

"Hmph," Hannah said. "It's no wonder they're all astir. They're bound to be with that little vixen come among them."

Abigail listened closely for more, "You mean the lady who captains the ship."

"Huh, yes, that tart. She's riled them up to something or another, I know not what. But I hear them scheming in the quiet corners, and once or twice the old Captain's made his way up to the Governor's Mansion itself. In these times I doubt that's healthy for the likes of old Stockett. As for that little strumpet—fie upon her!"

Abigail felt herself getting worked up along with Hannah, "Miss Hannah, do you . . . do you think she's . . . Nick?"

The tears overcame her as she broke down in sobs, falling into Hannah's ample body. A look of annoyance came over Hannah's face, but then it softened into real compassion as she let Abigail cry for a moment and then lifted her face.

"Listen, dove. I'll not sugarcoat anything. That woman can have her way with any man. I've not seen your young man go about after her myself, but I would be doing you a disservice for sure not to warn you that *she* might go for a handsome young thing such as him. I know it's not what you want to hear, but if you're smart you'll be ready to fight for him."

The words pounded on Abigail. She felt deeply grateful for Hannah's honesty, but she saw no way she could compete with that woman.

"What can I do, Miss Hannah?"

Hannah's eyes softened in pity more as she considered the young woman appealing to her.

"Be yourself, love. You're the dearest girl in the world. Any man can see that. So be yourself."

"Thank you, Miss Hannah," Abigail said, hugging her, and walking on down the stairs.

Hannah watched her go and muttered to herself, "What else can you do, sweetie? What else can any of us do?"

XXIII

Nick had become familiar with schooners since his arrival in the West Indies, and the *San Miguel* seemed typical in size and style, but it was more lavishly decorated than most. As he approached it on the dock, the figurehead caught his eye. He realized it was carved to resemble the Lady Evernia herself. His eyes followed the face and hair down over the naked torso, and he felt both embarrassment in doing so but also a kind of relief in being able at least to look at this facsimile of her. But instead of that release relaxing him, the vision of her unclothed ratcheted up his passion even more.

The Lady herself led him up the gangplank to the ship where men were swabbing the decks, mending ropes, and doing the thousand other things that must constantly be done aboard a ship. It felt good to Nick to step onto a vessel of any kind, and the smell of the salt air and the glitter of the sea all around excited him even more. He felt blood surging through his body so powerfully his fingers tingled. He felt he could have flown straight up into the sky and over to the blue mountains on the mainland and back again.

The crew looked up at him, their eyes searching, attempting to read who he was and what his purpose could be. Some of them had surely seen him before at the Falstaff, but he had not been very vocal, so they may not even have remembered.

As for Nick himself, he felt pride knowing he was accompanying this beautiful lady onto the ship. He knew he could not claim ownership of her in any way (at least not at this point), but he was enjoying pretending he did.

He followed her to the cabin and to the captain's quarters.

"Careful," she said in a mock-warning tone as she opened the door.

Immediately, yammering and barking started, and as Nick stepped inside he saw three small long-haired dogs come racing across the floor. The Lady Evernia shut the door behind her in time to keep them inside, and she knelt down to them as they leapt upon her and licked her face.

"These are my babies," she said, picking each one up and hugging it while the others yacked and vied for her attention.

Nick was not sure what to say, so he knelt down and pet them.

"You like dogs?" she asked.

"Yes," he said.

"Good. We will get along."

The words, though not unusual, struck him strangely in tone, and he watched as she stood back up, removed her hat, and tossed it on her desk while the dogs danced around her. Then she untied her wide black stash that gathered her coat at her waist.

"I have rum for you to drink," she said, removing her coat, her white blouse hanging loose and thin over her body, the curves of which rose against the material. "Go lie down," she commanded the dogs gently, and they retreated and quieted down, looking from her to Nick with their brown eyes.

167

"I do not drink rum," Nick said, hurrying to shift his own eyes from her body to her eyes as she looked at him.

"Neither do I," she said. "I don't take any strong drink."

He wondered why she did not drink. Did she have religious reasons for it?

A knock came at the door, sending the dogs barking again.

"Come in," she called in a strangely little girl-like tone over the barking.

The door opened and in stepped the tall man, Pew. He was smiling at her, his eyes narrow, but the smile vanished when he saw Nick. When the dogs saw him they quieted and lay back down again.

"Pew," she said and looked to Nick. "This is—what is your name?"

It struck him how emotionally involved he already was with her for her not to know his name and for him not yet to have spoken hers.

"Nick."

"Nick."

"Pleased to meet you," Pew said in a dismissive way, holding out his long, thin, pale hand but not looking at Nick. Pew moved in a snake-like way. In fact, Nick thought, there was something snake-like about his face, his narrow eyes, the small turned-up nose with the tiny nostrils, the thin lips from between which Nick expected a long thin tongue to dart.

Pew walked over to the Lady Evernia and stroked her hair and asked, "And why is he here?" as if Nick were a statue who could neither hear nor respond. The tone was not ugly, just a simple question that presumed Nick had no say.

"He's my new friend," she said, yawning as if she were describing a new dress she had just acquired.

Pew did not respond but rather knelt on the floor and started pulling the boot off her right foot.

"I can go," Nick said, turning.

"No," she stopped him. "We have a lot to talk about."

Nick stopped, standing awkwardly as Pew removed the boot and then started on the left one. It was all very awkward, and Nick did not know what was going to happen next. His body still was alive, so he looked around the room trying to take his mind off the situation.

That did not work very well, for the first thing he saw was a painting on the wall of a faun and a nymph. The faun's intricate muscles were all flexed and bulged, and he held a pan flute to his lips. Only a thin cloth just covered his groin. The nymph had no cloth of any kind to cover her, her pink flesh overwhelming, a symphony of freedom.

He looked away, his eye catching the Lady Evernia as she stood up and started shucking her tight pants off. Nick found himself hating her long blouse for hanging halfway down her thighs, and yet he also felt some distant voice in the back of his mind telling him he was not supposed to be in a lady's room at such a moment. He also could not understand how this man Pew was in here with her actually helping her undress so matter-of-factly. Pew set her boots down together as carefully as any housemaid would have done. Nick was confused—was this man her husband?

"Pew, bring me hot water for my bath."

"Yes, madam," he said and walked primly and authoritatively past Nick as if he were simply another piece of furniture, passing out the door and closing it carefully behind him.

"He's in love with me," she told Nick in a confidential tone and then she laughed, the sound of it like ice tinkling.

Nick could not figure out what to make of this situation, so he looked around more, trying to make sense of the room. He had been so overwhelmed by the dogs when he walked in that he had not been able to look the room over. Yet he realized that some part of him had taken note that the chamber was overfull, and now he looked at all the small things about, from women's clothing to small images and carvings all over the walls to table tops filled with all kinds of bric-a-brac that he decided must tumble all about when the ship set sail. Many of the items in this room gleamed in solid gold, and he could tell she had a distinct taste in what plunder she kept for herself—anything florid, any naked statue, anything garish, anything of high value.

"We need to do another lesson," she said. "You're learning quickly. You can see my swords," she gestured to them. "They're not my really nice ones. I keep them in a palace in Munich." She said this as if everyone in the world had a palace somewhere.

He walked over to the swords placed on a wooden rack. If these were not her nice weapons he could only imagine what the really fine ones looked like. There was a row of cupped hilt rapiers of the Spanish style. There were two matched pairs, their guards filled with elaborate flowery engraving. Three more were made of distinct style.

"You'll like the crew," she said lying back on a cushioned divan in the corner beside which, Nick now realized, sat a porcelain tub. "They're good men."

Nick stood utterly bewildered. Even in his dreams he had never imagined his being in a moment like this. He had absolutely no idea what to do, although again that voice in his head told him he needed to get out of here. Vaguely the Bible story of Joseph and Potiphar's wife came to his memory, spoken by his mother, and his ardor cooled for the first time.

As if sensing that, the Lady Evernia patted the divan and said, "Nick, sit down."

He stood unmoving, trying to force himself to leave.

"It will be a little while till they come back. They have to heat the water."

Still he stood, emotions rolling through him. He wanted more than anything in the world to sit right there and never leave, but he had held so hard to his principles, and that while literally surrounded with beautiful prostitutes. He had never gone beyond propriety with Sarah or with Abigail. But all that strength quailed before the power of this woman.

When he finally broke and took a step toward the divan he felt a totally new sensation of surrender. The deepest parts of his mind and heart raged at him, but on the surface he felt only excitement, thrill, and promise.

As if to reward him, when he sat down, she sat up and kissed him again. This time a hot flame seemed to issue from her lips. She made a soft noise and pressed her chest against his. He could not imagine himself more wound up.

Then she pulled her lips from his and looked into his eyes, her own sultry and blurred, the pupils tiny dots in expanses of watery blue. She smiled.

"Do you know my name?" she whispered.

His mouth opened, but nothing came out. His voice seemed paralyzed.

"They call me the Lady Evernia. But you can call me by my first name, Damiana."

He willed himself to nod. It was awkward and stiff, and she gave a little laugh.

A knock came at the door, sending the dogs into apoplexy again, although they quieted when the door opened and Pew

171

appeared. He assessed the scene quickly and gave Nick a cold stare. Nick returned it, desperately hoping the man would attack him so Nick could feel the release of combat. But Pew simply stood aside, and waved in men, who entered in a line with large vases of steaming water, the dogs barking and racing around.

"I had suspected you would return soon for a second morning bath," Pew said, his voice composed even if his face was not.

Second morning bath?

"Thank you," Damiana said. Nick tried to think of her as something other than the Lady Evernia. She had not taken her arms from around Nick's neck, and he stealthily glanced down her blouse. He knew it would add fuel to Pew's rage, but he did not care. He actually wanted that.

The men poured the vases of water into the tub and made their way quickly out. Their expressions seemed neutral, and Nick wondered what it was like to sail aboard the *San Miguel*.

When they had finished, Damiana spoke, "Thank you, Pew, you may go."

Pew simply closed the door as if she had not spoken and started walking toward her.

"I will help you get into the tub."

Damiana laughed, "I don't need help."

"Yes, you do," he said, his snake smile returning. He ignored Nick altogether, turning his body in such a way as to block him out.

Damiana laughed again, quiet, a little languid, "I'm fine."

"No, you're not," Pew said, reaching his hand down to take hers. "And you need privacy."

She looked at Nick and laughed, harder this time. Nick was not sure what to do. Rage built in him at this man ignoring him. It seemed to him that both he and this snake man should leave her to her bath, but he was not letting go, and Nick determined to defy this fop.

"Go, Pew. Leave us."

"My Lady Ev—"

"I'm all right, Pew. Now run along, and I will see you anon."

Pew looked at her, his eyes slits, his face in a kind of strange grin that did nothing to hide the sour look on his face.

"I will be just outside the door if you should need me," he said, his voice thin.

He turned and walked out. Damiana looked at Nick and laughed again. He tried to laugh with her, but the whole situation gave him an uncomfortable feeling.

When she stopped laughing, she looked into his eyes, still smiling. Then she cocked her head the way one of her dogs might have done and kissed him again.

She took her lips and arms away this time and stood up. Turning away from him to face the bathtub, she pulled her long blouse up and over her head.

Nick's entire body lurched as he looked at her body lit by the bright daylight. The curves were perfectly proportional to the length of her trim limbs. She stepped into the bathtub carefully and lowered herself, twisting as she did so to give him a full view of her front. He could not keep himself from looking at her body until all he could see was her face as she smiled at him over the edge of the tub.

"Come back tomorrow so we can do the next lesson," she said. "I've got to bathe now and have business to tend to later. I take several baths a day."

Nick was not sure what to do or even what he could do, his whole body on fire. He sat there watching her stupidly.

173

She laughed again, softly, "I'll see you tomorrow here aboard ship. No need to bring a sword. We can use mine."

He realized she was telling him to leave. He stood up slowly, her eyes still holding his in their teasing smile.

"Come here," she said, crooking a finger. He stepped to her, and she raised up out of the tub, her body streaming water, grasped his shirt, and pulled him down to kiss her again. He felt his knees weaken and was ashamed of himself for it.

"See you tomorrow," she whispered as she broke away again. Her nakedness on full display seemed not to bother her at all. Somehow it was different from the women at the Falstaff, who paraded about in such a way. Everything about this woman was different.

He made his way out the door adjusting his clothes. Sure enough, Pew stood just outside. The tall man's snake eyes locked with Nick's, and Nick wanted to start something. Wanted to beat this man to a pulp. But something far back in his mind whispered he should not do anything, so he walked on off the ship.

XXIV

L eesh looked past the graceful palms whose black fronds slatted across the silver shine of the sea under the setting moon. He was tired of being on land. He could feel its roots twining around his legs, transforming him into the kind of loathsome lubber he hated. It would be good to get back on the water again, to get some action and excitement back into his life.

Not that Hannah did not bring him enough conflict to keep him occupied. But he had lived so long and known so many women at this point that none could ever hold his attention so powerfully as those seven greatest women of the world—*los mares*, the mighty oceans of the world whose capricious moods far surpassed the capabilities of any human woman he had ever encountered. Even the most bewitching and unpredictable women Leesh had known paled compared to the sea.

Thankfully many things were afoot now, and Leesh could feel the excitement. He loved treasure, to be sure. He loved the feel of precious stones. He could look at rubies and emeralds and diamonds all day long and in fact considered himself an expert on them. He loved the smooth surfaces, the way the light caught and generated different colors. Translucence in such hard materials fascinated him deeply.

And he loved gold—ach, how he loved it! The very thought of it somehow spread his constant smile greater. Nothing had the heft of gold. All but the very tiniest bits of gold had it, sitting in a person's hand like an animal, its weight insisting upon its value in a kind of extra sense, as though it were a living thing pressing everything else on earth, living or otherwise, beneath it. Gold surely was the ultimately royalty, far greater than any potentate, of which Leesh had encountered not a few. The great rulers of the world may claim their power as coming from God, and Leesh was wise enough not to taunt or dare diety of any kind. But he well knew that all these powerful rulers owed fealty to great storerooms of bejeweled gold-encased relic casements, of mountains of coins, of fabulous accoutrements overlaid or solidly cast in this great entity, this beautiful yellow, gleaming, powerful, unending metal.

Not that silver should be disparaged. Oh no. Many a time Leesh had thrilled to its white grace, made all the more lovely when the tarnish was rubbed away. How many ingots of silver had he handled in his time? And those wonderful pieces of eight, how they shined! He was no musician, but if there were an instrument he had ever played it would have been letting them drop one by one from his hand, clanging against their brethren with their desultory, almost peevish tune, as though in their security at being fashioned of the second best metal they could whisper in the background of the truly visible dictator, over whom the real wars must be fought and at whom the most vicious criticism would be hurled. No, silver would never be cause for assassination; while its prettier sister must endure all the terrible trials and buffets of her position silver went right along enjoying its great position.

But it was not the precious objects alone that excited Leesh; also valuable to him was the movement of action itself. For reasons he himself could not explain beyond simply an accident of birth, Leesh possessed what he knew to be a very rare ability to see with tremendous vision. Most people he met in life could see only just in front of them. But he had always had the knack of seeing the motivations of many people involved in a situation and often having a reasonably good sense of what they might do before they actually did it.

He was not infallible at all. Not by a thousand fathoms. But it was that variable, that infallibility, that brought the excitement. There was something in the slippage between what he could see and predict and the fact that there were always things you could not see and that people so often did the unpredictable that quickened his nerves. What a splendid kind of jewel were human beings, the whole rotten lot of the lubbers. God bless them, they were the most beautiful ugly sorts of things on the whole blue and green earth. Who could say what they would do next? They came in inexhaustible supply and yet, remarkable as it seemed, never did one exactly resemble another. In his travels Leesh had known certain tribes to collect the shrunken heads of enemies and friends alike, and he had many times thought how nice it would be to save up the people he had met, stinkers and saints alike.

Well, the action had begun here now, and he was glad of it. Much to see of the field he now moved about on. Directives and bits of information were flowing all around, and he gathered it all and worked to fit the puzzle pieces together. He cooperated with Captain Stockett, to be sure, a man he trusted as much as any man might be trusted. But Leesh ultimately worked alone. Many times he had saved situations

177

through his own unique viewpoint and ingenuity. Stockett had downfalls, as anyone did—including Leesh himself—and so it was important to save the man from himself as well as from other forces.

Thus he had told no one of his trip out here. He had escaped in the earliest dark, having prearranged with the livery stable to hire a horse and have it tied to a tree on the outskirts of town, Leesh himself following the shadows of darkness in that slack time after even the biggest carousers finally collapsed into drunken sleep and before the industrious workers who kept this city in its everyday business began to stir. Thus he meant to slip out undetected. He was not sure if such secrecy was needed, but he well knew there were many people watching, and he determined to take no chances.

Once he found the horse and determined no one was hidden watching, he mounted and drove the animal hard down the path, hurrying as quickly as he could. There was little time, he knew, to accomplish what he must. It was a powerful stallion he rode, a long-legged creature far different from the squat ponies the Spanish had brought to this part of the world with them. Someone had probably stolen this one from somewhere in Arabia, and Leesh had paid a lot for his use. The horse was worth every penny, as he galloped along with incredible speed, his every muscle bent on motion. Leesh marveled at the thought of the size of this animal's heart pumping blood, his nostrils breathing in the air to fuel all joints, muscles, and bones moving and bending to attain speed.

Leesh had arrived quickly, slowing the horse as he approached to keep the sound down. There was a breeze here by the sea that kept the palms clattering, and he hoped that sound would mask his approach.

When he rode as close as he dared, he dismounted and, tying the horse up, crept up into the grounds. He had been here a few days ago with Hannah to visit the woman she had unloaded on the old owner of the plantation. That young lady, named Vivian, was a wonderful specimen herself, and many a time Leesh had thought to pay for time with her. But Hannah was a most jealous lady, and Leesh a most calculating man, who well understood how important it was not to threaten his own well-being foolishly. That said, if that young lady should be a sleep walker . . . .

But he was here on very urgent business, and during that trip here he had taken time to see how many dogs and other creatures sent to sound alarm he needed to know about. There seemed only one, a mastiff Leesh had made friends with, and as he made his way along the grounds his main aim was to keep the dog's fears allayed.

Not many men, especially ones of his age, could have pulled off such a thing. Few humans could ever approach a dog without the animal's knowing. But stealth was another of Leesh's gifts. It had been the first thing to distinguish him all the many years ago when he first fell in among cut throats and thieves, all the way back in old Cambridge town in 1638 . . . .

But there was no time for reflecting as he stopped again and gauged his situation. The moon was waning, but its light enabled him to find his bearings, and he could see the plantation house rising like a great white ghost against the backdrop of the mountainside. The windows were dark, as he had expected. He strained his eyes to see the dark shadow that would be the dog. He judged the mastiff was getting old, which would help, but still it would be difficult to sneak up on him.

Leesh's limbs might be remarkably strong and limber for his age, but his eyesight had suffered, especially recently. There was no beating old age. He could not see any indication of the dog. He would have to sneak closer.

He knew he was entering a dangerous proximity to the house and where the dog likely slept, and, though he hated to have to do it, he drew his knife from his sash as he made his way along. He did not want to kill the animal, but he would do so if necessary. He felt sure that if he could just reach the dog before he woke him then he could sooth the mastiff and all would be well. But there were no guarantees in this situation.

Then he heard the growl.

XXV

T he candles burned low, their wax rolled down like billows of the sea here in the dead dark of morning. Don Diego was awake as usual; he never slept at night when he had something afoot, saving all of his rest for the middle of the day, his cherished siesta, which he held to be one of the great trappings of civilization. The siesta had never been quite the necessary thing in Galicia that it was in other parts of Spain, so Don Diego saw it as a binding and bonding aspect of a civilized world that included all people of whatever rank.

But sleeping at night he had no time for at all. He generally finished all the letter writing for the day by midnight. Then the rest of those hours in the dark he spent developing various plans, moving pieces across a map in order to consider scenarios in which he might involve himself, with most of his efforts centered here in the Caribbean. He looked at a grouping of such pieces now, envisioning the ways the scenario might play out, giving particular attention to whatever contingencies he could imagine.

Scenarios and all the moving parts within them kept in constant motion, although it seemed at times that the entire situation would at times lurch forward. One of those seeming lurches had taken place today when he received the letter from O'Brien accepting his offer of cooperation. The letter had held little surprise for Don Diego, and it took him only a few moments to write out his reply and give it to the messenger.

To His Most Excellent Governor of Jamaica,

I have received your letter with pleasure and am glad to learn of your desire to cooperate. The date of August 29 agrees with me entirely.

There is no need for you to send a special ship to take myself and my delegation of a small personal guard to Port Royal. The Crown has provided me with a most inconspicuous ship—one reserved for just such purposes bearing none of the glorious marks of the Crown, unlike my usual royal vessel—upon which we can set sale at the appropriate time. The ship bears a Portuguese rather than a Spanish name, the *São Martinho*, and will raise no suspicion, having appeared on a regular basis in your harbor.

Assuming that all is well with this plan we shall proceed.

By the Grace of God and Our Lady

I remain gratefully yours,

Don Diego Pedro de la Figueroa

He had sent that letter away immediately by the English messenger. He doubted the Governor would agree very readily to his proposal of taking his own ship. He had already guessed during the night hours such as this very one tonight that the Governor would make such a suggestion. Don Diego would have been disappointed had he not. It was an offer that had the advantage of seeming guileless.

As Don Diego again worked through his plans he remained calm. He believed deeply in the principle of preparation. Having studied so many of the great conflicts of the ancients, he had always seen the power of preparation and planning. Certain elements were left to chance, no doubt about it. He could only pray for fortune to fall his way, and this he did every single day in his own private chapel here on the estate. But preparation could sometimes even mitigate fortune itself, and at least with correct and sufficient preparation many other impediments besides fortune could be removed.

He felt he had accounted for so much, but always there were surprises, and one must try to anticipate them all, for even the very least thing could put everything awry. Tonight there was only one thing he could think of that troubled him—something he could not seem to get out of his head. It was that messenger who had brought news of the *San Miguel* appearing in the Port Royal harbor. Somehow no one had ever found that messenger after he had delivered the news. Don Diego had ordered the ship detained and the entire island searched thoroughly. The latter was no easy task, however, for where Don Diego's estate stood on a clearing on a high cliff, the rest of the small island was dominated by thickest jungle rising against sheer cliffs, a single peak jutting high above sea level with only the smallest access at the dock. It would be easy for someone to disappear in that mass of green, and even the best search was unlikely to uncover every possible hiding place.

Had the man found such a place and remained on the island? Don Diego had decided on that being most likley and ordered a sharp look-out all around for the presence of any other ships in the area. When none were found he saw to it that the ship that had brought the messenger was searched—

that, at least, was possible—and, satisfied that no one had stowed away, the ship had been allowed to leave. Every ship that came and went thenceforward Don Diego kept a close watch on.

To Don Diego's thinking, it was best for the man to be hidden away out in this deadly jungle. All kinds of terrible beasts roamed the island to tear a human apart. As long as the man was prevented from communicating with anyone who left, Don Diego saw no way he could get any information back to an enemy. Meanwhile, Don Diego himself kept his own council, never voicing aloud his plans and thoughts, and sending his various orders through only the most trusted men.

Still . . . there was something disturbing about the idea of an enemy lurking somewhere in the darkness, perhaps this very moment. Thinking about it, Don Diego looked around him, as if perhaps he might catch the villain looking in the window.

It was the one thing he had not yet figured out how to account for. The man seemed to have been sent by Hector. At one time Don Diego had somewhat dismissed the little man as only an average swordsman at best and hardly a brilliant tactician and maneuverer. But he had been impressed with the man's resourcefulness. Don Diego well knew that Hector was entirely motivated by gain, both in money and power, and he wondered what the little man was about in sending a messenger who vanished into thin air.

Perhaps the messenger had been sent by someone else? Don Diego had considered that possibility. Could this pale-skinned Governor have sent the man as a spy? Did he have some way to communicate, perhaps via a pigeon? Don Diego had imagined the messenger camped on a ledge with a crude cage, sending off a bird trained to find Jamaica and return with other missives.

The thought was fantastic, but he had learned that here in the Caribbean the fantastic often became reality. There was a mysteriousness about this place. A man of weaker constitution might have been intimidated by it. Don Diego simply took it into account along with everything else that must be considered in his plans. Take it into account as he might, though, it remained a matter of concern, something he could not easily define or understand. He did not even know what the messenger looked like. The man would stand out on this island band of men all of whose faces Don Diego knew well, but in Port Royal, or anywhere else, Don Diego would have no idea what visage to look for as his silent and elusive enemy.

What was the ultimate impact of such a person? Don Diego had to admit that he had no idea. This mysterious messenger for the time being must simply be included with the weather, sickness, and other elements of fortune and misfortune that could either help or hurt Don Diego's plans. For now, Don Diego had time to consider the scenario, but with August 29 now set the speed would pick up and his time would start to run out. The period of planning was nearly over, and soon he must switch into full action mode.

XXVI

Leesh cursed in his mind at the sound of the low growl, but he remained calm, straining to figure out where the mastiff stood. The sound was so low Leesh thought the dog must be close by.

He stood still, holding his breath, as the growl died away. He could hear no sound of anything moving, no rustle of grass or pounding of paws in a rush to attack.

His neck rigid, his eyes looking about trying to catch any sign of movement, Leesh gathered his breath slowly.

"Arthur," he whispered the dog's name. "Here, Arthur. It's old Leesh."

Nothing. He held tightly to his knife, trying to anticipate the direction the dog would come from. If he could throw his left arm up to shield himself he could plunge the knife in. But if he could avoid it altogether . . .

"Arthur," he whispered again in as soothing a way as he could. Suddenly the wind shifted, blowing his scent toward the house. If the dog were there hopefully he would recognize Leesh's scent as familiar. But not knowing where the dog was Leesh could not know if that would happen. Who knew but that the dog had already caught his scent and did not care if they were friends already but simply considered him an intruder?

Leesh listened, hoping for something. Just the least indication.

He wet his lips to speak again.

Then he heard it. Puff-puff-puff, a stead lope, closer than he could imagine. He spun to where he thought it came from.

The impact knocked him on his back, hard, his knife flying from his hand.

Leesh felt the spit all over his face as the warm tongue licked him. He wanted to laugh out loud from the tickle of the swashing tongue and from his joy that the mastiff stood over him in friendly overture instead of tearing him to bits.

"Good boy," he whispered as quietly as he could. "Good boy."

He pushed the dog gently aside so he could stand. Then he found his knife and put it back in his sash. This was a good turn for him, but he was by no means out of danger, as the heavy panting of the dog well revealed. All he needed was for someone inside to hear that. He did not worry about the master of the house, but he did worry that the servants might set up an alarm. Of course, they were probably so worn out from work that nothing could rouse them, the poor devils. At least he hoped so.

He continued to move as quietly as possible, still sticking to the shadows, Arthur padding along with him and occasionally leaping on him, obviously thinking this a game. When Leesh had visited here with Hannah he had tried to get an idea of the house's layout. It was built in an open courtyard style, according to the Spanish model, with rooms end-to-end all the way around. This was good, much better than having to enter into a center hall and creep around the inside. He had figured out which rooms the master and his young wife kept, and he knew where the public parlor and dining room were. He was not entirely sure which room housed the person he sought, but he had a general idea.

The iron gate to the courtyard was not locked, and he hoped it was not too squeaky. He opened it very slowly, feeling its metal hinges grating. It would not take much to make a sound loud enough to wake someone here, so he eased it along, his goal to open it just enough that he could slip through. Thankfully he was not a big man.

He breathed a little easier when he got it to that point without it screeching. He slipped through swiftly and then immediately worked to pull it in to where Arthur could not come in. It seemed that Arthur did not care to. Perhaps he had been trained not to walk through the gate unless it was wide open. Or maybe he did not think there was much fun to be had inside where everyone was sleeping.

Leesh moved quickly away from the gate, hoping his doing so would not upset Arthur and send him howling or barking. The dog made no sound as Leesh darted like a shadow into the corner and stopped to orient himself.

There was the parlor and there the dining room and kitchen. These he was sure of. Above those in a second floor were located what he was almost certain were the bedrooms of the master and mistress. There were other rooms up there, but he doubted any were the ones he wanted.

Outside the house stood small huts where most of the slaves lived, but the man he sought would live in here, he believed. But which of the doors was the right one?

He had thought about this a bit and decided it was probably one of the rooms farthest from where the master slept. At first he had thought the master would have kept the man close by, but this man was not the head servant, just the driver. There was a small stable in the back, but another servant tended the horses. No, the man he sought was part of the household, trusted enough to bring people to and from the plantation but not the top person nor even the second or third. There had been a young light-skinned girl assigned to the new wife, and she was overseen by a fierce woman who also kept charge of the kitchen. The man Leesh wanted was probably under her.

But any of these doors could hold any of these servants. And Leesh could be altogether wrong in his surmising. Maybe none of these servants occupied these rooms. Who knew on these farms, which were self-contained little worlds to themselves where the logic of the larger world sagged like old thatching on an abandoned house. One heard of wild goings on out here, even between masters and slaves themselves. Perhaps that lovely light-skinned girl . . . .

Leesh focused. It was one of these doors, he really did believe. He looked them over for any sign to suggest their purpose or occupant, but they all looked exactly alike to him. It occurred to him for the first time that he should have swiped something belonging to the man he sought and enlisted Arthur's helping in tracking him.

Swounds, why didn't I think of that before?

Well, he must make the best of his situation. He tried to think what he could do if he got the wrong room. He could just hope he did not.

He approached the first one.

XXVII

O'Brien heard someone say the musician's name, but it was as unpronounceable for him as any other here in Bavaria. He watched the man stand, with his yellow stockings, the curls of his long dark hair glistening in the chandelier light.

Everyone was catching their breath, but O'Brien watched the man stand up, holding a strange little instrument. It looked like a violin but was shaped differently. Instead of f-holes, jagged tears stretched up both sides of the body's top. And there seemed to be far more strings—how many? O'Brien counted seven.

He was wondering at the instrument when someone appeared before him. It took him a moment to register who it was, as if he looked at the person and saw only a blurred form. Then the form resolved.

Katarina

She smiled at him, her white teeth small and perfect, framed by her full lips, the lower one pouting. Her porcelain smooth white skin molded over exquisite bones, and her eyes were pale blue, the pupils tiny. Her hair cascaded in long black curls.

"William," she said, with perfect elocution. "Are you quite ready?"

Her voice, so smooth and yet strangely childlike. Not quite right, though.

She doesn't talk this way. What is different?

He took her in his arms as he heard the first sweep of the bow across that strange instrument. Even as he swung into the dance, he looked up to see the musician playing, standing between the two people playing viola da gambas, the big instruments' bodies between their knees.

The smell of Katarina's perfume flowed through his nose, touching parts of his brain he had never imagined could be stimulated.

Where was Sean? Did he approve of his dancing with Katarina?

Of course he does. He's going to leave her behind anyway. He doesn't care. And anyway neither do I. I'm doing nothing wrong.

He abandoned himself to the dance as the instrument resonated throughout the ballroom here in the Residenz. Now this Bavarian hall, and even Bavaria itself, did not seem foreign anymore but filled with familiarity and everything he could ever want.

He felt her soft body in his arms as they turned and bobbed to the music. Her hand felt tiny in his own, the fingers delicate. And her eyes . . . they peered into his own in their pale blue, smiling at him, warm, excited.

Katarina

But something was different. Why had she come to him this way? Had she left Sean behind? She was always sweet and polite and talked to O'Brien, but she showered all of her real attention on Sean.

And the way she spoke. Why was it different?

And why did everything feel so strange, as if this all had already happened, and long ago, as though he were looking back on it even though it never actually happened? Something about the whole situation felt false.

On and on the music played. It seemed to last forever, and that was fine with O'Brien. He never wanted this to end. But just as the musician playing that strange little instrument never slowed or seemed to tire both O'Brien and Katarina danced on and on.

Then her eyes changed, a hot desire filling them, beaming a powerful new energy at him. They stopped their dance right there, breaking the rhythm of the rest of the dancers and not caring. She presented her mouth to him, that lower lip pouting so intensely he thought he would go mad. He was mad.

He lowered his lips to hers.

She's speaking English

The thought rampaged through his mind as darkness fell over him like a blanket and he realized his eyes were open. He was lying in a massive bed in the dark.

A dream

His heart was racing.

Of course

Katarina had never danced with him. She had never smiled at him that way in real life.

He knew exactly why he had dreamed of her—because he had seen her just this afternoon. Not Katarina literally, but her exact copy.

She had come to him, announced by the footman, "The Lady Evernia."

His knees had buckled when she walked into the room. The more he had learned of this lady—this pirate lady—who captained her own ship the more he had suspected. It seemed hard to believe, but he had lived long enough to see remarkable coincidences in real life.

He had not known exactly what her precise relation to Katarina was, but if the rumors were true they were of that same Wittelsbach family. Now that he saw her in the flesh he knew what that relation was.

"Please, come in," he said.

She walked in with ease, as though she had always owned this mansion and in fact himself. Ruefully he realized she had indeed always owned him even if they had only just met.

"Thank you," she said at last as he gestured to her to sit.

"Would you like tea?"

"Yes, please."

He ordered a servant to bring the tea. Then he sat looking at her, trying to hide the emotions her appearance inspired in him. He struggled to keep his thoughts clear. Vaguely he realized he should be wondering why she was visiting him.

"What can I do for you?" he asked.

She smiled, and it was a smile he knew well, although he had never experienced its full power turned on him. He doubted anyone on earth could withstand it.

"I wanted to meet you," she said. "I have heard many wonderful things about you. You are quite a renowned leader, maybe the greatest Jamaica has yet known."

The comment was absurd. He had done nothing particularly wonderful here. He had served in the English military and was a person of distinction, but he was hardly famous enough to warrant such a grandiose statement. It so obviously meant to flatter that he could tell instantly she was here to con him.

He smiled back in a mildly patronizing way, "I am only an humble servant of the Crown."

She kept her eyes on his—their pale blue heart-shakingly familiar—as the tea came. Her every movement was studied and careful, trained in the highest ways. She hardly belonged in this rough and raw part of the world. Something about her shined against the entire atmosphere of the place, including this Mansion, which was an oasis of culture here. She was almost otherworldy.

"You are a great soldier," she said.

He felt embarrassed for her that she should press on with this flattery, and that feeling increased as he saw her pull her chin in and curve her shoulders in a subtle figure-eight motion.

Poor girl. Yes, she's beautiful. But I've lived many years. I have the most beautiful woman in the world already. And Katarina . . . . is long in the past.

She held his gaze a moment, then she looked around the room, her eyes alighting on the book shelves. She stood up, again her movements easy, and walked toward the shelves.

"*The Great Cause of Liberty Conscience*," she said. "Do you agree with Mister Penn?"

The question caught him off guard, and his mind quickly reset as he reassessed her. He had formed an opinion of her as simply a beautiful ruffian, a rich young woman sewing her oats in the West Indies. He was shocked to see her mention this treatise on religious tolerance. He recovered quickly, however, remembering the tools of a con. He doubted she had read it.

"What do you mean?"

"Well, it strikes me that from his Quaker standpoint he offers a cogent and quite vital defense for our conscience dictating our policy."

O'Brien was stunned. Again he reassessed, deciding to press her.

"Do you not think there is a flaw in trusting too much to conscience?" he asked. "After all, scripture is written down. We can point to words, divine words. But conscience can be wrong."

She delayed a moment, looking at the other books on the shelf, and he was surprised to find himself feeling he had perhaps spoken out of turn and without full authority, so added, "Not that I am an ecclesiast, of course."

She remained silent still but now raised her hand to point to another volume, a folio of plays written by the late Shakespeare.

"I feel within me a peace above all earthly dignities, a still and quiet conscience," she had quoted from *Henry VIII*. O'Brien recognized it, and his nerves quickened with excitement as a different Shakespeare quote sprang to mind, and he spoke the lines:

> "Conscience is but a word that cowards use, Devis'd
> at first to keep the strong in awe:
> Our strong arms be our conscience, swords our law.
> March on, join bravely, let us to't pell-mell;
> If not to heaven, then hand in hand to hell."

She delayed a moment, and again he felt he had gone to far—ashamed that he had played unfairly against her. But she showed no sign of being daunted as she spoke, "Richard III had no conscience to speak of."

"But you see my point. A conscience can misguide."

She turned and looked at him, her pale eyes catching the diffused sunlight in the room, "You're assuming something stable to misguide away from."

The comment took him aback. He was not quite sure how to answer for a moment but then recovered, "We have the divine revelation."

She smiled and then laughed, a single light sound that softened everything in the room. It confused him. Now she seemed to be the one who knew things he did not. Was she questioning revelation itself? That was ridiculous. And yet . . . .

He realized the confusion on his face and that she saw it, so he recomposed himself. It was then that she walked slowly toward him in a brazen gait that made its purpose clear. With servants right there in the room watching, she put her hand on his gray hair and curved her hand smoothly along the side of his face. Then in a smooth motion she glided into his lap.

He looked at the servants, his pulse racing.

Katarina

He knew he should tell her to stand up. She was so small and light he could have picked her up. But he felt paralyzed.

He looked up into her eyes, which peered back at him with a strange blend of hot and cold.

"It is a pleasure to meet you," she said, and the way she said "pleasure" weighed heavily with promise.

She left then, and for the rest of the day he had been able to think of nothing else but the encounter—how she looked, what she said, the way she had turned the tables on him so effortlessly. Somewhere in the back of his mind warning bells rang, but far overpowering them was the great gushing sound of his desire to see her again, to talk to her about what she read. Elizabeth, the fairest in all the land, suddenly looked like a peasant girl to him, and her silly unread way showed just how empty and false she was. Now he had encountered the real thing, a truly wonderful woman just like

. . . .

He had not thought to inquire as to her parentage. He already knew. This must be Katarina's daughter.

And now she had returned. Stood here in this room.

In his dreams.

XXVIII

L eesh opened the door slowly, feeling carefully for any sign of resistance that might make a creak. He had little time, but he knew he needed patience.

Finally he opened the door just wide enough and glided through. The moonlight poured through the window, casting the entire room in blue. Immediately he could sense this was not the room where the man he sought slept. He could not explain how he knew but he did. Still he must make certain.

He neared the bed and discerned a woman sleeping between two children. The sight struck him. He did not think much on slavery—it was simply part of the world he lived in. But at moments such as these, looking at a mother and her two children sleeping, the thought passed through his mind that while they may not live such hard lives as the slaves working in the fields they nevertheless faced little opportunity for freedom. The same was the case with the peasants of England and other parts of Europe he had been to. All over the world there were people who may have been born with talent and ability, often far more than their betters, but most of them would never have the chance to use those talents and abilities in meaningful ways. The world was built the way it was built, and it was very difficult to advance beyond one's starting point.

It was not impossible, though. Piracy offered one way to break out, and Leesh had seen many do so. But at what a price? The constant threat of death, the necessity of living as an outlaw. No wonder many of the men who gained treasures took themselves out of harm's way and built plantations such as this one. But killing and thieving followed you, hanging about you like the fumes of rum. You might think you have enough money and that you want to settle down, having secured a new position in life. But so often you cannot escape your deeds.

Leesh lingered for a moment, listening to the quiet breathing of the mother and her children as they slept. For a moment he felt himself transported in time and space away from Port Royal to Canterbury in his own little bed as a child, in the blue light of the moon, his little world small. For a moment he recalled what it was like to be innocent, far from the ugly acting of humankind. He had not been like these children; opportunity had abounded for him. And what had he done with it? He felt a tremor in his cheek but steeled himself. This was no time to dawdle.

The Devil take it

He started to back away carefully.

"Um-hm-ugh."

The sound came from the bed and Leesh froze, watching.

The mother had started. He could see her moving. She was turning over, putting her arm around her daughter.

Leesh narrowed his eyes. It seemed the mother was looking right at him. It was hard to tell if her eyes were open here in the dark. Surely she would have reacted if they were.

He started to back away again. He reached the door and shut it softly, relieved. Had the woman screamed he would have had to silence her and the children, and that would have been unfortunate.

Moving quickly in the darkness he came to the next door and again eased it open.

This time he knew he had the room he wanted.

Again, some kind of inner sense told him the man he sought lay in the bed here. Leesh moved toward it swiftly. There was so little time.

Looking around to make sure no one else slept here Leesh bent over the bed and put his hand over the man's mouth.

The man jerked awake, but Leesh held him, exerting as much strength as possible.

"Shh," Leesh whispered in his ear. "Mo wa ore."

The man jerked again, and Leesh could see his eye rolling upward in the dark trying to see him.

"I am not here to hurt you," Leesh said. "I want to give you freedom. Ominara."

Leesh saw the man's eyes roll back to a forward gaze. He had no idea if he was having any influence over him.

"I need help from you. You can be free if you come with me. A slave no more. Se o mo?"

Leesh waited for a reaction.

"I hate to come to you this way, but you must trust me. We must leave at night. To show I mean no harm I am only asking you to come with me of your own free will. There are other ways to make you come. You can have freedom, wealth, anything else you want. I know you're not happy here."

Again Leesh waited for a response. None came.

"It's a pirate's life I'm offering, mate. A life where you prove yourself, and you get whatever you work for. No more being a slave. I can tell you're not happy here. You know who I am don't you?"

Leesh waited a moment, and finally he felt the man's nod under his hand.

"Good, mate. I know some African words because I sailed there many years before the mast. I am asking you to trust me. I need your help, and I can help you. Come with me and you never have to come back here again. You can become part of our crew, and we will see to your protection. That's what I offer you. Your help for freedom."

The man made a noise under Leesh's hand.

"Don't talk too loud, mate," Leesh warned. "If I let you go and you bellow I'll slit your throat sure as rain. Do you understand."

No response. Time was running out. Leesh jerked him violently, "Se o mo?"

The man nodded. Leesh took his hand away from the man's body first and grabbed his knife. Then he took his hand away from the man's mouth. He said nothing, so Leesh said, "What did you want to say?"

The man lay still for a moment, then whispered, "What happens if I no go with?"

"Well, mate, I come to you with this fair offer you can take or leave like a man free as any gull. If you say no then I'll be on my way. I *do* kindly request you to say nothing of this meeting in that case. If you do say something, then you'll surely die. I tell you this as two men, not as free and slave. I'd say the same to any. By the heavens, I think that a fair and even deal to be made between mates."

The man lay there, apparently thinking.

"One more thing, friend, "Leesh continued. "There's not much time. You must make your decision quickly and we

201

must hurry away. You'll have just time to dress. So you must decide one way or the other now."

Again the man delayed. Leesh could sense him wrestling.

"How do I know you tell truth?" the man asked. "You are pirate. You are slaver."

"No slaver, mate. I'll admit I've trafficked in living people, but only as my general business. I'm no trader."

He knew it was a weak response. Likely this man would not be much impressed with such a fine distinction. Leesh knew something else too—that if this man did indeed refuse to go with him he probably *would* have to kill him here in his bed.

"What is your freedom worth, mate?" Leesh said, the compassion in his voice genuine. "Do you want to spend the rest of your life a slave or a man?"

Leesh meant it. He really did not want to have to kill him. But he needed a response. He waited still.

"I'm going to start counting down from ten, mate," Leesh said.

"Ten."

The man lay still.

"Nine."

Leesh gave a pause.

"Eight."

Still nothing.

"Seven."

Leesh's grip tightened on his knife.

"Six."

Leesh shook his head in pity.

"Five."

Still nothing.

"Four."

Nothing.

"Three."

"Wait."

"No time left, mate. Coming or going?"

A pause, "I go."

XXIX

Nick tried his hardest to get back to sleep, knowing that having to try was a sign he would fail.

He had been distracted from the moment he walked out of the captain's quarters aboard the *San Miguel* yesterday. His nose was filled with the Lady Evernia's—Damiana's—perfume. His eyes were filled with the vision of her. His brain could not seem to focus on anything else.

He had wandered around Port Royal, hardly aware of where he was going. It was as if he saw the world anew, this woman bringing it to life in fresh ways. Now that he knew the sound of her voice and had interacted with her she seemed more real to him, but somehow even that familiarity had not lessened her mystery or the aura surrounding her. Now he wanted even more to know her, to be a part of her life, to . . . possess her. He wanted the world to know he was with her and that she was with him.

It was the first time in his life he had ever been intoxicated, and the feeling of it charged through every part of his person. For awhile it was a wonderful, powerful, energized feeling. But then that feeling started to subside, replaced with a kind of dull ache. Being apart from her dimmed life. And a part of him actually worried a little. He wondered what kind of thing she might be doing this moment with that Pew. He imagined him with her as she bathed. What all had he done with her? Who was he?

Nick sensed that Pew was hardly a rival for him. He was not good-looking or attractive in any way. Nick recalled her saying he was in love with her and her laughing dismissively. The memory of that disturbed him, and he could not exactly explain why.

Now he was walking through the city not sure where he was, trying to work out this disturbed feeling, trying to understand the way he felt and who this woman was.

He reached the Falstaff and went in, getting himself a drink of water.

"Nick," he heard and looked up to see Abigail. His heart immediately warmed. *She* never gave him an uneasy feeling at all. He knew where he stood with her, and it filled him with gladness to see her green eyes.

"Hello!" he said and hugged her. She felt soft and solid in his arms, a stable presence that put everything in a familiar and welcome place. "How is your day so far?"

"Well," she said, her eyes laughing. "And you?"

"I'm doing very well, especially now that I'm seeing you."

She blushed and tucked her chin, an innocent, endearing gesture that gladdened Nick even more.

But then he felt something else. A small scratch of guilt. He had a feeling he had betrayed this sweet soul.

But I did nothing out of line

He *had* kissed, Damiana. But really she had kissed him. And he had done nothing, well, sinful. But . . . .

"Are you all right?" Abigial asked, her green eyes concerned.

"Yes," he said, tamping that guilt down and smiling. "Let's eat. I'm starved."

In the afternoon he went with the crew to prepare the *Tetrarch* for setting sail. He did not know many of the details, but he knew word had come to weigh anchor soon. He saw the *San Miguel* and thought about her there.

Damiana

Again the uneasy feeling came to him, and his guilt brought him to think about Abigail. Then, strangely, he found himself feeling very good about both women being in his life. He had not necessarily thought of himself as a man whom ladies would be distracted over. He had always loved Sarah alone. But his mind cast back to that night in the tavern in Bristol when he had first met Leesh. He remembered the beautiful women there and the feeling the place had given him. His mother's religious teachings had caused him to recoil from that scene, but another part of him had longed for it. How he had wanted to be part of that world, those women all around him! He had not seemed to catch the attention of the bawds at the Falstaff for some reason. Perhaps because he did not offer to pay, and they had plenty of men bringing them business. And he did not think paying to be with women to be a very legitimate thing.

But Abigail and Damiana had both approached *him*, not the other way around. And maybe he was some kind of man to be desired. The feeling that he might hurt one or the other nagged at him, but it did not outweigh the more pleasant feeling of being wanted.

In fact, as he worked he felt his muscles bulging and growing with his gaining strength, and this made him feel all the more manly. He imagined both of the women going about their womanly business. He imagined Abigial awaiting his return. Then he imagined himself with the Lady Evernia and his crewmates in awe of him by being with her.

He went back to the Falstaff with that feeling in his body and heart, and when he arrived he basked in Abigail's attention. He could tell it brought her joy to wait on him, and he let her do so. He also found himself talking in ways he was unaccustomed to, a little saltier than usual, and peppering his language a little more with slang.

But not too much. He caught himself doing it and wondered to himself,

Who am I?

He toned it down then and recovered his usual self, escorting Abigail upstairs, the men taunting him gently. He kissed her before she went into her room, an innocent, soft, quiet kind of kiss. Very different from the kisses he had received earlier.

"Good night, dear," she said, smiling up at him.

"Good night."

He watched her smile vanish behind the door as she closed it behind her. The guilt set in immediately.

Two in one day I've kissed

It was hard for him to believe. He got in bed and thought about this day. Who was he, indeed? He replayed the different scenes, and it struck him that he was not being fair with these two women. They were both giving him their affection, but he was splitting his. But, then, he felt differently about both of them. Abigail was so loyal and solid and sweet. Damiana was . . . he did not even know how to begin to describe her. She was exciting, provoking, mysterious, utterly unique.

He was still unaccustomed to the physical work, so his tiredness did not take long to overtake him. He slept deeply, but once again he awoke in the dead of the morning, his body more alive than ever with lust for the black-haired woman, only now she was "Damiana," a named entity whom he had interacted with, whose body he had seen, whose lips he had kissed.

Strangely, he heard footsteps down the hall. Someone walking quietly out. That was not so unusual here at the Falstaff, as men came and went throughout all hours of the day and night. Still, most men who had paid up for the night were sleeping at this point. This was the only quiet time in the city, and even these hours were not so quiet everywhere.

It took what seemed an eternity, but finally Nick went back to sleep, and when he awoke again it was broad daylight. His body felt worn from his labor aboard ship yesterday as well as the fitful night of sleep.

He tremored at the realization that he would see and interact with Damiana again today, and he dressed quickly and headed out the door. Hurrying downstairs he ran into Abigail.

"Good morning, Nicky," she said.

"Good morning."

"Nick," she caught his arm.

"Yes," he heard the mild irritation in his voice.

"Are you all right?"

She had asked him the same thing yesterday, and now it seemed too much. Why was she asking him this? It irritated him more, which he tried to hide.

"Yes."

"Good. I was wondering if . . ."

"What?" he tried not to sound so curt but was not succeeding.

She looked at him, reading his eyes, "I was wondering if you would like to go out to the beach. It's a very pretty day."

Nick looked at her eyes watching him innocently, and his irritation subsided. He felt he had planned to commit some kind of sin (and perhaps he was), and now he saw he should not.

The pleasures of sin for a season

Gladness welled in him. This very good woman was keeping him from mischief. He did not need to be around that other woman if he was going to be tempted to do evil.

"Yes," he said, "Let's go."

"Not now, lad," a man's voice said.

Nick turned to see Captain Stockett walking through the doorway that led upstairs.

"The crew needs to meet now. Out with you, Miss."

Abigail looked at Nick, smiled and curtseyed, and headed out the door into the street to the market where she had been headed.

"Sit down, Nick," the Captain said, directing Nick to a table.

XXX

When O'Brien read the letter from the Special Counsel he pondered what it meant that he would take his own ship to the city. It brought less control of the situation, which O'Brien did not like. But he also did not want to do anything that would put Don Diego on guard or give away his own plans.

Time was moving swiftly toward August 29. Now that events were set in motion he found himself questioning the plan again and again, trying to find flaws in it. He could only hope he had been correctly informed. It was so difficult to be completely sure. In all his days at war he had been plagued by the reality that information, timing, and so many other factors could and in fact almost always did alter even the best plans.

Meanwhile, the woman had been on his mind. The Lady Evernia, as she was called. She looked so like Katarina. That resemblance affected him mightily, as had her personality and her way of interacting with him. The whole encounter gave him pause and made him think through whether he actually liked his plan. Indeed, he had more or less decided to make some changes that he alone would know about. Best not to let a band of pirates in on every step of that plan.

A knock came at the door and a footman entered, announcing, "Lady O'Brien, sir."

"Show her in," O'Brien said.

She entered, fluttering her fan over her delicate face, "Oh, Willie, it is so very hot outside."

"Yes, it is," he said, immediately feeling the mix of anger and disappointment in her that pained him like a dull endless toothache. "What do you want me to do about it?"

"Oh, hahahaha," she said, a fluttering laugh that matched the motion of her fanning. The laugh enraged him. She was really a very flimsy person in every way.

"Elizabeth, I am quite busy at the moment."

"Oh, I know. I just wanted to stop in and say hello."

His eyes narrowed. She did not usually disturb him this way.

"Has something happened?" he asked.

"No."

He watched her, "Very well, then. I hate to be rude, but I really must tend to my duties for the day."

She still stood there. Then she spoke, a little breathlessly, "There is something, Willie, dear. I am wondering if you might send someone down into the market there to buy me a little something?"

"What?" he raised an eyebrow.

"Well, Martha said she saw the most delicate lace there, and I so would like more lace."

"Martha."

"Yes, you know, Martha. My maid?"

"Yes, yes, I know Martha. I was just thinking . . ."

"What?"

His mind raced, trying to decide if Martha was some kind of enemy. Surely not. Surely she had just been shopping as she naturally would.

Ach, calm down. Too much fear and suspicion only cloud things

O'Brien took out his purse, "How much?"

She hesitated, "I don't want you to give it to *me*?"

"What?" he could not hide his irritation and bewilderment as he looked up at her.

"I don't want to go buy it. I want to send Martha."

"Well send her then."

"She must have money."

"Well, give this to her," he extended his hand.

"No. I must not touch it."

"This is preposterous!"

"Please, Willie."

"Don't call me Willie!"

He realized he had stood up on those words, and he saw her shrink, tears filling her eyes. She turned and ran out of the room.

Regret filled him. He had treated her too roughly.

But I'm a rough man. A warrior

He pushed the emotions away with ease, having done so for years during combat when he saw men maimed and killed. This was hardly as severe as that. Large matters needed tending to.

Sitting back down, he shifted a piece of paper in front of him and wrote.

> Most Excellent Special Counsel,
>
> I am pleased to receive your letter and to know that our cooperation will soon be realized. I quite understand your desire to spare me the trouble of sending you a ship. For the sake of hospitality, however, I would like to offer that service once more. As our proposed date of August 29 quickly approaches, I realize there will not be time for you to reply, so if you would like to accept my offer

please feel free to return on the ship by which I send this missive. I look forward to greeting you in person soon.

With Gratitude I Remain Your Humble Servant,
William O'Brien

He blotted the paper and folded and sealed it. He had already briefed the captain of the ship he would send, so he had the message sent with instructions for the ship to set sail as soon as ready.

Then he called for the Admiral.

XXXI

The crewmen made their way into the Falstaff. Nick felt restless, eager to get out to the *San Miguel*.

The Captain told Edward Corbyn to keep a watch out and not let anyone in while they met.

"Where the devil is Leesh?" the Captain asked. No one knew. Nick thought about the old man probably off fornicating. Then Nick imagined himself doing so and immediately tried to purge the thrill the thought gave him.

"Well, I'll say what we need to say and be quick about it," the Captain said. "We've gotten word to set sail tomorrow."

Sounds of surprise erupted in the room.

"That's a bit soon, Cap," one of the men said, a short fellow named John Black.

"You know we have been preparing to leave at a moment's notice," the Captain said.

"Can you tell us where we're headed?" Nathan Birdsong asked.

The Captain nodded to Stuart, who spoke, "We'll set a course due east."

More sounds of surprise, and Nick himself wondered what such a course meant. A third man, John Wheeler, spoke up, "Due east? But are we not after gold on the Main?"

The Captain put his hand up to silence the men.

"We'll be sailing with the *San Miguel*. I will tell their captain of this plan as soon as we have finished here."

"Can't you tell us anything, sir?" pleaded George Larson, a hulking beast of a man who had only recently joined the crew.

"You will receive further orders in due time," the Captain replied, and then shifted his head to see as someone entered.

It was Leesh. And a man accompanied him.

"Hello, ladies all!" Leesh said, making his way inside and toward the Captain. The man with him was black, his face severe. He looked gaunt, weak. But there was something about him that suggested he was stronger than he appeared.

"I have a new mate to introduce," Leesh said, bringing more surprised responses, and Nick looked at the Captain, who registered surprise even on his face.

"This is Izegbe. He is going to set sail with us. He's a good man. A very good man to have aboard ship."

"Asking leave to speak, Captain," said John Wheeler.

"Aye, man," Captain Stockett said, even as his gaze searching Leesh.

"Well, sir. It's just that . . . things being, you might say . . . well, the winds not blowing in our favor lately, well . . ."

"Well, what?" the Captain thundered.

"Well, sir, we don't know whose been . . ."

"Who's been what?"

"Well, sir, I guess there's no better way of putting it. We don't know who's been ratting on us. And now . . . there's this new fellow."

"See here," the Captain said, and his voice dropped to a low register. "We all know knavery's been afoot. I don't blame a one of ye. And I'm asking you to trust me now. If you cannot do so I will understand and there'll be no hard feelings. But you need to walk now if you don't want to sail with us. I'll brook no doubtings of me before the mast. Those of you who've sailed with me know I'm straight with you and I'll not steer you wrong."

"It's not that, Captain," another broke in. "Nobody's doubting you. It's whoever the traitor is."

"I'm not believing there's a traitor among us," the Captain said, authority projecting through his voice with a power just short of harshness. "I've been investigating the whole matter. There's knavery afoot and maybe more."

A murmur stirred among the men.

"But we mean to carry on as we will," he went on. "No one ever said treasure came easy. We sail together to gain our own. So, I say again, if you are doubting at all you can leave now and all is well. But I'll not tolerate any insurrection once we set sail. You may be spared a bootless trip, but then again you may miss out on a more than fair take."

Nick looked around the room at the men, reading their faces. He had already decided the Captain was withholding information until they were at sea so that no one could leak their destination. Now he wondered if the Captain also was looking to weed men out. But then would a spy leave now not knowing what would happen? And would a spy have some other means to communicate from aboard ship?

His interest in the moment relieved the pulsing desire within him to get out to the *San Miguel* some but not entirely. He knew he should be going with the crew to make the ship ready, but he wanted badly to see Damiana.

First one man, and then two others turned and walked slowly out of the Falstaff under the Captain's watch. Only three, all of them new to the crew. Nick looked at their faces.

"Anyone else?" the Captain asked, his voice and facial expression neutral, nonjudgmental.

No one moved. All held their chins high and their gaze locked on the Captain.

"Very well, then. You know what to do."

The men scattered, heading out to the ship. Nick stood up to go with him, but heard the Captain say to Leesh under his breath, "What have you got us into now?"

"You see we're shorthanded," Leesh said, quietly, sidling up to the Captain.

"Can he sail?"

"He can do better than that. We need to talk."

"Yes, we do," said a woman's voice.

Nick looked up to see Damiana standing there with Pew.

XXXII

"A bird told me you all were meeting," Damiana said, her voice level.

"Yes. And my bosun and I were about to come tell you exactly what we said," the Captain replied.

She watched him, "We should have met all together."

"Aye, lady, perhaps you're right at that," the Captain said, and Nick detected a note of condescension and was a little surprised to feel anger rise in himself at the Captain for it.

"Well, what is the news, then?" she asked.

"We sail tomorrow."

She looked at him a moment, and Nick noted how capable she appeared.

"Very well," she said and turned to go. Then she stopped and pointed to Nick. "This man I want to sail with me aboard the *San Miguel*."

Nick felt the Captain, Leesh, and the new man all look to him. A strange mix of feelings came over him—surprise blended with embarrassment that gave way to a kind of pride.

"We're short-handed, miss," the Captain said. "I cannot spare him."

"I will exchange two of my men for him."

The Captain looked at her. She looked at Nick, her eyes giving him a warm—was it loving?—look. She went on, "I think it good for our crews to mix so that we all know we are truly working together."

She looked back at the Captain as she finished, her look clearly conveying that he had broken her trust.

The Captain returned her look and then let his gaze drop as he pondered the offer. After a moment he looked up at Nick, "What do you want to do, lad?"

Nick felt himself redden. He was not exactly sure what he wanted, not entirely sure he understood everything that was happening.

"You're the Captain, sir," he said and immediately regretted it. It was then he realized just how much he wanted this lady.

"This man is not equipped to cross swords with the Spanish," she said. "I have begun to train him, and that will make him an asset to your crew."

Nick felt his reddening deeper as he felt the questioning gaze of the Captain and Leesh on him.

"It is difficult to argue with her reasoning," the Captain said, finally. "So I ask you again, lad. Will you go aboard her ship or your own?"

Nick looked at the Captain and then at the woman. He thought he could see something in her eyes—the beginning of disappointment.

"I don't know that he is quite at liberty to go aboard your ship, my lady," Leesh said, as though he had awakened from a deep sleep. Nick saw her turn her eyes on him. "You see he has a lady of his own. And I believe she is a jealous one, to be sure. So I imagine he is probably not much at liberty to sail with a different lady, if you understand what I mean, and begging your pardon, miss."

219

Damiana had cocked her head as Leesh spoke, looking down at him, the heels of her boots lifting her above him. Leesh himself beamed his smile upward at her.

"She's not my lady," Nick said, a little more frantically than he normally would.

As soon as he said it he was sorry. But then he felt something else. A kind of shift in the room. His heart sank. He hated to turn his head and look, knowing what he would see. But he must, and he did.

There Abigail stood.

Nick saw her green eyes well with tears, and he felt himself the meanest person in the world.

"Abigail," he said. "I—"

She started shaking her head slowly, then turned and ran away.

Nick wanted to chase her. Guilt spurred him to do so. But he did not want to do anything to lose Damiana, to whom he turned and looked. Her cold eyes peered at him with a new understanding.

"Now that I consider it," Captain Stockett's voice broke in. "I recall that this man *is* recovering from a wound. I don't believe he is fit to sail as yet. Better to stay and strengthen yourself, lad."

"I'm fine to sail, sir," Nick said.

"It's all right, sweetie," Damiana said, her voice now condescending to Nick. "She's a sweet girl. You should stay with her."

Nick looked at her, feeling he was losing her.

"Sir, I am fine to set sail in the morning. I am not attached to that lady."

"We'll see you in the morning, gentlemen," Damiana said, and Nick thought he saw tears in her eyes as she turned to leave. Somehow Nick had forgotten that Pew was standing there, but now he saw the man looking at him with triumph in his narrow snake-like eyes before he turned and followed her out the door.

Nick looked at the Captain and Leesh, who smiled at him in his usual way.

"You might want to talk to the young lady," Leesh said.

Emotions surging, Nick turned to head upstairs.

Nick cursed in his mind as he stalked up the stairs. How could things go wrong so quickly? Just yesterday he had been basking in the experience of having two women in love with him at the same time. He may have felt a little guilt, yes, but that hardly compared with his feeling of elation.

But now the whole situation had toppled. He was not sure exactly how to fix it. Both women were hurt, he could plainly see, but something in him guided him toward Abigail first even though he thought he saw a softer side of Damiana that also hurt. He thought then maybe he should run out and catch her instead.

He was here now, though, at the door to the room Abigail stayed in. He knocked.

"Abigail."

No answer.

"Abigail."

Nothing. Fear seized him that maybe he would not be able to fix this situation. He decided to speak through the door to her.

"Abigail, I'm . . ." he was not sure what to say. He was definitely sorry for what he had said, but saying he was sorry would also bring it back up that he had said it in the first place. He burned even more with shame and regret. "Abigail, I'm so sorry. I wouldn't . . I wouldn't hurt you for the world."

The catch in his voice surprised himself, and as he spoke memories of the past weeks flooded over him. The sweetness of her voice, her green, green eyes, the frolics and flirtations they had, that complete belief in and loyalty to him. He felt like a monster: selfish, uncaring. He could hardly believe himself.

"Can you please open the door?"

He waited, listening even for just some kind of movement. Still nothing.

Turning to go, he heard the door unlatch and turn. He stopped and looked as Abigail opened the door, her face red with crying. Seeing her that way he felt awful. He hugged her and she came into his arms sobbing.

"I'm so sorry, Abigail," he said, stroking the back of her head and holding her, feeling her sobs. He wanted to say that if he could have unsaid what he had said he would. But somehow it seemed best to stay quiet and hold her.

Finally she pulled away enough to look up at him, the green of her eyes set off by the red around them, "Nick, I—I loved you."

The past tense of her statement hit him hard.

"Abigail, I—" his hesitation told him volumes but he willed himself not only to say it but to believe it completely. "I love *you*."

She squeezed her eyes as though in pain, tears spurting out and rolling down her cheeks, "Then why did you say what you said?"

"I . . ." he had no idea how to answer. Nothing he could think of to say came anywhere close to sounding right. "I'm just a fool," he said bitterly.

She put her arms around his neck, drew his face down to hers, and kissed him. He could feel her passion gathering through every part of her body and spirit and directed into her lips. He had never been kissed that way before, not even by Sarah. The kiss communicated to him how completely he filled up this woman's life. Its power awed him, bent him backwards. Through the mist of the moment came the conviction that no one would ever love him this much again and that he must hang on to this woman. She may not have the mystery or beauty of the Lady Evernia, but she was true as true could be.

Here was the full key to happiness, and maybe the Captain was right in saying that Nick should stay behind. Obviously the Captain and Leesh sought to keep him from Damiana, and perhaps they had the right idea. It *was* true that he had not entirely healed.

And worse yet, he had the feeling that the Lady Evernia— Damiana—had some kind of strange and bad effect on him. Somehow he was less of himself around her. Integrity seemed less important. All that really seemed of value was to possess her or at least be perceived as doing so. This realization gave him a vague sense of fear and a conviction that he should stay away from her or face dire consequences.

In Abigail's arms he felt safe, secure, wholesome, clear-headed, *himself.* He felt no excitement, but he did feel the pleasure of potential contentment.

But had he lost her? She had not changed that past tense to present tense. He was not sure if this was a parting kiss or one to signify their bond growing stronger.

When she finally broke her lips away from his she pulled back again, looked up into his eyes, and smiled. Then he felt that everything would be all right.

"I look a mess," she said, putting her head down.

"You look beautiful," he said and really meant it. She really was very beautiful, not just pretty. And that beauty shone out from within her to illuminate her lovely features. He was very fortunate to have such a woman love him.

"I must wash up," she said, and then she lifted her face and kissed him again quickly on the lips and turned back into her room.

Nick felt great relief and happiness. He would not dally around with the likes of the Lady Evernia again. A calm life of peace and love was his.

Within five minutes he was already questioning the very idea of a calm life of peace and love, though, the impulse rising in him again for something more.

XXXIII

H ector made his way through the streets. Although night had fallen, it was still relatively early, and all the taverns were rollicking. Folks inside sang the same songs every night to the point that Hector could have sung any of them by heart himself even though he had never actually stood shoulder to shoulder with the people to sing along. If he went through certain alleys he would hear other sounds of vice, from vomiting to literal fighting over gambling victories to the grunts of men with prostitutes.

Thirty paces would take him out of this scene and into the quiet of the warehouses, and he quickened his step as he saw the welcoming maw of darkness. When he reached it he paused a moment to relish the quiet before he proceeded into the labyrinth of warehouses. He turned one corner and then another and another, stopping finally at one of the big doors.

He did not have to wait long before a man emerged on a ship docked hard by and walked down the gangway to Hector.

"Good evening," the man said in a French accent.

"Good evening. You have the shipment?"

"You have the money?" the man asked immediately.

Hector glared at him for a long moment before he spoke, "I see the goods and then I pay."

The man shook his head in the dark, "That is no good."

"That *is* good," Hector said. "Payment for services rendered."

"Le Nez en Laiton," the man said. "You have a reputation."

"Not for cheating."

Hector found this kind of a talk a waste of time but understood it was part of doing business. He had had this very conversation with new business connections so many times now it bored him.

He waited for the man to relent but was not surprised when he did not.

"All right," Hector spoke, putting a note of resignation in his voice. "You win. Here. I pay you now."

He brought out one purse and handed it to the man. Then he reached for the second one, but it was not there. He patted around on his person then looked at the moment, a trace of worry on his face, "O Dios, I . . I don't have the other half."

The man's eyes narrowed, "You're a fool."

"I know, I know," Hector said. His personality had changed entirely. Gone was the authority and defiance as he continued to feel around him frantically. "I don't know what happened. I-I had it."

He looked at the man in a questioning way.

"Hmph," the man grunted.

"Please!" Hector said. "Please! I need this shipment. I must have left the other purse at my office."

The man looked at him, disgusted, "How do I know you did not *lose* it along the way here?" The sarcasm in his voice stung.

"I promise you. Even if that happened, I have more money in my office. Here is half. Why don't we go ahead and put the shipment in the warehouse and then I can go back and get the rest of the money."

"No," the reply came quickly. "You've paid for half, you get only half. You won't go get the money yourself. I'll go with you and make sure you get it."

Hector could see the man forming his plan. He figured to get more than the other half.

"All right," Hector said. "We can do that. But we need to hurry. I don't want anyone to know about this. Can we at least be getting that first half loaded while we're gone?"

"I am in no hurry," condescension filled the French man's tone.

"You don't understand," Hector said, panic flooding his voice. "This city is crawling with royal troops. They make the rounds here every night. They will be here on the hour."

"So?" the man asked, shrugging.

"So," Hector wet his lips. "You and I cannot be caught here. The authorities suspect me. We're running a risk standing here so long. Normally . . "

"Normally what?" the man's interest was piqued.

"Well, it's just that usually this all goes more smoothly. Men just pay and then we go our separate ways."

"But the shipment must be loaded."

"Yes, well, you see the warehouse master lives here and oversees that. He is an honest man the soldiers love. He is quiet and gentle. No one suspects him of anything."

The man looked at him, his expression thoughtful.

"He holds the key to the warehouse not me. Can you imagine if I were caught with it?"

"Where is this man?"

"He is up there," Hector pointed to stairs leading to a little hut built atop the warehouse. "I must go get him," then added under his breath, "He's probably sleeping."

"I go with you," the man said. "Let's go."

Hector hesitated.

227

"I *go* with you," the man repeated, his tone threatening now.

Hector threw up his hands and led the way up the stairs, knocking on the flimsy door of the hut.

Nothing happened for a long moment. Then a stirring sounded and the door opened. Inside stood an older man bent over, his long moustache white. His clothes hung on his thin frame, and his hands shook.

"Yes, sir," he said in a trembling voice.

"Get your key, Simpson," Hector said with authority in his voice again. "We have a shipment to load."

"All right, sir," the man named Simpson said and turned inside to get his large keyring. He led the way slowly back down the stairs and went to the large lock on the doors and started trying the keys.

"He doesn't know which key works?" the French man from the ship asked.

"He is . . " Hector spun his finger at the side of his head to say the man was crazy.

The Frenchman nodded and turned up the gangplank. Then he returned with two men carrying the first of the wooden crates.

"They know this old man is in charge if he ever gets the gate unlocked," the Frenchman said. "Now let us go."

"All right," Hector said and led the way.

Hector took the man the long way around, keeping the darker areas along the shore. They were nearing the church.

"We'll go around the back way so we'll not be seen," Hector said, making his way behind the large structure.

There came a sound of something hitting the ground.

"Wait, you dropped something," the Frenchman said, kneeling to pick it up.

Hector turned quickly, the dagger already in hand, and as the man stood up he plunged the knife in his stomach.

Surprise and pain brought the French man up short. Hector withdrew the blade quickly and slid it into the soft flesh again before the man could recover. As the man bent over cringing in pain Hector slipped around behind him and drew the sharp edge across the man's throat, pulling his head back so that the blood spurted in a fountain away from him into the darkness.

"French fool," Hector said in a gritty tone and let the man fall, kneeling to wipe the blade off in a patch of grass beside the path. Then he took his own purse off the corpse. After doing so he took the man by the wrists and dragged his body over to an overturned dinghy nearby. Letting the body go, he lifted the edge of the boat and dragged it over the man.

Killings were common in Port Royal, and another dead body would hardly raise alarm. Certainly the man's crew could well guess what had happened, but Hector did not worry about that. He knew that as soon as he had gone out of sight that Simpson, the seemingly benign little warehouse operator, had removed his false moustache and oversized clothes to show himself a healthy younger man who would announce himself as the new captain of the ship.

The crew might want to rebel, but this young man would immediately produce a purse full of coins to be split evenly among the crew, each member getting an amount far greater than he was accustomed to. That amount was only a little more than half of what Hector had agreed to pay this man, which meant that Hector was getting contraband and his own ship and crew for just a little over half the price of the contraband alone.

That is business, Hector thought, as he started walking to his home, which was not far away now. The swords, guns, and powder he had just obtained at a great bargain would be needed when the new war between the Spanish and English started, and he intended to demand top prices from whomever was willing to pay the most. He had been working quickly to position himself for maximum gains once war began. He imagined the coins he would have all stacked in neat towers, and the delirium of that vision made his walk seem only a moment.

He went into his building and walked up the stairs to his door.

Powerful arms pinned him.

XXXIV

The night was shaping up to be more raucous than usual. A vessel had just come in that had apparently raided a merchant somewhere not far from Virginia, from what Abigail could make out. The men came bursting into the Falstaff flush with money, making for brisk business.

She hated all those loud men, cursing, drinking, laughing boisterously at each others' vulgar jokes. They were taking their turns with the ladies of the house, and the sounds of their grunting and howling could be heard coming from the many rooms upstairs.

Abigail had been trying hard to put on a pleasant face and cheery mood as she worked, but it had been too hard for her. Nick's words kept ringing in her ears. He had apologized, yes, and her love for him was so strong she had already forgiven him. But the hurt just would not go away. Nor would the fear.

After apologizing to her and telling her he loved her he headed out to work with the rest of the crew to get the *Tetrarch* ready for departure. She suspected it would be late when he got back, and she was determined to put on a brave face for him.

But she also remembered his slight hesitation when he told her he loved her, and the more she brooded over it the greater and more significant that hesitation seemed. It made her feel cheated. She had given so much to him and so quickly. And he had seemed so completely devoted to her, so happy to spend time with her, so much *in love* with her. Could she have misread him? Was she *crazy*?

The problem perplexed her so much she had difficulty doing her chores, which brought Hannah's wrath down on her over and over again until finally Hannah ordered her out. Abigail was grateful for it, but she did not quite know where to go because all the rooms were being used for business, including Hannah's, which was never used except in such moments as these.

It occurred to Abigail to go down to the docks where the ships were. Part of her knew she would probably torture herself doing so, but somehow she thought that if she could just get a glimpse of Nick it could bring her assurance. Her legs trembled like a pudding every step of the way. She did not want anybody to see her, so she blended with the crowd always milling about the docks.

It did not take her long to locate the *Tetrarch*, and when she did she kept a watch, catching sight of Nick as he worked. She really did love him so earnestly; it was a pleasure just to watch him moving about the ship, up and down the lines, tending to the myriad jobs to be done.

She did not know where the *San Miguel* was, and she did not want to. Seeing it would make her sick. As she watched, she felt better. Something about this perspective of seeing the man she loved helped, bringing her a kind of pride and stirring her ardor. Several times she thought she wanted to go and throw herself upon him. As the time passed and the sun began to descend it almost seemed as if this morning had not happened at all, and she let her mind run with that idea and with the belief in his love for her.

When she finally left her perch she was feeling quite good, and she walked back in a bouncing step and returned to work. For awhile all was well, but then doubt crept back into her like a dull pain. As darkness fell she began to worry about his being away so long. Her brain told her he had much work to do and may even stay aboard ship for the night. But another part of her wondered if he was with that woman. Then images of his being with her filled her mind and knifed her heart.

Hannah began to snap at her again as Abigail's concentration waned, and again Hannah ordered her up the stairs. Things had quieted a bit up here, many of the men having slaked their thirst for women and now satisfying their thirst for rum downstairs.

She went to the room she shared with Susannah. It was dark inside, and Susannah spoke sleepily, "Humhu, Abigail?"

"Susannah."

"Sweetheart, can you leave me be? I'm completely worn out from these fellows."

"Oh," Abigail said quietly, her mind growing more distracted still.

"I made plenty of coin, but now I'm fagged. Do you mind, love?"

"Mind?"

"I've got to get some sleep, dovey. Stuart will be back later, and I need to be fresh for him. He'll want some sport sure since he's soon to sail away."

The words seemed to float to Abigail in a fog.

"Oh, yes," she replied, finally.

"Thanks, dear."

Abigail walked out, closing the door behind her. She was so distracted she did not notice when another girl passed her with a man.

She stopped into Nick's room, remembering his words.

I'm not with that lady

Her eyes burned as she walked in and collapsed on the bed, crying. She loved him so much. If he would just come back she would be all right, she knew. She knew she was being unfair to hold him accountable for being gone.

The thought occurred to her that maybe he wished he were with her and was missing her this moment while he worked. A small measure of comfort came over her. Her fear that maybe she would not see him again before he left faded slightly. That fear had taken deep root and with it the even worse fear that something might happen to him at sea.

Surely he would come to see me before leaving

She began to imagine what such a meeting would be like. She envisioned him taking her into his arms, and she could smell his natural, masculine odor strengthened by sweating in the hot sun. He would tell her he loved her with no hesitation at all this time, and he would kiss her with overwhelming passion, so powerful she would swoon.

She closed her eyes feeling that swoon now. She could feel his lips soft and moist, the strength of his arms and body, his smell, his breathing.

Something came over her head and pulled roughly over her face, smashing her nose. Her eyes flung open in surprise, and she opened her mouth to scream, but whatever it was yanked down over her lip, around her throat, and tightened before the air could pass through her vocal cords.

She felt herself pulled roughly upright, her breath stuck in her throat against what she realized now was a tightening rope, its sharp hemp scratching her skin. She tried to speak, but no air came, and she felt her eyes starting to bulge.

Then came a terrible jerk, and suddenly she was free of the ground and could feel herself swinging, her throat gagging. The already dark room darkened even more, everything clouding over, her consciousness slipping away.

As if in the far distance she heard a woman say, "Sorry to do this, honey. But you're in my way."

XXXV

Hector tried to reach his dagger. His arms were pinned tight, and whoever held him lifted him bodily as they made their way inside his own chamber. He tried to stretch his hand to reach his weapon, but then he felt it slip out from his belt.

There are two here. Maybe more.

He tried to think how to get out of this situation and who this was. He had plenty of enemies.

"Now, mate, you've been a bit sloppy in your dealings."

He knew the voice but could not place it immediately. He thought through all the men he had manipulated or cheated, trying to match a face to a name.

He tried to work free, but the strength of whoever held him allowed not even the least movement. It was strength almost beyond his imagining. He would have tried to call out, but his body was clamped so tight he could not get up enough breath to do so beyond a kind of whisper, and the sound of his wheezing voice filled him with a sensation of terror— something he rarely experienced.

Then a man stepped in front of him, and Hector recognized him immediately as the little bosun of the *Tetrarch*. The tightwire walking drunk. The man was smiling at him, his teeth gleaming in the single bar of moonlight that fell through a crack in the furnishing in front of the window.

Hector tried to think how this man found him. Had he been following him? That seemed impossible.

"You see," the little man said, still smiling as he always seemed to, "son, we've had some mysteries to unravel. We are what you might call a close-knit family."

Hector tried to speak again. He wanted to ask exactly who "we" were, not because he did not know but in hopes of slowing down the rapid pace of this situation and maybe finding a way to turn it to his advantage.

"And being such," the man went on as though he had all the time in the world. Hector saw the man holding his own dagger, turning it in the moonlight so that it glinted a silvery blue. "Being such, we do not at all appreciate a man spreading falsehoods among us and, you might say, steering us in poor directions in what you might call our business endeavors."

Something about the man's tone comforted Hector. Surely if these men had come here to kill him they already would have done so. Likely they simply came here to scare and warn him, and Hector could deal with that. He felt his heart rate slow down and his body relax in the iron embrace. The thought flashed through his mind that he might relax enough simply to slip out of this hold, but then the man's powerful arms tightened around him.

Stay calm

"You run quite a business here, lad. I must say I'm impressed."

Clearly this man *had* been watching him. Hector's mind cast back to that day when this fellow walked the tightwire. Could he have been watching Hector that day? Could he have actually followed him, somehow scrambling down off that wire and keeping him in sight? A pang tore through Hector as he realized he may have underestimated this man.

Just like that woman

Doubt tugged at him. He had always prided himself on being smart—the smartest man maybe in the entire world. It was true things did not always break his way, but he had chalked that up to fate and happenstance. Nothing had ever really shaken his faith in his cleverness until that woman cut his nose off. Now this was happening.

As if thinking about his nose, the little bosun reached and tore the nose off his face.

"Ah, my friend. This will be a good souvenir for me. I've collected such treasures over the years, I have. If any man should discover my little hoard he'll be mighty surprised. I've imagined it as a kind of joke. There are pearls there, to be sure, and emeralds, and not a little gold, as my mate, Stuart here, knows, having sailed with me many a year. But along with it are glass eyes and wooden legs, aye. And a bunch of body parts from the world over. Maybe it came of my doctoring days before I even thought to go before the mast. Who knows?"

The man's smile faded a little with this soliloquy, and Hector again dared to think he might survive this. He had weapons all around this chamber he could put his hand on in a moment to defend himself. If he could just get to one of his swords.

As you did against her

He pushed his doubt away. Not everyone could be a world class swordsman . . or woman.

"Well, that's enough talking, lad, no? I wish I could set you off on an island somewhere and let you think on things for a hundred year. But alas we're not at sea. And a rotten thing it is. I've grown so sick of the land I have thought I really might just finally die."

The little man's smile beamed brighter yet, but now it seemed sinister, and Hector's heart sank.

"Then again, you'll have far more than a hundred year where you're going, mate. You'll have forever to think it all over. All the things that might have been. All that money you might have had. You will replay it all over and over again, wondering where you went wrong. And then you'll go mad, sure, for you see . . ."

The man drew close to him, so close he could smell the strong aroma of rum from his breath. Hector's heart began to beat wildly again, and he could feel his body stiffen. He heard the man laugh softly.

"For you see, lad, worry over it as you might through all of eternity, but you'll . . never . . . find . . the . . answer . . . . why."

Hector felt the cold blade slice upward just under his breast bone and knew when it pierced his heart. He could feel the gush of blood within him and the rough twist of the blade as his life passed out of him.

XXXVI

Nick felt good. His body felt strong from the work he had done aboard ship, and he realized how great that activity was. Work somehow washed away the trouble he had brought on himself earlier.

He had left the Falstaff in a bad mood, and he was not having any cheering up. At first it was difficult for him to do anything. He kept thinking about what he had said and how it had hurt Abigail. He felt very badly about that and was glad he had talked to her. But then oddly he also felt bad that he had fixed the situation with her because she began to feel like a drag on him, a barrier holding him back from the woman he really wanted.

There was just no denying it. He really and truly hated to hurt Abigail, but the deepest chambers of his heart told him he simply did not want her as badly as he wanted Damiana.

He recalled Damiana offering to bring him aboard her ship, even to the point of trading *two* of her own crew for him. This new sign of her affection for him had thrilled him. But then the whole business with Abigail happened, and now that offer seemed to be gone and, more important, the Lady Evernia with it.

"Hey, mate, you've got a far gaze," Nick heard John Black say, and Nick reddened as he realized he had been caught looking over at the *San Miguel.* He tried to get back to work, but John pressed more, "Have we a love bird here?"

"No," Nick shot back, surprised to hear his voice come out as a snarl.

John laughed, "Oh, now. Tell us the truth."

"Tell us what?" Edward asked.

Nick reddened more.

"We have a young man in love here!" John said.

"Really?" said Gavin Parson, a man of middle age whose cherubic face looked like that of an adolescent. "Who is the lucky lady, mate? Is it that green-eyed elf at the Falstaff I'm always seeing you with."

Nick did not know how to respond; John broke in, "Aye, mate, I saw him stealing glances over at our sister ship."

"Oh-ho!" Gavin said. "Now then!"

"What?" Edward asked, drawing near as well, mop in hand. "What's it all about?"

"Our dear boy, Nick, here," Gavin said, his voice taking on a cultured sound, as though he were a wealthy merchant in London, "he's a-fallen for that most luscious goddess, the Lady Evernia."

"Really, now? Is it true?" Edward smiled at Nick. "She's the tastiest morsel of all, by thunder."

"The Lady Evernia?" William Brownstone said, also stopping work. "Nick? Well done, you dog!"

On and on the teasing went, at one point John Wheeler acting out the role of the Lady Evernia flirting so ludicrously that Nick could not keep himself from laughing. At that moment Stuart appeared on deck and yelled the vilest kind of curses at them to get back to work.

Nick felt that good feeling of camaraderie as he bent into his work. Before long Edward struck up the song "All For Me Grog."

>And it's all for me grog, me jolly, jolly grog
>
>All for me beer and tobacco.
>
>Well I spent all me tin on the lassies drinking gin
>
>Across the western ocean I must wander.

Nick listened to him sing the first verse with a growing sense of comfort in familiarity. Maybe these women problems were not quite so bad as he thought, and he listened to Edward's voice,

>Where are me boots, me noggin, noggin boots
>
>They're all gone for beer and tobacco.
>
>For the heels they're worn out and the toes are kicked about
>
>And the soles are looking out for better weather.

As he swung into the refrain, some of the other men joined in, and on "Well I spent all me tin" so did Nick.

They went through the verses they knew; then Edward started in on another song they all loved. Nick felt the singing lift him, and before he knew it he was tending the ropes and sails in rhythm with the singing. Then they sang another song and another, their energy focused, all sense of time lost, everything focused on the working of their lungs and limbs. High aloft at one point Nick looked down to see some of his mates dancing a jig while Stuart only looked on and gave one of his rare smiles, knowing that this energy would carry them forward with the work and bring them together.

Right in the middle of this moment appeared Leesh, and watching the men dancing he too went to work leaping about, which brought a cheer from all the men. Watching it all, Nick felt the pride of being a part of this family. What was left of his real family was far away, and he would always care about them. But these men formed the vital community of his life. Even the memory of his mother did not make him sad, and when some of the songs they sang were ones she had sung it did not sadden but gladdened him to be a part of life as a pageant.

They all worked late into the night, long after the Captain, Leesh, and Stuart had gone. It had been hot, and Nick felt a burn on his skin, having worked shirtless through the day. But he did not mind. All his troubles seemed swept away, and he felt himself strong. He wanted to pick up the first lady he met and kiss her. And he looked forward to returning to the Falstaff and seeing Abigail, with her warm smile and deep love for him.

He and the men walked through the streets to that establishment, hearing the carousers in the various taverns, stopping several times to speak to men they knew. What a great thing it was to be knowing people here, and what a free thing it was to be among these brethren!

When they finally reached the Falstaff he was surprised and gladdened to see it so rollicking with new customers. He almost wanted to try his first sip of rum, but he fought that desire off as he sought Abigail. She was not down here working, and he pulled one of the women aside and asked about her. The woman said she was not sure where Abigail was. Nick asked another woman and go the same answer. Well, she was probably upstairs.

He ran up the narrow stairs as quickly as their steepness allowed. Finding her door closed, he knocked but received no answer.

Maybe she's worn out, poor heart

He turned and walked to his room.

The sight did not register immediately. It seemed to take him a long time to make sense of legs hanging so still just beyond the foot of the bed. He felt his head tighten behind his eyes, which themselves snapped into alarm.

What . . .

Something in him knew already, and he realized his mouth had opened and that his entire system was bracing. He tried to will his eyes not to look up, but he failed, and he saw Abigail's face leering down at him, those green eyes that so often flashed now cloudy and unfocused, the face blueish, the head turned at a painful angle, the tongue hanging out slightly as though she were a blubbering drunk.

He fell to his knees, feeling he would vomit. He shut his eyes and opened them again, trying to think this was not real. He wanted to reach out to someone for immediate comfort, and then he felt the slash of horror and grief that the person he wanted to reach out to was . . . .

He realized he had blacked out for a moment. He was still on his hands and knees. He looked up again but quickly looked away. This was so horrible it was hard to imagine it was real. He had seen death before, and he had killed. But this was different. She was so still, and so . . .

He stood up, his knees weak. He needed to tell someone, to do something. He turned to go, but his eyes caught something, a piece of paper on the bed. He turned back and picked it up.

Dear Nick,

I cannot go on without you. You have broken my heart. I do not want to stand in your way of having the woman you truly love. I want you to be happy.

Abigail

XXXVII

Nick had no idea how much time had passed. Reading the letter, he had fallen back to his knees and finally crumpled onto the floor all the way. He had not moved. Pain seized every part of his body.

The feeling was not unfamiliar to him. He had known it with his mother, with Sarah, with Gowan. He realized how foolish he was to think he had left it behind back in England and that being here in the New World he would be better.

Many people had passed the open door to this room and not bothered to look inside while he lay here. Nick did not care if anyone ever did.

But now he heard footsteps and his name spoken in a familiar voice but as if from half a mile away. Nick could not bring himself to move. He heard the footsteps come inside and then a reaction, not a gasp exactly but a kind of softly-voiced reaction. Then he felt the body close to him, kneeling beside him.

"I'm here, lad."

It was a voice that usually brought him comfort. But now he felt rage creep up through him.

"I'll be back," the familiar voice said again, and Nick could hear the footsteps away and the yelling for help.

But the rage continued to build in Nick. He could not make sense of it at the moment, but he knew it made complete sense.

Still he could not move, and he stayed crumpled on the floor as other men rushed into the room, more familiar voices. They lit candles and voiced their reactions to the grisly scene before them. Nick could hear them working to get the body down from the rafters, and even though he did not look and did not move at all he could envision them taking her down, her soft feet knocking against each other, her arms falling lifelessly, the hands . . . he thought of those hands touching him, rubbing his neck, strong yet soft, full of care.

How could this happen again

The words resolved themselves, and grief fueled his anger like air to fire. He did not move from his crumpled position.

He felt that familiar presence kneeling beside him again, knowing it was Leesh. "Hey, lad, you must be up. We sail at sunrise and must be away. She's gone, now. There's no more you can do for her. You must move on."

Nick's mind went back to that day in Bedlam, Sarah locked away forever, and this same man talking to him, saying these very same kinds of things. Sail away, leave grief behind. Nick had been comforted by Leesh then and had come away to this place. But he had just gone from one grief to another. Now another woman was destroyed because he had not stayed with her, had left her behind, had . . .

The rage reached the surface. He brought himself to a sitting position slowly and looked at Leesh, who for once had no smile on his face as he knelt.

Nick shook his head, feeling his lips tighten and wrenching. He wanted to curse, to say all the words he had learned aboard ship and here in this God-forsaken place.

Maybe the whole world was God-forsaken. What was the point of trying to be good or find happiness?

He moved before the old man could react, hurling him on his back. Then Nick leapt to his feet, looking around at the men in the room—men he had sailed with and just hours ago had believed to be his family. But they all looked rotten and terrible to him.

He dashed out of the room, down the stairs, and out of the Falstaff.

The tropical night air was so hot and humid it threatened to suffocate him. How could anyone stand to stay in such a place? He longed for cold air, the refreshing taste of frost on his lips and the exhilarating rush of chill into his lungs with a deep satisfying breath. Mosquitoes swirled all around him, the bites coming on his sweaty skin as he ran up the street. He slapped at them hard, hurting himself and glad of it.

They had done it. Leesh and Captain Stockett. They had brought him here. They had made him part of the pirate life. They had meddled in his business. He could have handled the two women on his own, but Leesh and Stockett had decided to take charge of him as if he were a child. If they had not forced him to say what he said, Abigail would not have been devastated. Nick could have gone off on the voyage and been with the Lady Evernia, and by the time he got back, if he ever came back, Abigail would have surely found someone new. She may have had her heart broken, but it would not have been as bad as this.

As this

He stopped short, right in the middle of the street, his feet kicking up the sand. He looked around at the buildings lining the street and rushed toward one and pounded the wall as hard as he could. The pain raced through him, bringing him a strange relief momentarily. But then it fed his rage again, and he started running toward the docks.

The *San Miguel* loomed quietly in the darkness. Nick climbed aboard and started toward the captain's quarters.

He did not get far before men leapt before him, swords and pistols drawn. In the center stood Pew, towering over the rest.

"What do you want here?" Pew asked. "No one invited you here, you rogue."

The rage pulsed higher still to a fever pitch in Nick. Again he felt himself hoping someone would attack him, especially Pew.

"Out of my way," Nick said. "I'm here to see your captain."

Nick could see Pew smile by the light of the moon, "I don't think so, poppy. I think you've assaulted our ship. And now we will fight you like any other enemy."

Nick braced himself, glad for a fight. He had no weapon with him, so looked at the men, decided who he would attack and disarm. He did not care if he died.

They stood facing each other, tension building.

"What's all this?" a woman's voice broke in lazily, followed by a yawn.

Nick saw the Lady Evernia step out in a robe fallen off one shoulder, its pale blue curve forming a lush wave in the moonlight that descended darkly down her chest into the next swelling blue wave of her breast.

The tension remained but shifted somehow, its tenor changed.

"This man," Pew said in a way that now sounded peevish. "Has come aboard our ship in a menacing way."

"Nick," she said, smiling and walking to him. She put her arms around him and kissed them in front of all the men. Then she said, "I invited him here. Carry on as you were."

The men stood for a moment, bewildered but also obviously accustomed to having no idea what their captain was about. Then they turned and moved toward their various sleeping places.

Except for Pew, who stood unmoved, still glaring.

"Come on," she said to Nick, taking him by the hand, using her other hand to lift her robe as she walked. "Good night, Pew."

"Good night," he forced himself to say with an equally forced smile at her. But the smile vanished back into that cold glare at Nick as he passed behind.

Damiana's dogs broke into yelps and barks when they entered the captain's quarters, but Damiana called them down and led Nick to the bed.

Each tortured rapid step along the way here he had thought he would be saying something to her, although he was not sure what. Now that he was here, talking seemed ridiculous. Everything here in this place at this moment was purely physical. There was no time to think of explaining Everything was rushing so quickly, it felt out of his control. Only one thought formed in his mind

This is one woman I'll not leave behind

XXXVIII

Ah, Governor. You tip your hand so easily.

Don Diego set the letter aside, smiling, and took up his own blank page to write on.

To the Honorable Governor of Jamaica,

I have received your letter with the gladness and warmth it is accorded. Your generosity endears you to me even more.

Of course the trusting and beneficent nature of your gesture requires that I refuse it, if for no other reason than courtesy. I will arrive in your harbor in the aforesaid Portuguese ship, the *São Martinho*, no later than August 28.

Upon arrival, I hope that we may communicate via inconspicuous messengers so as not to arouse suspicion.

By the Grace of God and Our Lady

I remain gratefully yours,

Don Diego Pedro de la Figueroa

Folding and sealing the letter, he gave it to a messenger to have it sent back on the ship that brought it. When he was alone he sat back in his chair and looked up at the ceiling, once more playing out in his mind how things would proceed, trying to account for every contingency for the thousandth time.

He did not know how long he sat in the quiet, thinking, but at last the scenario reached its end in his mind, and he saw himself victorious and imagined how it would feel to relish his success.

That thought spread out into a feeling, and as he sat perfectly still his vision slowly focused back on reality, so that he saw the ceiling for what it was. His eye locked in on a spot here and then one there. Roving over the expanse of the ceiling he saw in the corner a cobweb. It was so impossible to keep those away, and these ceilings were so very high. He would need to get a servant in to clean it.

Then he became aware of the ceiling itself as a solid entity, an existence complete with its own being. He became fascinated with it and worked truly to see it as it was.

He did this often, focusing on his surroundings, on other people. He had learned over the years the importance of looking not just inward but outward. Doing so provided understanding profound and far-reaching. Always he discovered something new and startling, however infinitesimal it may be.

But he did not gaze and study the ceiling for long. He could return to that at a later time. For now, he must be up and away. The time of planning had ended; the time for action had begun.

XXXIX

Hannah lingered while the slave shoveled clumps of dirt into the grave, his skin glistening darkly with sweat under the hot sun. It seemed the Christian thing to do to wait here. Not that she spent much time trying to be a Christian.

But Lord knows I should do a little extra something

She surprised herself in needing to fight back tears, for she had not thought herself any longer capable of having them. She worked to firm herself up. Maybe age was finally softening her? Well, she did not mean for that to happen.

But it was so easy to fall into a soft, weak way. It was not good business, and she really did not need a man ordering her about. Her first husband had been a terror that way, and when he died and she married again her second husband died young. She decided then and there she would not marry again.

She was in London, then, a poor woman living in a snug but poor dwelling near the bank of the Thames. She had grown up with her first husband, and they had married because that seemed the most natural thing to do. Even though he was a slight man who avoided any involvement with the civil war that erupted hardly a year before they were married, he was a perfect monster under the influence of

252

strong drink, and the alcohol killed him. He seems to have gone staggering into the night after an evening at a public house; the fog had settled unusually thick, and in his drunken state he had lost the way to his own home and was so disoriented he actually stumbled into he river and was carried away by the current, later found among reeds, his body mangled.

The second husband was an actor. A charming, handsome, winking fellow, he had swept her off her feet. She loved being introduced to the theater, with all its strange splendor. Something about men dressed as women charmed her, and the whole lot of theater people were so outlandish they brought a color to life she adored.

But that very outlandishness she loved was what outraged the Puritans, who had gained control of Parliament and banned theatrical productions in 1642, three years before Hannah met her second husband. At first the ban was hardly enforced, but with each passing month the authorities cracked down more and more, arresting actors, stagehands, writers. It became increasingly difficult to get work acting. Unfortunately, that was the only kind of work her husband knew. Not only did he have no other kind of experience, but regular work seemed to diminish him, as though he were a splendid flower able to grow only in very specific soil and light.

He moped for a time, but then his rage at his situation flamed, and he determined to enlist to fight against the Puritans who had deprived him of his livelihood. He reasoned that his great skill as a swordsman on stage perfectly prepared him for real combat. He thought perhaps he could be a spy, as well, and indeed he came to life with the belief that acting prepared him perfectly for many aspects of warfare. He sallied forth, leaving Hannah proud but in tears.

He was killed in his first conflict, the story being that he flourished the sword beautifully but evidently did not understand that on a field of battle someone could stab him from behind.

Hannah's poverty had been deep all her life, and her second husband had only made things worse, for while he might wear the most splendid costumes on his beautiful body he had no good clothes of his own. In her grief and desperation she sealed off her heart from ever loving again and instead formed a plan of action to support herself and the four children she had borne with her two husbands. Having learned something about acting from watching her husband and theatrical friends with whom she now lived and who raised her children as a community, Hannah began to practice the oldest trade. She found it really very easy to perform, and to pretend she enjoyed the men who paid to enjoy her in the most intimate way.

It was not an easy time, and more than once authorities threw her in prison. But she seduced guards and found ways to pay off judges and so made her way again and again to freedom. She grew so successful she gained a reputation and even a measure of fame as a jolly bawd who could make it worth your while to help.

Then in the later 1650s rumors spread in the theater community that a person could migrate to Jamaica, which had become a pirate hangout. "Anything goes," the word was, and Hannah and many others made the trip, leaving her children behind well-healed and prepared to succeed. Hannah herself had grown hard as flint, although her beauty at the time hid it. She established the Falstaff herself, of her own funds, named for the character her husband most loved—the old knight John Falstaff, created by Will Shakespeare.

And here she had remained, the most famous bawd in the city. She had maintained her freedom and seen to her business, arguably one of the shrewdest business people of either gender or any race. She rarely indulged herself physically with any man anymore. There was more money and less labor in having young beautiful women working for her.

But the little man with the devilish smile had appeared one day almost twenty years ago. There was something about that smile. She had tried to resist but could not. She regretted getting involved almost immediately, worried that now he would become a weight in her life. But he had simply sailed away. She was surprised to find herself missing him.

Finally he appeared again, and the gladness that filled her at seeing him was genuine. That feeling returned every time he did, and she came to cherish it. But she had always refused to call it love. And she treated Leesh rougher than any other man, which made her treatment very rough indeed.

But she knew deep in her heart that she had long since given it to him, and now she worried that as her age advanced she actually both wanted and needed him more. Her heart, mind, and body had long accustomed themselves to fighting for herself and her business, and she did not foresee any weakening in that way. But the nights felt lonely now without Leesh there, and she could not imagine being with any other man anymore.

And now she had allowed herself to pity this little waif of a girl who had shown up at her door with a sad story. Who was Hannah to fret over sad stories? She knew them well. Was there really something so especially pathetic about this girl? Or had Hannah herself changed, growing more sentimental?

The fierce anger she felt toward the so-called "Lady" Evernia told her she had not softened all the way. That Nick was a nice lad, and he had showed genuine affection for Abigail, God rest her soul. But then that black-haired beauty—no one could deny her beauty—had appeared and the boy had gone wild. Hannah had watched the whole scenario play out. Nick should not have succumbed and hurt Abigail, but from long years of learning how easy it was to seduce men Hannah laid more of the blame on the woman. Her expectations of men were very low: Leesh was a rare man.

Still, manipulated as he may have been, the lad had hurt this dear dead girl. Hannah knew how fragile she was, and it did not surprise her that much when she took her own life. Yet she could not remember when she had felt this sad and desolate, made all the worse by Leesh's sailing away this morning. She had never asked him to stay behind for her, and she determined not to do so today. But she wished terribly that he had not left, not on this day. She felt so very alone, and something about this young woman being put in a cheap box and lowered into the dirt in the pauper's cemetery, her only marker a wooden cross, pained the deepest recesses of Hannah's heart.

But she managed to keep the tears in. It would never do for anyone to see her cry and send the story of it around. She twisted her lip, setting it as though in stone. She was Hannah. No one and no thing would put her off.

She turned and walked to the carriage where the surprisingly large group of people waited for her. The group was not actually that large but seemed so given how little time Abigail had actually lived here. The assembled people were whispering among themselves but turned and faced Hannah when they saw here approaching.

A big man of strange coloring Hannah had never met before spoke to her, "Miss Hannah, I am very sorry about Miss Abigail's death. She was a bright flower."

Hannah looked the man over, "How did you know her?"

"I am a butcher. Matheeus by name. She came to buy meat from me in the market."

"Very well," Hannah said, making to walk on but then stopped. "Why aren't you in the market now? Are you rich?"

She enjoyed putting people off, especially men, with her brusque questions. But he did not even flinch. Rather, his face spread into a smile, "I am taking a holiday. Just today."

Hannah tried to think what Saint's day it might be, "This isn't a holiday, is it?"

"It is for me."

"Why?"

"It just is. Let us say for the first time in a long time I can afford to take the day off. Not because I'm rich. No, just because today is a day of freedom for me."

His answer confused her. She wondered if he was a slave who had just been set free. There was something strange afoot, for she had heard of runaways of late, including one Vivian had told about when she arrived to ride out with the rest of Hannah's lot to the graveyard. Vivian could have simply met them at the paupers' cemetery, having passed it on the way into Port Royal, but she wanted to be with these women she loved.

"I'm glad you don't have that insolent driver," Hannah had said to Vivian.

257

"He's no longer with us," Vivian had replied. "He ran away just two nights ago."

"You're a slave," Hannah said now to this big man, Matheeus.

"No, Madam. Not any longer."

XL

Nick looked over at the *Tetrarch* alongside the *San Miguel*. They were sitting still, halted in their course due west, straight for the Main, apparently to a fortified town named Nueva Lebrija where, as with other such missions, treasure allegedly had been hoarded. The two ships had embarked together as planned, heading east just far enough to be out of sight of Jamaica. Then they had turned south, describing a half circle below Jamaica and toward their destination.

They could have reached the place already, but the plan was to arrive on August 29, so they had anchored to wait here in a patch of relatively shallow water. Climbing high aloft the mainmast Nick could see that the two ships now sat in the center of what was almost a perfect circle of teal blue surrounded by the darker blue of far greater depth.

Seeing the *Tetrarch* and the men moving about on deck filled Nick with conflicting emotions not unlike those he experienced almost a year ago when he had first voyaged on that vessel, boarding her out of frustration, anger, pride, and a sense of adventure. That experience had nearly killed him, but he had emerged from it far stronger than he began, and he had bonded with those men. When he returned he faced the terrible ordeal of his mother's illness and death only to find that the girl he had always loved—whose heart he had broken but whom he had come to reclaim—had gone out of her mind because of a terrible deed. Leesh had convinced Nick to sail here into these beautiful waters and begin a new life, which Nick had done. And he had fallen in love again here in this place, with a lovely, sweet girl. But that had not been enough for him because another woman had come along who moved him more than any other had before. And when the sweet, lovely girl found her heart broke she killed herself.

That night when she died he fled from her and from those men and that cursed ship. He wanted nothing to do with them. In rage he blamed them, but he knew ultimately that he himself felt and deserved all the blame for what he had done. He had not appreciated Abigail's love but had crushed it as though it were nothing.

And so he had rushed to the other woman. He could not entirely explain why. His body drove him frantically to her. She had been thrilled to see him, her happiness emanating with powerful warmth. Even as Pew's hatred lashed out, she had taken Nick that night into her quarters. There she taught him the ways of men and women, and as she guided him through the portal of that experience he was lost in the massive wash of humanity itself, outside of time and meaning, the past dulled to oblivion and the future opened up, as though the grand secret of the universe had been revealed and another ocean existed upon which he could sail into heaven itself.

He did not feel so much that way when he awoke late the next morning, the movement of the ship on the waves telling him they had already embarked. The pleasure remained, to be sure, but with it came a hard-edged sensibility that with his new knowledge some part of him had been lost for which he immediately pined. Somehow the world seemed a bit more complicated and ugly than it had just the day before. He had experienced this feeling aboard the Dutch ship the *Tetrarch* attacked illegally back in the winter: then he had killed for the first time, and the guilt and terror of that act had changed his core. Now he realized he had retained some innocence from that moment, but now that innocence was gone, and he wondered if he had any left to lose. He had tried to so hard to follow his mother's strictness only for it to come to this, a night with a woman he barely knew.

A new kind of seriousness drew his face, and he could feel himself older mentally, physically, and emotionally. He felt it just made everything worse for him to linger in her bed, with its perfumed sheets, and he hurried up and dressed and made his way on deck.

When he emerged he found the ship slicing through blue sparkling water, the wind at their backs. Looking up he saw Damiana's flag—black with a red rose on it—whipping smartly. Then he looked over to see the *Tetrarch* sailing alongside. It was strange to look over at the ship and not be on it himself. The crew was going about the business of sailing as would be expected, but when Damiana saw him she called out his name and came to him, kissing him again in front of the entire crew. Embarrassed yet proud, his eyes open, he noticed with disappointment that no one paid any attention except for one—Pew.

It was no secret that the tall man was his mortal enemy, and Pew quickly settled into a passive-aggressive pattern with him. Again, this was familiar ground to Nick, for his first voyage had included an enemy, albeit that hulking man had been far more formidable than this dandified figure. Still, Nick stayed on alert, always wary for when this man's hate and jealousy went from passive-aggressive to full-on aggressive.

Meanwhile, Nick did nothing to ease the situation, for even though his guilt had driven him from Damiana's quarters that morning, as the day went on, his memory of the night and of her combined with his sense of pride at being associated with her this way. Although he felt wicked for what he had done, the pleasures of it filled his senses and drove him to a fever pitch, so that when night came and she took his hand to lead her to her quarters again he not only did not resist but hurried along frantically with her.

Then the ships came to a halt and anchored here in this beautiful circle of water under the down-beating sunlight only occasionally dimmed by a fluffy passing cloud. The light blue water dancing made the whole world seem joyful to Nick, who felt the strength of his limbs fully returned and an all-new sense of manhood he had never been able fully to imagine before. Also, although the sun grinded down here on the water, burnishing everyone's skin into a deep tan, a steady breeze kept up, stirring the air with freshness that combined with the light that filled Nick with excitement.

Now that they were anchored, Damiana came to him, rapiers in hand, "Here, love. Let's take our next lesson."

Her eyes looked paler yet in this bright light. He took the sword, saluted her, and raised his point.

"No, not that way. Loosen your arm. And point your front foot at me at all times. That is key."

Nick adjusted accordingly.

"Imagine this circle. It is, you might say, a magic circle. But you do not stay on it but rather interact with it."

They moved now, and she guided him in the ways of the steps, explaining how he must use angles along that circle to change the distance. The concept of distance was one he understood but in a backward, forward, and sideways manner rather than in the way she was explaining. It began to dawn on him that this form of movement was based in a kind of philosophy very different from the one he knew and that that philosophy was deeply entrenched within Spanish thinking.

This movement came naturally to her, but she also clearly grasped the style of movement *he* knew as she labored to explain the differences between them. At times it was difficult for him to pay attention, however, as the sweat caused her blouse to stick to her to the point of transparency.

When she finally declared this lesson over he wanted to embrace her, kiss her, haul her off to the captain's quarters. But when he stepped toward her to do so, she only shook his hand and then passed him, already reaching down to pull that sweaty blouse over her head. She turned as she tossed the blouse aside and then shucked her boots and stripped her pants en route to the larboard gunnel, where she stepped up and dove into the sparkling blue water.

It all happened so quickly, and the image of her naked body in full daylight so shocked him that it took him a moment to recover his senses. Then he looked around to see if the other crewmen had noticed. But none seemed to care except for, as usual, Pew, who was busy gathering her clothes up and hurrying to the captain's quarters.

Just like a nursemaid

Pew hurried back out with fresh clothes just as she climbed aboard. Nick watched her dry off and put on a new blouse that hung to her knees.

Then he heard the hallo.

He turned and walked to the starboard side of the ship where he saw a dinghy pulling up alongside. There stood Leesh, smiling as usual, having rowed himself over. Seeing him filled Nick with a strange familiarity. Suddenly Leesh seemed wholesome and safe compared to the lady who had just exposed herself to everyone, not even caring how Nick felt about her doing so. And why should he care? He did not own her. But had they not been knowing each other in the most intimate ways? Did that not entitle him to have some say about her?

"Ahoy, Nick. How are you, lad?"

Damiana came up beside him, her blouse hanging open, exposing most of her chest. Part of Nick wanted to cover her up while the other part felt pride in Leesh seeing what he had access to.

"My lady," Leesh said to her. Nick noticed Leesh did not give her the appraising look-over he normally reserved for beautiful women, and it bothered Nick. He felt cheated somehow, as though the older man was not acknowledging this beautiful creature Nick had captured.

"Good day," Damiana called out, smiling in a way that Nick realized disturbed him. It was a flirtatious smile, not one she had ever given him. "And what can we do for you, kind sir?"

She had never spoken to Nick this way, and he looked hurriedly at Leesh, expecting him to return the flirtation, but instead his smile, remarkably, had an almost fatherly cast to it, something Nick had never seen before. Part of Nick felt relieved, for deep down he doubted he could ever really compete with a man as charming as Leesh. But another part of him wondered if somehow he was wrong in assessing this woman as the greatest one in the world. Why was Leesh not making a play for her? More importantly, why was *she* making a play for Nick? Or was he just imagining she was?

"Not much, my lady," Leesh replied, not in his usual insinuating tone but almost in the way of a town crier. "I just came along to check on me young man there. Old Nicky. He's had a bad time of it lately. And I wanted to see how he is holding up."

Nick had told her all about Abigail's death the second night he was with Damiana, after their passion had subsided. Tears had filled her eyes with her expressions of shock and horror, and she had held him while he sobbed. He felt a deep connection with her, that she understood the depths of his heart and sympathized with him completely.

"She was your true love," she had said, with a hint of sadness in her voice.

"No," he hastened to say. He did not want her to think he loved anyone more than herself. "But she was very sweet and one of my greatest friends. And she was there for me when I needed her to nurse me to health."

"You will never get over her," she said in a flat way.

He felt a rush of insecurity. Why had he spoken so?

"No, no, it's not that way at all," he said. "When I met you everything changed."

He could see she had tears in her eyes, but when he said that she smiled and drew him close to her. He determined never to mention Abigail again.

"I am fine," Nick told Leesh now.

"I'm glad to hear it, mate," Nick said. "The Captain and I are wondering if you're ready to come back aboard the *Tetrarch*?"

Part of Nick *did* want to go with Leesh. Now that his initial emotions had subsided, the *Tetrarch* and its crew represented home to him. He was not mad at Leesh or the

Captain anymore. But now he was intoxicated with Damiana and did not want to leave her. Also, he felt a dim uneasiness about her that maybe if he left she would summon Pew to her quarters.

"Thank you, mate, but I'll stay here for now," Nick replied, finally.

Leesh smiled for a moment, his eyes seeming to say something to Nick. But that passed quickly and the little man shrugged, "Very well. Glad you're mended, my boy."

He sat down, grasped the oars, and took a surprisingly strong pull for a man of his age. Watching him, a funny feeling arose in Nick, driving him to call out before he could stop himself, "Give everyone my best!"

He felt ashamed as soon as he spoke. Leesh seemed not to hear him, but worse yet Nick could sense a silent recoil from the woman standing beside him. He should not have said it, but something in him felt he was being untrue to Leesh not to. It made him feel small and childlike to say it. Then it occurred to him what it sounded like to her.

Now he stood looking across at the *Tetrarch* again, feeling all those conflicting emotions. He had worried at first that he had hurt Damiana by showing allegiance to his old crew, and he had been careful to hide it. She had not shown any reaction, and things had continued as they were. Now they were having another lesson, and he knew it would not do to be staring across at the other ship when she came on deck.

He looked away and saw one of the *San Miguel*'s crew swabbing the deck aft. Nick had done very little work aboard this ship, and he could sense resentment not just from Pew but the rest of the crew. Strange that only Pew seemed bothered by his involvement with the Damiana. The rest seemed more peeved that he was getting what surely looked like a free ride.

Damiana emerged from the cabin, walking barefooted, wearing only her long blouse and her hat, which shaded her eyes. She took her position, and he took his. Then they saluted and went on guard as usual, practicing the footwork, Nick frustrated that he could not quite seem fully to get it. He understood the basic idea, but it was very difficult to make himself take advantage of angles, especially in a situation of parrying in which he normally would step back. As if reading his thoughts, she stopped and spoke.

"Today we will learn about blade work. It is not like what you are used to. You tend to make contact with the blade."

Shifting into a stance closer to the kind *he* usually took she brought the forte of her blade against his foible in a light click.

"Like so, yes?" she said. He nodded.

She stood back up into her regular stance, "But the Spanish do not make contact in that way. Instead they do what they call an *atajo*."

Nick listened to the exotic word, wondering what it meant.

"It might look like contact, but it's not," she went on. "Watch."

Still keeping the blade parallel with his she brought her blade against it in a definite way that differed from what she had done before, although he could not explain exactly how.

"Feel the difference?"

He nodded again. He could indeed feel the difference, and he realized again how thoroughly this style of swordplay was entwined with a Spanish way of understanding the world.

"The idea is not to contact the blade and establish a line of defense," she explained. "Instead you are gaining a kind of leverage. That is not it exactly or entirely, but that is part of it."

She did it again so he could feel the difference and try to make sense of it, "Imagine that there are degrees to the blade. You are gaining degrees."

She watched him struggling to understand.

"Follow me," she said, making another *atajo* and moving as she did, and he felt that sinister glide toward him, effortless, like a whisper, so that she had closed into range to kill him. His mind went back to that first day when they had done their kind of dance in the alley. Instinctively he stepped back.

"No. You're parrying and stepping back again. When you do that you lose distance. Meet my *atajo* with your own. Don't back away but respond by changing the angle and threatening me back."

Something clicked when she said this, but he realized this maneuvering was easier said than done. He would need to work on this as he had been during his time sitting here in the middle of the blue sea every day.

A horn sounded, and Nick saw her stop and look past him at the *Tetrarch*.

"Time to go," she said. "Vamos!"

XLI

S pies had kept a close watch on the progress of the *São Martinho*, keeping O'Brien aware of its every move. She had sailed directly from the Special Counsel's private island and headed directly to Port Royal, plodding through the sea in a stately, unhurried way just as the Special Counsel himself walked and moved. O'Brien thought about that man and his pride.

She had eased into the harbor and docked quietly at midday. Nothing suspicious here. Just another vessel coming into Port Royal. She brought no goods and seemed not to be warlike—so people took little notice of her and showed no concern as they went about their usual business.

That had been August 27. A message came to O'Brien directly:

> To the Honorable Governor of Jamaica,
> We have arrived in the harbor. Please advise us as to how you wish to proceed.
> By the Grace of God and Our Lady,
> Don Diego Pedro de la Figueroa

O'Brien wrote out detailed instructions. He explained that he wanted to apprehend the criminals under the cover of early morning before daylight when the rogues were likely to be most vulnerable. The Special Counselor was to walk to the

269

Governor's Mansion with his delegation (it gladdened O'Brien to imagine dictating that the Special Counselor must walk to *him*). O'Brien would greet the delegation at the gate of the Mansion with his own troops, and together they would proceed to the known hangout of the pirates in question, the Falstaff. There they would apprehend the thieves and make a public proclamation of cooperation, a draft of which O'Brien included for the Special Counselor's perusal.

A swift reply came saying that all was well with this plan. The next day O'Brien stayed alert, getting updates practically every half hour. He hoped he would catch someone from the *São Martinho* heading to the Falstaff in an attempt to jump the plan. But the day passed quietly, if tensely, and night fell on the city in peace.

Throughout the night O'Brien envisioned where the *Tetrarch* and *San Miguel* would be now. If all went as planned they should be arriving at first light at Nueva Lebrija. He envisioned the crews of those ships arming themselves and pulling for shore.

He sat in one of the great chairs in his study fully dressed for the occasion, waiting for the clock to tell him it was time to meet the delegation. When it finally did, he arose. Moving quickly he passed out into the courtyard, his eye taking in the troops standing to attention. Satisfied with what he saw, he ordered the gate opened and positioned himself in the entry.

Minutes passed, he and the rest of the men standing still, the air humid. He thought he heard the sound of marching, but it was not. Just his ears playing a trick on him.

Again he envisioned the carnage at that village on the Main. He imagined each part of the plan carried out. He could see Captain Stockett leading his men alongside the woman . . the girl . . . the . . .

This time he really did hear marching. Realizing he had relaxed slightly he straightened again, clenching himself for this moment. Everything must be pulled off correctly.

The marching grew louder, still punctuated by the cry of roosters.

Again he played out in his mind once more how he would proceed. He imagined the conflicts that could arise.

The delegation approached, the individual sound of the boots sounding on the sand-dirt road.

And now the small group stood before O'Brien, who looked at their leader.

Concern gripped O'Brien

This man was not the Special Counselor.

XLII

This situation felt familiar to Nick. The slog through thick jungle, the anticipation of the attack, and the fear that this would be another bust.

But this time was also different. He was not among the crew of the *Tetrarch*, and he felt keenly that he was now among enemies. For the first time, he wondered if he had been unwise to attach himself to Damiana.

The two ships had arrived at the Main together and had agreed to attack at dawn. But Damiana woke him when it was still black dark.

"Whu, wha?" he said, disoriented.

"Get up," Damiana whispered. "We're going now."

He shook his head and blinked his eyes. Unable to clear them, he opened one eye and saw that she was fully dressed and armed. The sight jolted him.

It's earlier than agreed

His heart clenched. Something must have changed. He got up quickly, fully awake now. He dressed as fast as he could and strapped on two pistols and a rapier.

When he emerged on deck he saw the crew of the *San Miguel* getting in the boats to head ashore, and he looked across the water, dark under the black new moon, for sign of activity on the *Tetrarch*. But he could not see the ship anywhere.

"Where's the *Tetrarch*?" Nick asked aloud, his voice shattering the silence.

A chorus of shhh's sounded, and Damiana appeared swiftly at his side.

"We must keep silence, Nick. Follow me."

"Where is the ship?" he whispered, looking around again.

It occurred to him that the *San Miguel* had shifted her own position in relation to the Main.

"*We* have moved away!" he said aloud.

She stopped and looked at him, then pulled him close.

"Come," she whispered and pulled him with her by the hand.

Suspicion built with anticipation in Nick. What had happened? Had the captains changed plans while he slept? Had the *Tetrarch*'s crew gone ahead ashore? Or was the crew of the *San Miguel* breaking the plan, leaving the *Tetrach* behind, and . . . .

Comprehension dawned on him.

She means to get the treasure herself

He pushed the thought away. He could not know that for sure. It was only a suspicion. He must be patient and watch. Many times he had not been privy to inside information and so did not fully understand what was happening. He got into the boats with the rest and helped pull silently for shore.

Gentle waves rolled onto the beach as they came ashore, dragging their boats into the sand and beginning the chop through the jungle in the dark. Nick positioned himself at the back of the group. He wanted no one behind him and kept his eyes sharp to keep track of Pew.

273

It seemed to take an eternity to chew through the greenery. More than once he felt something move along the ground, and he imagined anything from giant snakes to crocodiles stirred up by their progress and ready to strike.

Finally they halted, apparently right at the village.

Nick heard a whisper snaking its way through the party toward the back, the word reaching him, "Quiet."

Everything went silent.

And then, apparently at some kind of signal the crew began to slip out of the woods for the village.

Nick hesitated for a moment, his sense of danger very great. He tried to listen within himself to what he should do. He considered returning to the beach, getting into a boat, and rowing back to the *San Miguel* in hopes maybe that the *Tetrarch* would come along. The feeling that he was taking part in a betrayal of the Captain, Leesh, and the crew was growing in him.

But something else inside him pressed him to raid the village. He did not know what this impulse was or what caused it.

He stood a moment longer, watching the shadowy forms of the crew steal up a hill toward the village. The hesitation ended.

He ran after them.

XLIII

O'Brien hid his surprise as best he could as he peered into the eyes of the Spaniard at the head of the delegation.

"The Special Counselor?" he asked.

The head of the delegation had a strong face.

"Don Diego is not well. He must remain aboard the ship. He has sent me in his stead."

"And you are?"

The man lifted his chin slightly, a move the projected the unique pride of a Spaniard, "I am Agustín de Robles, Captain of the Personal Guard to the Special Counsel."

O'Brien allowed his gaze to linger for second on the man's eyes, which glinted in the light of the two torches in the mansion's courtyard. O'Brien tried to calculate what this all meant. He was not sure exactly what to think or believe. He had not been so foolish as to think he was the only one laying a trap, for he knew the Special Counselor to be a dangerous and intelligent man. It may be that he really was sick, but it was also possible that he was only claiming to be. But what advantage did he have for remaining aboard ship at this moment? He surely would know that O'Brien would not attack him personally, for that could have larger ramifications and possibly even lead to war between their two nations.

O'Brien could not afford to stall. Everything must go on as if the Special Counselor were here.

"Very well," O'Brien said in his firmest and most authoritative tone. "Let us proceed."

He gestured to his next in command, who called out for the soldiers to fall in line as O'Brien and the delegation walked ahead together.

O'Brien was glad this Spaniard did not attempt to make conversation as they headed down the street. If he had tried to talk to him O'Brien might well have a made a mistake. His mind raced with thoughts and scenarios.

And concerns.

Could it be the Special Counselor had orchestrated something far larger than O'Brien had thought? O'Brien had never assumed that the Special Counselor did not have his own angle, but something did not quite seem right here. He could not pinpoint any one thing or really even a collection of things that suggested a problem, but he could feel it in every nerve in his body.

He did not sense conflict coming right here and now in Port Royal itself, although he did wonder what might be aboard that Portuguese ship. A flash of horror struck him at the thought that perhaps the ship was filled with gunpowder and that the Special Counselor intended to have a Guy Fawkes kind of surprise for the city. But that thought passed on. The Special Counselor would not blow *himself* up.

Unless . . . .

No more time for thought as they turned the corner and the Falstaff came into view.

XLIV

Nick ran up the hill, over saw palmettos, tripping once but quickly leaping back up and running on, the humidity blanketing him even here in the early morning so that already sweat poured off him.

The silence of the village lay like an eerie quilt, and that sense of familiarity grew stronger.

He reached the edge of the village, ducking into the shadows, unsure if anyone had yet awakened. He had his rapier drawn, ready to attack whoever appeared.

He saw what seemed an indication of light and noticed shadowy figures darting toward it. Alert to danger, he made his way quickly and cautiously, his adrenaline pumping in a way that made him feel shaky and out of control.

Stopping short at the corner of a stucco-walled building he peered around at where the light seemed to be located.

He could see torches driven into the ground, their flames caught in a small, hot gust. Several of these were lined up along the front of the village's coquina stronghold, and he could see the lights of that building also lit, their yellow-orange warm against the black of the night.

He wondered who had lit the torches. The crew would surely not want to call attention to their activities. Did this town simply leave these torches lit through the night? That made no sense.

Nick looked around, trying to assess the situation.

His eye caught movement. Something in the warm glow of the flames. He made out shapes emerging in the darkness, a line of them running along the line of torches. Then he realized what he was seeing.

His heart sank.

XLV

O 'Brien looked around the Falstaff. Its owner, the famous Hannah (no one knew her last name), stood before him. Behind her stood a line of the women who worked for her as prostitutes, some of them haggard from years in their profession, others young and beautiful. Lined up too were the servant women, of all different shades of skin color. Also standing were the few men here, except for one who in his drunken stupor could not be roused.

The smell of the place, the feel of it, actually warmed O'Brien's heart. In his position of Governor he did not feel it appropriate to mix with the rabble in such a place as this. But all his life he had loved such places, even as a nobleman, sharing the warmth of their vulgar talk and jokes, the convivial feel of the alcohol working in him, and the general sense of gladness and freedom such a place brought. It would be nice to be a part of all this.

Maybe I shall turn to piracy

This was no time to reflect, however, and he was well aware of the delegation at his back and the soldiers flanking him.

"Miss Hannah, as you are commonly known," he said. "In the name of the Crown and in cooperation with the sovereign nation of Spain I demand that you hand over two rogues you are known to harbor, known commonly as Captain William Stockett of the ship commonly known as the *Tetrarch* and Captain Damiana Evernia of the ship commonly known as the *San Miguel*, also commonly known as the Lady Evernia, to be tried for unlawful acts of piracy."

The old lady had seen and done much in her life, O'Brien could tell, and his being here intimidated her not at all. He noticed she held a wad of tobacco in her mouth, which she now spit, leaving behind a small splatter of brown on her lips.

"We don't have any such as you name," she said, her voice hard.

"Can you inform us as to their whereabouts?"

"No."

"Do you deny knowing these two rogues?"

"Yes."

O'Brien looked over the women, "So if we question you and these ladies and others who come and go commonly in this establishment they will all say the same."

"I have not a clue what any of these vagabonds will say or any of these bawds. I cannot control the word of such. I can only tell you I know nothing of these rascals you name."

"I see," he turned to the Spaniard in charge. "Well, now the questioning must begin."

The Spaniard looked at him with those yellow eyes, and O'Brien waited for the response he expected, which was that the Spanish well knew that neither the *Tetrarch* nor the *San Miguel* were in the Port Royal harbor and might quite naturally ask why had he let them go. If the Spaniard did, O'Brien was going to reply (lying) that he had not known the vessels had departed, to which the Spaniard would reply he was either lying or incompetent. To which he would reply that if they already had this knowledge why did they not report it to him?

280

Whatever to distract and delay

"Very well," the Spaniard said. "I will apprise the Special Counselor of the situation."

"I should like to accompany you," O'Brien said.

The Spaniard looked at him, and his yellow eyes seemed to gleam, "Are you sure, Governor? The Special Counselor is very ill. He would not want you to have the same sickness."

"I will take care to keep my distance."

"Very well, Governor," the man said, turning to go.

O'Brien signaled the men flanking him to accompany him. Seeing this, the Spaniard halted, "Soldiers would be neither necessary nor wise. It is important that neither Spain nor England seem hostile, you understand."

He spoke the words in the kindest and most benign tone, but O'Brien's suspicion catapulted.

"I've just remembered," O'Brien said. "There is a law— an obscure one—that the Governor must oversee the questioning of witnesses in Port Royal. Please give the Special Counselor my regrets."

"As you wish," the Spaniard replied and walked out the door.

XLVI

Nick realized what all those shapes were: people.

Just as before, the entire village was lined up as if to receive the intruders. Except instead of rushing to this spot in the middle of the day they had apparently already been standing here waiting for the crew of the *San Miguel*.

Nick walked out into the open, still alert but suspecting what would happen next, seeing children leaning half-asleep against their mothers, men slouched and looking at him as though they knew a joke he did not, teenagers pushing each other in their barbaric style of flirting.

He knew this situation so well.

He wondered who had spied on whom. He also wondered about the *Tetrarch*'s crew. Where could they be?

He turned to see Damiana coming out of the stronghold.

"Prisa! Hurry," she said, no longer whispering. "To the ship."

Two men appeared carrying a chest. Nick looked at them in surprise.

"Wait," he said, stopping them. "Is there really treasure in there?"

"Sí, señor."

The Spanish struck Nick and with it the sinking feeling that he had been incredibly stupid. He had been so caught up in Damiana he had hardly interacted with the crew.

So stupid . . . I've been on a ship with a Spanish name, captained by a woman who is part Spanish, and have not been the least bit worried.

"Why are you cheating the *Tetrarch* out of this loot?" he demanded.

Damiana looked at him, "We're not. We will split it up with them."

"Then why are we here without them?"

"I don't know. They left us."

Nick did not know how to respond to that. It was true the *Tetrarch* had not been there by the *San Miguel.*

"What's going on here?" he asked.

Damiana urged on another pair of men carrying a chest, "What do you mean?"

"I mean," Nick said, his anger rising, "the whole town is lined up out here to watch us take *their* treasure, just like every other time we have tried this. Except this time there *is* treasure here."

"I guess we got it right this time," she said, looking for the next chest to appear.

Nick felt himself on the verge of full comprehension, but somehow could not quite get the situation clear. Information was missing here, and he could not figure out what was happening or why it was. This familiar set up made no sense, had no purpose.

But now it was not familiar. The people were here, but this time the treasure *was* here, too.

This was a twist in the script. Would there be another?

He knew what usually came next.

XLVII

I deally Leesh would have waited until all the boats had reached shore and the crew had disappeared into the narrow strip of jungle between the beach and the village. But there was so little time that as soon as he judged that the *San Miguel*'s crew had all reached the breakwater he gave the signal to pull for the ship itself.

The crew of the *Tetrarch* had turned in early claiming to need rest for the attack at dawn. But it was a ruse. They all waited as Leesh watched the *San Miguel* quietly pull away, maneuvering into a different angle in relation to the village of Nueva Lebrija. Leesh knew they would later claim they had not properly anchored and so had drifted away. The darkness of the moon made it easy enough to maneuver easily, and the *Tetrarch*'s crew, who was not at all asleep, doused all the lights and also changed the ship's position. There was an island triangulated between the two ships, and the *Tetrarch* swung around behind it. Her masts reached higher than the low island's tallest foliage, but that would not be a problem with the moon dark.

Once positioned, most of the crew dropped boats and pulled alongside the island within its low mango branches and waited. Stuart, the Captain, and a skeleton crew remained on board while Leesh led the men waiting in their boats close around the island.

Leesh watched as the *San Miguel*'s crew unloaded into the boats, just as Leesh knew they would, courtesy of information obtained by Izegbe. In fact, Leesh knew the entire ugly plan and its ramifications. He had followed Hector that day, watching him from high on the tightwire when he followed the Captain to the Falstaff. Then Leesh had taken a quick bow, scrambled down, and rushed to the tavern just as Hector was slipping away. Leesh followed him to the door full of scratches in the narrow alley, watching him go in and come out.

Then Leesh went to that place himself, met that mysterious entity within. Leesh had sailed the world's seas enough to know that fantastic things were to be found everywhere that defied what civilization thought to be impossible. He did not know exactly who or what that entity was, nor did he take time to wonder at it beyond trying to figure out its characteristics and motivations. The latter he still had not figured out, but he did detect something in that voice and the strange mix of different languages. He recognized the African tongue, and he knew who maybe could help him.

And so he had gone to Izegbe, to spring him from slavery and offer him a life of freedom and wealth. There was only one condition: that he speak to that strange entity.

Leesh took him to that door with the scratches, and when they went inside and began to speak in the African tongue Nick was glad to see the true plan come out. He saw now what information had been leaked and by whom and for what reasons. Hector had played an integral role in setting up the strange village dramas on the Main. But he was not the only one involved.

It was powerful knowledge, and Leesh sought to turn it to his advantage. The Captain had struck a deal with the Governor, but that plan depended on faulty information. It was important to fend for yourself, especially when playing with such a devilishly clever bunch.

And the Lady Evernia was clever indeed. He could not help but admire her ability to manipulate, although it was hardly fair to do so with such a young pup. Then again, Leesh imagined there were few grown and so-called smart men who could withstand her either. Who knows, maybe he himself would have faltered under a full direct attack.

Of course it was impossible to know whom to trust, Leesh well knew, so he watched with open and careful eyes. So far, things had proceeded as he expected, the *San Miguel* positioning itself to attack early, take the loot, and run.

Leesh's little fleet of dinghies pulled quickly to the *San Miguel*, and he hoped no one noticed. Quietly they scaled the low side of the schooner and crawled on deck. There they slipped up on and overpowered the small crew left behind. They tied them up and gagged them. It would have been better to slit their throats, but there were larger forces at work here to watch out for, so Leesh settled simply for incapacitating the men and taking them below to the sound of barking dogs. Leesh located them in the captain's quarters and puzzled about what to do with them. He hated to kill needlessly, but the situation was critical.

While the *Tetrarch*'s crew spiked the guns ranged along the deck (the schooner's low draft did not allow guns on a lower deck), Leesh signaled by lantern for the *Tetrarch* itself to come up. It glided swiftly from behind the island and drew up as close as possible to the other ship. Hopefully in the dark it would not be noticeable that there were actually two ships close together until it was too late to do much about it.

"A-ho," whispered John Black. "The first of the quarry comes."

XLVIII

Draw your sword, you whoreson knave! I've waited long enough to paint the ground red with your blood."

So it comes to this

He looked around to see Pew stepping forward, his tall shadow casting an even longer shadow in the torchlight, his hand on the hilt of his rapier.

Nick's consciousness registered his bewilderment. This challenge coming with this clearly pre-planned drama now all mixed with the awful feeling that Damiana was somehow on the inside of the whole thing.

But there was no time to think. Nick gripped his rapier. He had no idea just how much Pew knew or how good a swordsman he really was just based on the demonstration he had watched in Port Royal. Nick also could not say he had any truly strong grasp on the Spanish style he expected now to face. He would have to do the best he could.

Nick glanced quickly at Damiana and saw a strange smile on her face.

A devilish smile

Pew drew the sword and saluted Nick. Nick did the same and watched as Pew raised his sword hand in the expected way.

Nick too raised his sword, his mind racing, trying to remember what he had learned. He knew he had made the mistake in the past of letting his opponent dictate the moves and did not want that to happen again, so *he* took the first step.

As he did so he tried to execute the *atajo* in the way he had learned, trying not so much to displace Pew's blade but rather to gain an advantage on it.

Pew glided into his response, and Nick recognized it for what it was—no parry, no stepping back, but rather a redirect, an *atajo* of Pew's own, that quickly turned the tables.

Nick responded with what he knew, parrying and stepping back out of harm's way as the blade's point just missed his body in a cold, smooth, gleaming advance.

These devils don't even thrust

Nick anticipated Pew's next step, this time in the opposite direction, turning the circle backwards with the back foot and then stepping forward with the front foot while dragging the blade in a slice to the stomach.

Nick stepped back, which was fortunate because he missed the parry, taking the wrong guard position and so not meeting the angle of Pew's blade correctly.

Nick caught the movement of Pew's lips twisting into a thin, sickly smile.

"Remember what you've learned, Nick," he heard Damiana say.

Her voice struck him in breaking the silence, and he realized how bizarre it was to fight this duel in front of a mute audience in the deadest hour of the morning. At the same time, her words bolstered him.

He must not stay on the defensive. That would defeat him. He must attack.

Staying in the bent-kneed stance he was more accustomed to he passed forward into an attack.

The move was rash, not befitting the style of swordsmanship he had taught himself. It depended on surprise and strength.

And it fooled Pew not at all.

Still walking calmly on that invisible circle, Pew evaded the attack altogether, and only Nick's athleticism saved him as he twisted away in an ugly move that sent him sprawling into the sand.

Pew's blade had just caught him on the arm, but it was a only a scratch, and Nick sprang to his feet. As he did he heard a hissing sound, and his eyes cut over to see Damiana's mouth set in an open snarl, her upper lip curled in an h-shape, her teeth showing. The look and sound mesmerized him for a second.

He forced his attention back to Pew.

XLIX

Back at the Mansion O'Brien tried to think what this new turn could mean. What could the Special Counselor be about? It was no surprise that Don Diego did not trust him. Who could be trusted in such a place and time? But O'Brien had a gnawing suspicion that the Special Counselor was not aboard that ship at all.

And if he was not here in Port Royal where was he?

A knock came at the door.

"Come in."

The footman entered bearing a message.

"For you, sir."

"Thank you."

O'Brien opened it.

Dear O'Brien,

I regret that illness confines me to the ship this evening. My second in command, Agustin, has informed me of the situation. I regret to hear that neither of the ships in question are here. I hope you can provide an adequate explanation for why they have escaped under your watch, especially when *you* have arranged to have me brought here. I fear knavery is afoot. I hope you do not intend to detain me.

> By the Grace of God and Our Lady
> and the Crown of Imperial Spain,
> Don Diego Pedro de la Figueroa

O'Brien pondered the letter a moment, his mind working through scenarios again. Then he opened a desk drawer and brought out the packet of letters the Special Counselor had written in the past so he could compare the handwriting.

It did seem to come from the Special Counselor's hand. But something seemed off. It got the message across, but it lacked a certain specificity, and the salutation was curt, although that could be expected under the circumstances.

He considered how best to respond, and after a moment took up a clean sheet of paper and a new quill, which he dipped into the ink. He would much rather be fighting, but he must fulfill his role as Governor.

He began to write.

L

Pew closed before Nick could realize it, and again Nick resorted to his athleticism to dodge his head just out of the way of the blade.

Nick backed away several steps and stood, his heart beating quickly. He felt out of control, and Pew was so tall he could not only close quickly, but if he should suddenly decide actually to lunge and thrust, his reach would have been very long indeed.

Nick judged that distance and took two more steps back.

He needed to catch his breath. More importantly, he needed to calm down, to engage his mind. He had no control of the situation at all but was simply reacting, even when he attacked.

"Kill him, Nick," he heard Damiana say. At first her words heartened him. But then they rankled. He had no time to figure out why.

He took a deep breath and focused, forcing his mind and breathing to slow down. He must relax and remember his long experience. He had not yet learned to fight in this style, and he could not learn it now. He knew how deadly and cold it was, but trying to match it would not work. Pew clearly knew the style far better than Nick did.

The better approach was to do what *he*, Nick, knew, using his new knowledge to anticipate Pew's attack. This Spanish style had a cold-blooded grace to it, but then so did the French style Nick had learned. This rapier was hardly a smallsword, but then its greater length made an advantage.

Maybe Pew did not know the French style, but Nick realized he would be foolish to depend on that possibility. Rather, Nick needed to find his own advantage somehow, someway. There was nothing unbeatable in swordplay, he knew. The only hope he had was to be himself and to do what he knew as best he could.

His mind played back to that day long ago when he had watched the man in gold defeat his true father, Lord Furth, there in the woods outside Naunton. The man had been completely confident in himself, while Lord Furth lumbered about. Nick realized with shame how he himself now resembled Lord Furth.

He shut the ugly image of himself out. He was still alive, could still do something.

Feeling his heart pounding, he threw his left hand back in the languid French style and went on guard in tierce, in the way the French did the smallsword.

Pew had already begun his next attack.

LI

The second boat arrived laden with treasure, and the men called up to the crew on the *San Miguel* to throw down ropes to hoist up the chests. Then the men themselves followed and were surprised when strangers stood there pointing muskets and swords directly at them.

"Tie them up," Leesh said, smiling at the *San Miguel* crewmen while men from the *Tetrarch* continued walking the chests on planks over to their own ship. Leesh figured there was a high likelihood someone was keeping watch from shore, so he wanted to make sure that everything looked normal from the starboard side of the ship which faced the land.

"I still want to cut these bloody cheats' throats," Edward whispered to Leesh.

"Aye, mate. But they're only following their orders. It's their captain's the bad one."

"Aye," Edward said quietly, thinking.

Leesh watched Izegbe helping herd these new prisoners down below deck to join their mates. The man was a quick study, having already gained an understanding of the rudiments of sailing. He would be a good sailor, and Leesh thought about how he had picked another good one just as he had with Nick. But Nick was young yet and had much to learn.

Leesh had known it would be only a matter of time before the Lady Evernia made her play for Nick. He was as helpless as a lamb before her. It may be that Leesh had helped her along, priming him with his description.

Maybe he and the Captain had not been so wise in dealing with the lady that day. There was a risk of driving Nick closer to her, sure, but it was a risk he had felt worth taking at the time. But then came that business with that young lass hanging herself. That was a bad turn, no doubt about it. One could not tell what kind of imbalances were in a person, and since finding her hanged Leesh had thought back over the many years of his life and all the times people had broken. He hated to see her break, and he hated to see what it did to Nick.

The situation was even more delicate than ever now. Leesh had tried to read Nick when attempting to coax him back to the *Tetrarch*, but it was clear that Nick's resentment worked hard against Leesh. It could be that Nick had completely bought in to the Lady Evernia's scheme. He certainly seemed to be on board with what the *San Miguel* had done. But then it was also possible Nick did not sympathize, and Leesh could imagine the boy—for really he still was a boy—torn and unsure exactly what to do. Nick had a sense of equity and justice, so it may be that he was beginning or would soon begin to doubt the Lady Evernia and even turn on her. Several of the men had asked about what to do about Nick—should they make an effort to "rescue" him? Part of Leesh wanted to try that, but another part of him could not keep from calculating the risks it would bring to their situation.

A situation rather dire

LII

he key is counterattack

The words clarified in Nick's mind as Pew made this new attack, advancing with that infernal *atajo* that seemed to crawl up Nick's blade like a snake, as though it were an extension of Pew the snake himself. Indeed, when Nick again heard a hiss he realized it was coming from Pew this time, and his mind registered that it probably had the first time.

But this fight was everything now. He needed to take control.

This time he was ready and calm, taking the *atajo* as given in his position of quarte and then binding into seconde, a strong move with the palm down. As he did so he stepped forward, grabbing Pew's sword arm with his left hand and striking as hard as he could with the pommel of his rapier.

Nick aimed for Pew's forehead but did not execute well. The pommel hit on the brow-bone above Pew's left eye but glanced down, doing little damage to the skull. But the force of the move thrust the pommel forward still, and it slid down into the eye socket and dug in behind the eyeball.

Nick yanked down viciously, a new anger driving him. The move caught the back of the eyeball and squeezed it out of the socket, and into the sand below, a glistening jelly ball.

Pew cried out and tumbled forward onto the ground himself as a collective gasp arose from the crowd.

Nick watched Pew as he managed to keep himself on his knees then on his feet, stepping forward, growling and hissing, holding his hand over his eye. Pew whirled, facing Nick. This was a man who had the presence of mind to stay alert and on guard even as he was going through the shock and pain of losing his eye.

It gave Nick pause as he watched Pew's face contort, its snakelike features tightening with hatred. Nick watched emotion take over as Pew advanced again quickly, still controlled but a little less so. His stance changed, so quickly Nick almost did not perceive it. The style changed with it, and Nick recognized the movements as being closer to the style he knew.

Then Pew made a mistake. His sword arm had bent when his stance changed, and now he lunged before extending it again. It was a fatal mistake.

Nick extended his sword into the attack.

Pew stopped short, but it was too late, his arm still bent. Nick's guard overpowered Pew's blade and pointed straight at his heart.

LIII

O'Brien finished his short letter and blotted it:

My Dear Special Counselor,

    I am saddened to hear of your illness and wish you a speedy recovery. I regret that the *Tetrarch* and *San Miguel* managed to leave without my knowing. They must have left sometime in this very night.

    Whatever the case, I assure you that those pirates must somehow have been informed of their perilous situation. I further assure you that you and your crew are completely safe and will be in no wise harmed.

    I had hoped to catch the rascals, but we can still do so at a later date. For now, rest. If you should like to return home and wait for me to let you know when the two ships return I will gladly do so.

    With humility in the name of the Crown I remain,

    William O'Brien

    Governor of Jamaica

O'Brien folded the letter and sealed it. He wanted to keep the *São Martinho* here tonight, but not for much longer after that. It would not do for her to be here when the pirates returned.

If they did return . . .

O'Brien felt uneasiness growing stronger and stronger in him. He told himself he had provided enough protection for the *Tetrarch*, but had had an increasingly disturbing feeling that the crew was in trouble. Not that it should matter to him. These pirates were a curse on the city.

But he *had* made a deal with Stockett, and he *did* envision a future of cooperation among the pirates, maybe finding some new way to make them legitimate as Letters of Marquis had done for so long.

There was no feeling good about the situation, though.

LIV

A t the last second Pew shifted his body so the blade pierced his shoulder instead of his heart. Still, even in his pain, the man returned to his usual composure, raising his sword arm and replacing his other arm behind him in his usual way of the Spanish.

Now, however, he grew less aggressive as their fight continued. He still applied the *atajo* with the same sinister maneuvering. But now the moves were probing, and he rarely lost contact with Nick's blade.

Nick too worked with care, impressed by this man's grit and well aware of how dangerous this man was.

Move and countermove, a conversation, each man trying to understand what the other was saying, trying to find the weak spot without committing himself. Both driven by emotion, which both knew to be unwise and the cause of the injuries they had sustained.

Finding a weakness in this man's defense was no easy thing. The aggression was gone now, but Pew seemed even more deadly, and something in Nick warned him not to abandon himself to an attack but to stay patient.

In a *salle d'armes* this bout would have been textbook, the French style with its defensive posture against the Spanish maneuvering, Pew wheeling around Nick, who let his instinct take over to grasp Pew's working that invisible circle of death.

Even at full strength again Nick was starting to feel some fatigue as he held the rapier and kept his knees bent. Nick could not remembering fighting someone for this long, and impatience began to work in him.

This is to the death

If he could just find another chink in Pew's armor, or if the man could just make another mistake.

But it was Nick who made the mistake.

He mistimed an attack, creating a situation of simultaneous attack, having lost his concentration for a fraction of second. Pew sensed it. He caught the blade against his guard and started the lightning-fast move to wrench the sword out of Nick's hand.

Nick raised the point swiftly, taking the blade back, then thrust.

It all felt like luck, a mistiming that managed to turned into perfect timing.

He felt the blade pass into soft flesh, and he felt the body give.

LV

Nick could tell he had not pierced any vital parts as he pulled the blade out. But Pew had dropped his sword and now fell to the ground.

Nick looked down at the man, his anger turned to a feeling of victory, the scores of times the man had made snide remarks and other passive-aggressive attacks over the past several days at sea passing through Nick's mind. It would feel good to get this man out of the world and not have him meddling with him and Damaina.

Then that lady spoke.

"Finish him," she said. "Finish him, darling, and let's go."

Pride filled him at once to know he had this wonderful, beautiful woman and had fought off another man devoted to her.

But immediately another feeling crashed in as he looked at the man on his knees awaiting the death blow. As though a cloud blew out of the way Nick suddenly saw the man differently. Somehow now he did not seem a real rival. He was just a fussy man who annoyed but who never really had a chance with a woman like the Lady Evernia.

Which made her words strangely sickening to Nick. He looked at Pew and thought that it would be beneath him to kill him. Unfair, really, for the man to die for a woman he could never have anyway.

But then not killing him did not seem right either, for that felt like an act of disrespect somehow.

A new anger filled Nick as he thought about being in this situation that offered no good way out. Partly, Nick was mad at Pew. But he grew angry at Damiana herself. She had broken her plan with the *Tetrarch*, and she had egged on this fight.

Again, Nick felt that suspicion that she had some inside awareness of what was happening in this and the other villages.

"Morning comes! We must go to the ship! Avast, Nick!"

Nick stood and looked at her, "Are you going to leave this man here?"

She stopped and looked at him, malice glaring in her eyes, "He's nothing to me."

She turned and walked into the woods with the other members of her crew. Her move horrified Nick yet also struck him with awe. He looked back down at Pew, who was crying now, obviously not for himself but at what she had said.

Pity filled Nick. Part of him wanted to put the man out of his pain. But the man had fought so hard, even after losing an eye. He deserved to live.

Nick turned and ran into the woods.

Occupied in his fight, Nick had not noticed that day was breaking. Now he could see the first orange light on the horizon as he ran to catch up to the boat with Damiana in it. No sooner had he climbed aboard than he realized Pew had too, apparently running just behind him, even in his pain.

Nick jolted away, afraid Pew would try to stab him. But the tall man appeared to be unarmed and was clearly fighting to remain conscious.

Still, Nick could only feel uneasiness. Remaining alert to Pew, he turned to look at Damiana's back, her long curls, the wonderful curves of her hips, thinking of making love to her. He had thought such intimacy created a bond that was wholly unique and unbreakable. It had changed him forever, and he believed he would be inseparable from her from now on.

But now she seemed distant, strange, as though they had never shared the deepest parts of themselves. He could not understand how she could do that. He felt as if he were in the way. She had urged him on against Pew, yes. And he had thought when he ran out into the water and caught her boat that she would be happy to see him as she had been when he had gone to her after Abigail killed herself. But now she seemed indifferent to him altogether.

She's occupied. It will be different later

But the thought rang strangely hollow. He could sense something different going on.

As they approached the *San Miguel* he heard her curse under her breath, and the sound of it shocked him.

He looked where she looked.

It looked as if the *San Miguel* were splitting into two ships, the one pulling away from the other. What was this hallucination?

But it was not an imaginative fancy. There was another ship starting to drift away.

The Tetrarch.

LVI

Nick wanted to shout for joy, but his emotions conflicted too much and also the situation was confusing as he heard Damiana curse again and yell something in Spanish to the men rowing.

Finally they came aboard ship and she climbed up the low hull with amazing speed and catapulted over the starboard gunnel. He hurried up and over too and was shocked to find the deck clear of any crew.

He looked and saw the *Tetrarch* picking up speed, getting away. All around him men were yelling in Spanish, nothing he could understand. Then more of the crew came up out of the hold, speaking rapidly.

"They've taken the treasure!" Damiana yelled in English "After them! Vamos!"

The crew leapt into action, but Nick did not. He refused to do anything, simply standing there unsure what to do as the ship started to turn in pursuit, the sails unfurling quickly and catching the wind. The *Tetrarch* had a good start, but this little schooner had great speed and a good shot at catching her.

Nick's alarm grew as he saw the crew working to maneuver the guns but then realized they had been spiked. He could feel the anger growing aboard ship.

Then just as the *San Miguel* was building momentum toward its top speed, Nick felt her slow down and he heard a new outburst of Spanish. He tried to make sense of it as they pointed. Then he looked, not at where the *Tetrarch* was making a getaway, but to the north.

There sat a line of ships, menacing in advance. Nick could see the flag of England flying aloft on these ships.

Royal navy

Again Damiana barked orders in Spanish. She had always spoken in English before. But now she seemed a different person altogether. Her voice became lost in the sound of the ship's bell ringing.

The *San Miguel* was turning, giving its larboard side to the advancing fleet. If those ships attacked, this one would suffer major damage. Regret tore through Nick for having put himself on this ship.

He did not hear the sound of the first shot. Instead he heard the water splashes a mere twenty feet away. Then the sound of the shot came rumbling over the water now turning from morning purple to blue as the sun fully appeared over the horizon, turning the advancing ships into silhouettes.

He looked again at the *Tetrarch* hurrying away from this scene. How had the navy known to come here?

More shots followed quicker and closer as the *San Miguel* turned and headed in the opposite direction. Fast as this ship was, it was not moving quickly enough, and before it could turn fully, the first cannonballs smashed into the hull and tore across the deck. Nick felt the ship shudder and heard the lead whistling by, glancing off the main mast with a cracking pop.

Damiana encouraged the crew to greater speed while Nick just stood there. He did not look forward to being caught aboard this ship. And he wondered, had this whole thing been a setup?

Nick remembered Leesh paddling over to try and get him to come back to the *Tetrarch*. Had the old man been trying to save Nick? Had Nick been too foolish to let him?

Shame filled Nick as he thought about how Leesh had always been so good to him and was surely only looking out for his own good as usual. What a foolish idiot Nick was.

More iron smashed into the hull, and the ship shook with the impact. Nick thought he could smell wood burning and looked around for a flame.

In looking, though, his eyes happened to alight forward, past the bow directly ahead.

There another line of ships was advancing.

All this for just one ship?

Then he realized.

These ships were Spanish and were advancing quickly.

The *San Miguel* headed directly toward that line, picking up speed.

She's with them

His heart gripped as he truly realized how stupid he had been. He looked back at the English ships pursuing. They surely saw the Spanish.

Turning around again he watched the rapid convergence of the *San Miguel* with the Spanish galleons. He could see the men working on those decks, and he could see the guns bristling.

The cannonfire roared, deafening, just as the *San Miguel* passed through the line of ships. His ears ringing, Nick looked back to see sprays of popping water all around the English ships, some of them hit. Their line was breaking, and they were turning to flee.

They don't want war. But does Spain?

These were national matters. More than Nick could understand. What he *could* understand was his own danger. Turning back he saw ahead a massive man-o-war and felt his entire person sink with dread.

LVII

We pulled up as sharply as we could upon sight of the enemy," the Admiral said to conclude his account of what had happened. "My judgment was that the priority was the preservation of peace between our nations."

"And they fired a round?" O'Brien asked.

"Yes, sir."

"One volley only?"

"Yes, sir."

"And they did not pursue you?"

"No, sir."

"Very well, Admiral. You did the right thing. Leave me for awhile to ponder this situation."

"Yes, sir."

As the Admiral left the room, O'Brien worked his way through what had happened. He already understood that the situation had been a set-up, but now he realized the high stakes. It was clear to him that the Special Counselor had devised the whole plan and deftly maneuvered himself, O'Brien, into its accomplishment. It was Don Diego himself who had leaked Nueva Lebrija just as he had the other locations as strongholds with treasure. O'Brien was not sure if this location actually did have treasure, but he doubted it.

The *Tetrarch* had not yet returned to Port Royal, which suggested that maybe they *had* found treasure. On the other hand, if she had stopped to see what would happen with the *San Miguel*, the crew might have seen the encounter of the two navies and so now laid low to stay out of the fray.

Then again, maybe not—for if war were to be reignited it would be a perfect opportunity for privateering.

War . . . .

Was this what Don Diego wanted? Had this whole thing been an elaborate ruse to start war? If so, then why bother? Why not simply attack Port Royal?

No, that would point the finger at Don Diego himself as a war monger. Better to work this thing through the pirates who lived in that space in between legitimate and illegitimate. With that bunch everything became murky, and it was difficult to tell who was really in charge.

But O'Brien could see the Special Counselor's hand at work in everything. He had obviously put the Spanish-named schooner in play in order to draw an attack, which he could then use to lift this seemingly cooperative effort to the level of conflict between kingdoms. He had even pitted his own people against each other in order to make the whole thing believable. And, most bizarre of all, the ruses he had used had been so not believable—whole villages gathering to watch their own plundering, the strange duels like ancient single-warrior challenges of old, the treasure always missing. The man was devilishly clever, O'Brien had to admit. On one hand, the whole business was so fantastic as to seem silly. And yet that very quality and the mystery and strangeness surrounding it had served its purpose of piquing the interest of the pirates and of O'Brien himself.

And O'Brien had played right into the Special Counselor's hands. He had played along in the cooperation plan, and when O'Brien had tried to create a distraction, he was simply establishing the very distraction Don Diego himself wanted. O'Brien was certain the Special Counselor had not come here on that ship at all, and O'Brien had not been surprised when she set sail out of Port Royal after the early morning encounter at the Falstaff. Don Diego had coopted O'Brien's ruse to use for his own plan. Don Diego had set up his own navy there at Nueva Lebrija to meet the English navy, which O'Brien had sent to apprehend the *San Miguel*. The idea had been for the *Tetrarch* to allow the *San Miguel* to carry all the treasure, and the navy would apprehend the latter ship while the English one got away. That was the deal he had struck with Captain Stockett. So it did not surprise him that the *Tetrarch* escaped, only that she had not returned to Port Royal yet.

More importantly, who could possibly know how Don Diego had leaked the false information that set up his plans? This remained a mystery to O'Brien, but his mind went more and more to that young woman with the beautiful black hair who had visited him . . .

Katarina

He almost felt relief that things had not worked out the way he had planned, for he did not know if he would have had it in him to punish her. His plan had been to capture and hang her and the rest of the *San Miguel*'s crew for their acts of piracy, thus showing cooperation yet preserving the pirates he had cut his own deal with.

But I could never kill you, Katarina

Even now he awaited a letter to clear up exactly how the beautiful woman was connected to the woman he loved. Could she actually have been *Katarina*'s daughter? He had heard so many rumors about the woman's parentage he could not tell which one was true.

But she must be

Meanwhile, other letters were flying about as O'Brien worked to deal with this new international crisis. He was proud of the Admiral for having the presence of mind not to attack. But he also knew it was the English word versus the Spanish word. He was not sure exactly what motivated Don Diego. Perhaps it was money, but from all he could find out the man had no need of riches nor any particular interest in them.

It may have been power. Or maybe it was simply glory, the desire to distinguish himself in war—when there was no war to fight in then it must be manufactured.

A knock interrupted his thoughts.

"Come in."

A footman entered, "My lord, the Lady Elizabeth is here for tea."

"Show her in."

LVIII

L eesh sat alone in the cave, the roar of the falls echoing around the damp rock walls and rolling back through the dark caverns. This was Leesh's personal hideout.

This entire island was a secret haven Leesh had made use of for many years. Few maps included it, but knowing ones called it Fan Island because its jagged jungle-covered cliff rose in a great fan shape straight up out of the sea. It appeared to have no natural port because years ago a pirate captain had devised a false island of trees to hide its narrow entrance. This was the pirate captain with whom Leesh had first sailed, and only Leesh remained alive to know the entrance, having shown only the crew of the *Tetrarch*. And not all of them even had known of it, with many having sailed on missions without actually visiting this place. In fact, while they may not have realized it, all of the crew knowing about this place (save Stuart and Stockett, who had known about it for some time) put themselves in a precarious position, for the sea was littered with skeletons of those who had disaffected and had been killed for their knowledge.

After fleeing the scene along the Main they had sailed here careful to see they were not followed. They moved aside the false island under cover of night and squeezed carefully through the narrow but short strait that led to a deep pool right in the center of the island. When daylight arose the sun revealed the high peaks surrounding the pool like a great green ring. The men new to this place wondered at the sparkling blue water and the falls that plunged hundreds of feet into it, the winds that swirled here catching the falls and turning their hair-like strands of water into puffs of white vapor.

Buildings had been built on the cliffs for the men to stay, but after the treasure had been divided and when night fell again Leesh slipped away and made the careful climb via a series of concealed ladders up to this cave, which could be entered through a conveniently wide entrance that curved far back behind the falls. Making his way into the deep caverns he added his recently acquired treasures, including the brass nose, to the store he had been amassing for years. He had thought many times of retiring to enjoy it, but he was a social creature by nature and could not stand to give up adventure for as long as he could be a part of it.

Once he had settled everything in its hiding place, he slept on the bed he kept in a different cavern along with some fake treasure meant to throw prying intruders off the trail (for who knew if this island and cave should be discovered? hiding places needed hiding places). He slept well, his mind emptying to the drowsy overwhelming sound of the falls.

He awoke before sunrise and made his way back to the cave's opening, and there he sat listening to the falls, his head tingling and his spine chilling to the sound. For a man whose mind was always working it was nice to empty it.

That worked for awhile, but eventually images and thoughts made their way into his consciousness. He thought of that night with Izegbe . . .

315

. . . there in that place with the heavily-scratched door where that person or entity or whatever it was lived. Izegbe and that entity spoke in their language, Leesh only able to follow bits and pieces of it.

"What is he saying?" Leesh had been unsure about this entity's gender so just used the standard male reference.

"Says this Nueva Lebrija really is the place."

"There is treasure there?"

More communication, then, "Yes. Treasure there this time. But this is all part of a plan."

"What kind of plan?"

More communication, a pause, and then more. Then Izegbe spoke to Leesh in English again, "Says big leader of the Spanish has a big house and is planning a war. Says leader knows Governor O'Brien's plan to attack. Says part of Spanish leader's plan. Says all a trap so the English will attack a Spanish ship and the Spanish fight back. Start a new war."

Leesh processed this information. Then he asked the question he had been trying to answer for so long.

"Who is the spy? Is it the woman?"

No need to communicate with the entity this time, "Says the woman is big Spanish leader's woman. She leaked Nueva Lebrija as target by his orders. Says the Brass Nose is the real spy. Says he's positioning himself to grow rich on war."

Leesh digested this information too. He had been wary of the Lady Evernia from the beginning, but now he saw how dangerous she really was. She had carefully manipulated the Tetrarch's crew. She had a gift for bringing men together.

A thought occurred to Leesh, "Izegbe, can I ask how does he know all this? Just from the Brass Nose?"

More communication between the two African speakers. Then Izegbe, "Says partly but also he has investigated for himself."

Leesh leaned forward, "What do you mean? Has he interacted with this Spanish leader?"

More communication, then, "Not exactly. Says was there on the island. Sent a message for Brass Nose and stayed on island to watch the Spanish leader for a time. Learned the man's whole island and where he lives."

Leesh was confused, "The Spaniard just let him stay there and run around the island?"

Again the words between the indistinct entity who seemed almost not there and the African man who had until an hour and a half ago been a slave, then Izegbe, "Says no, Spaniard never saw him."

"How did he do that?" Leesh asked.

His words met with a low laugh, eerie, otherworldly, followed by slowly articulated sounds. But before Izegbe could speak, the entity itself did,

"You—of all men, Archibald Leesh—know it's unwise to reveal all your secrets . . .

. . . even here in the blue light of early morning, enjoying the pleasant tingle of the atmosphere, Leesh's blood ran cold at the memory of that mysterious entity speaking his own full name even though they had never met before and Leesh had not revealed even so much as one of his nicknames. Leesh well knew there was magic in this world. He did not know if this entity came from Africa or somewhere else, but he well understood how powerful the magic was. And he respected it deeply. He would make no effort to deceive or cajole this person, if person it was. Leesh had treated this entity with respect and would continue to do so.

Just as he would Izegbe. He was proud of the man, as he was of Nick.

Nick . . . he hated to leave the lad behind. He really did. But young men had to make their own choices, come what may. That Leesh had learned from experience.

And always there were choices to be evaluated and made, for good or ill, often for both at once. That was the great challenge—to try and find some sense in the moment, which would end so quickly but would bring consequences that last forever. That was why it was important to enjoy peace of mind when it came at moments such as this one when he could let go and listen to the roar of the falls.

Which he did, letting his mind go numb as the day accomplished and the gray curtain before him turned to sparkling white.

LIX

The musty, cold, clammy atmosphere of the dungeon seemed permanently stuck in Nick's system. His wrists and ankles were chaffed by the cold metal shackles, and the smell of his own bodily fluids from not being able to move filled his nose.

For the moment, he had managed to position himself so that the wounds on his back did not hurt quite so bad from the lashing. That was the latest round of torture he had gone through. He had no idea how much time had passed since that had happened; here in the dark, with no sense of sunrise or sunset, it could have been hours or days.

It had fully dawned on him just how terrible his situation was as soon as he saw the Spanish ships that morning and the *San Miguel* passed through their line, the whelming firing of the guns sending a shudder through him. He did not know the significance of the massive man-o-war flying a Spanish flag, but he knew something bad awaited him. As they pulled up alongside the ship, some of the crew grabbed Nick. He looked to Damiana, but she seemed to have forgotten he existed.

Two of the crew pushed him roughly to board the massive ship just behind Damiana. When he came on deck he saw Damiana in the arms of a tall Spaniard, watched as the man kissed her and she arched her back inward to curve her body into his just as she had done with Nick.

The sight of it sliced through his guts worse than any sword. He could not grasp what he was seeing. He tried to cope with the emotions tearing him to pieces inside.

When the kiss finally ended, the two began speaking to one another in Spanish. She gestured, and the man's face registered surprise. She pointed to Nick, and he looked at him, his face clouding. The man gestured at Nick and spoke louder, obviously angry. Then he barked an order, and the crew men pinioned his arms as Nick felt ropes come around his wrists and tie tightly. Then the crew shoved him roughly to the floor and tied his ankles together.

But Nick did not feel any physical pain. His pain came from the idea that this woman with whom he had spent time and given himself to as he had no other woman was actually kissing and clearly involved with this other man. Nick just could not process this or the emotions that arose in him.

He had lost track of what was happening outside of himself and only vaguely registered that the guns were not firing. He assumed the English had not engaged in the battle. But that all seemed as nothing to him.

Then he saw the Spaniard walking to him, his uniform resplendent. The man knelt before him, "I hear the two of you have been making love to my woman." Nick realized Pew lay beside him, also bound. "For that you will pay, English dogs."

Nick closed his eyes when he saw the man about to spit. When he opened them again it was just in time to see the man's leg swinging forward, the boot crashing into his skull once, bringing an explosion of stars, twice to send him slipping away, a third time with no sign of stopping as Nick faded away.

He had awakened in a different part of this dungeon on a rack, already feeling his limbs pulled in different directions.

"Wake up, cur," a voice said full of malice but also sinister patience. "Tell us where your mates have gone."

"I—" Nick's throat was dry. He swallowed, "I—I don't know."

"Tell us, or you will experience great pain."

"I don't know."

A creaking sounded, and Nick felt the hard inexorable stretch, the pain skimming through him first along the surface and then settling deep. He forced himself to keep from screaming. It was not much of a pull, but the pain was horrible, and he could tell that much worse was to come.

"We try again," the voice said. "Tell us where your mates have gone."

"I tell you I don't know."

A moment of silence. Then came the creak, and the pull seemed to wrench his joints apart. This time Nick could not hold back the scream.

As it continued, Nick lost track of how many times that terrible machine had been cranked, and he was surprised when he awoke still in one piece. But the pain was the worst he had ever experienced in his life, and his whole body felt as if it might collapse at any moment. He was shackled, and the cold damp was all around him.

He had little time to think or make sense of his situation, however, because he was immediately taken to another round of torture, this time with water. Again he passed out, and again when he awoke men came to haul him off, clearly having been watching for when he awakened. Then came the next round with the whip, and he had passed out, awakening chained here again.

He had been allowed to lie here awake longer this time, and he reflected as well as he could on his situation. He labored to puzzle out the events to find the truth of what had happened. As he thought, he wondered how long he would have until the torture began again.

Time seemed to have passed, but he had no idea how much. He heard what he thought was Pew's voice in the distance crying, "Woolded! I've been woolded! God pity me!"

Then he heard a jangling and a cranking of iron, followed by footsteps.

He smelled her perfume even before he heard her footsteps, and knowing she was coming jolted him. He saw warm light from a torch.

Then she was there, close to him, her face ruddy in the light, her blue eyes sparkling even in this dreary place. Hatred for her throttled him, but that hate was filled with longing, for which he hated himself.

"Nick," Damiana said, concern in her voice.

He did not answer, wanting her to go yet not wanting her ever to leave.

Then she put her arms around his neck, pulled him to her, and kissed him. He did nothing to reciprocate, but she seemed unbothered by that as she let him go.

"I'm so sorry about this, Nick. I didn't realize they were hurting you."

He could hear a catch in her voice, and the thought wandered up that maybe she *did* care about him.

"I want to get you out of her, darling."

He looked into her eyes. They projected warmth and care now, but he remembered being on deck on the *San Miguel* and their looking at him with no recognition, as if she had forgotten who he was.

"You're with that man," he said.

She looked at him, still projecting that warmth in her eyes, "No, I'm not. He shouldn't have told you I was. He is very jealous. I love *you*."

She sounded convincing enough that Nick struggled to reconcile her words with what he had seen.

"You can get out of here," she said, running her hand over his face and down his chest. Even in his pain his body came alive, and images of being with her abrupted into his consciousness.

Was this a new kind of torture?

Again she kissed him, pressing her body to his, bringing him memories of being with her, and he seemed transported out of this place and back to her quarters on the ship.

But something struck him differently now. Even as his body yearned for her, a part of his mind seemed to stand apart and assess the moment. And that part of his mind detected something—that she was trying to control his reaction, to control *him*.

Still, he could not help himself; he started kissing her back. Energy mounted.

Then she pulled away and caught her breath, whispering, "I can't resist you."

It sounded too good, but he could not believe she was lying.

That man can't give her what I give her

A thin pride in that idea propped him up. But the props were thin and wobbly, and doubt tormented him.

"You can get out, Nick. They just want to know where the *Tetrarch* has gone."

Suspicion crashed into him, cooling his ardor. He looked at her a moment, then spoke:

"They sent you."

"No," she said it in an outraged way, as if it were the worst thing in the world she could be accused of. "Nobody knows I'm here."

Maybe she's telling the truth

His mind flopped back and forth even as her beauty—and that other extra something she had—registered in his brain. Part of him wanted to lash out at her, but the other part of him could not.

"Damiana," he felt close to her speaking her name.

She waited for a reply, then quietly said, "Yes?"

"I swear to you, I really don't know where they are."

"Nick, you sailed on that ship. Did they have a hideout?"

"Not that I know of. I haven't been on it for very long."

She seemed to consider this, "If you can just tell them anything they will let you go. You have my word."

He tried to hold up his hand, but the chains were heavy, and his wrists hurt, "I would if I could. I promise you."

Now she seemed to go away, not by moving physically but by abstracting herself somehow. She kissed him again, but this time there was no passion in it. Yet, she let out a little moan, which suggested she was fighting against herself. Then she stood up.

"I'll see if I can do anything," she said, and she seemed to be crying softly, a sound that pierced him.

She turned and walked away. He watched her proud straight back, her black curls.

Then she was gone, and it was dark.

He wished she had stayed. Then again he did not want her here. The image of her kissing that man, of her being naked in front of her crew, of her ability to go so far away all returned to him in the dark. Somehow, she was inside him— her perfume, her image, everything about her—and he did not know how to get her out. She brought danger and pain, but, for no good reason he could explain, he felt privileged to experience the suffering she brought.

But of course it would be far better not to be suffering. He thought about when life did not have this suffering, when his mother was alive and they still lived in the house in Naunton.

And Sarah was there. With him.

Sarah . . .

He longed to regain innocence and to turn back time so he could be with Sarah again. She would never have been this way with him—not like . . . .

But he had treated her so terribly, just as he had Abigail. Now one was mad and the other dead. He was determined not to hurt another woman. It was better that he suffer than that he make her suffer. He deserved it.

Then the thought clarified in his head

I'll love her til the day I die

The syllables pronounced in his head like an iron bell of eternal doom, a judge's sentence full of exquisite pleasure and unimaginable pain.

Not that that day is very far away

Epilogue

The dark garden full of the aromatic flowers sang the same endless tune. Always behind one of the big trees she saw the shadowy form of a man. Even though she could not see his face she knew he was familiar, but how? Who was he? Where had she known him from?

When she tried to sneak up on him he vanished into thin air. Sometimes he would stay gone a long time. But he always appeared again.

She tried to speak to him, but when she opened her mouth it was not English that came out but some other language she could not even understand, herself. This frustrated her because the man could not understand what she was trying to say. *He* never spoke.

There was another presence there, also very silent. Somehow she could not quite talk to this presence, and something about it filled her with both fear and pity. It never went away, never moved. She felt she knew something about this presence but could not tell what.

Then that presence did go away. She waited to see if it would come back, but it did not. Its going away seemed to mean something to her, but she could not quite catch what it was, and when she tried hard the darkness seemed to fragment into bursts of orange and yellow light.

She had no sense of the passage of time, but she waited patiently for that other form to appear just as the man did after he would disappear. The man did not scare her. She just wanted to know who he was. He seemed maybe to be two people in one. And she seemed to know one or both. But none of it really made any sense.

Meanwhile the other presence stayed gone. No sign of return. She began to fret about it, although she could not say why. She began to become frantic, wanting the presence return. But it did not. She began to think that maybe that presence never would return, and the thought sent her into despair. The despair grew worse the harder she tried to understand it.

Then a moment came when she accepted that the presence had gone forever. And in that moment her eyes seemed to grow wide and the darkness began to lift. The big trees went away, and with them the flowers and their aroma.

She found herself in a room of gray walls and a high window through which gray light drifted in. There were bars on the windows. She felt very cold, looking around the tiny room and finding herself alone. She had no idea where she was, but she had a new awareness of herself, and it was as if something snapped back into place inside her. She opened her mouth and spoke in English.

"Sarah," she said. "That is my name."

The End of Book Two

Thank you for reading *Port Royal*!

I hope you had as much fun reading it as I did writing it.
If did you enjoy it, please take a moment to rate the book
on Amazon. If you have an extra minute or two and would
like to write a brief review about it, that would be great!
Also, feel free to recommend this novel and the *Pirate's Life*
series to others. Together we can get this story out to more
people.

For more exclusive material, including updates and short
stories, go to
www.fountadams.com
and sign up for free membership.

Sincerely yours,

Fount Adams

www.ingramcontent.com/pod-product-compliance
Lightning Source LLC
Chambersburg PA
CBHW021532250626
47154CB00006BA/2082